TRANSLUCID

DRAGONFIRE STATION BOOK 1

ZEN DIPIETRO

PARALLEL WORLDS PRESS

COPYRIGHT

TRANSLUCID (DRAGONFIRE STATION #1)
COPYRIGHT © 2016 BY ZEN DIPIETRO

This is a work of fiction. Names, characters, organizations, events, and incidents are either products of the author's imagination or used fictitiously. Any resemblance to actual events, business establishments, locales, or persons, living or dead, is coincidental.

All rights reserved. No part of this publication may be reproduced, stored in a retrieval system, or transmitted in any form or by any means (electronic, mechanical, photocopying, recording, or otherwise) without express written permission of the publisher. The only exception is brief quotations for the purpose of review.

Please purchase only authorized electronic editions. Distribution of this book via the Internet or via any other means without the permission of the publisher is illegal and punishable by law.

ISBN: 978-1-943931-15-6 (print)

Background Illustration © 2016 Maciej Rebisz

Published in the United States of America by Parallel Worlds Press

DRAGONFIRE STATION UNIVERSE

Dragonfire Station Book 1: Translucid
Dragonfire Station Book 2: Fragments
Dragonfire Station Book 3: Coalescence

Intersections (Dragonfire Station Short Stories)

Selling Out (Mercenary Warfare Book 1)
Blood Money (Mercenary Warfare Book 2)
Hell to Pay (Mercenary Warfare Book 3)
Calculated Risk (Mercenary Warfare Book 4)
Going for Broke (Mercenary Warfare Book 5)

Chains of Command Book 1: New Blood
Chains of Command Book 2: Blood and Bone
Chains of Command Book 3: Cut to the Bone
Chains of Command Book 4: Out for Blood

To stay updated on new releases and sales, sign up for Zen's newsletter at www.ZenDiPietro.com

1

Drifting. Safe, wrapped in layers of gauze and dreams. Not quite aware, yet not fully oblivious either. Just tucked into a pleasant pocket of numb vagueness.

Until sharp sounds and bright lights pierced her sanctuary. Disjointed assaults on her senses made her try to twist away, but she was too swaddled in the ether to move. She wished the barrage would just leave her alone. Beneath the tumult, an insistent sound repeated, catching her attention. The more she tried to ignore it, the more demanding the noise became. With a burst of irritation, she focused on the sound and followed it up, away from the pleasant gauze.

"Em. Em. *Em.*"

She lifted her eyelids and blinked, trying to clear her hazy vision. The voice stopped its litany. Pale blue eyes stared at her from less than eight inches above.

She turned her head to look past the stranger. She saw medical equipment. Techbeds. Three nurses on the other side of the room, talking to patients. A doctor, watching her.

Why was she in the infirmary? Was she sick? She didn't remember being sick. She ran her hands down her chest and over her stomach. She didn't feel any wounds. She clocked a single exit on the far side of the room and tried to estimate how long it would take her to get there. Hard to tell without knowing her physical condition.

The doctor stepped closer and the blue eyes withdrew slightly, providing a better overall view of the pink-haired woman they belonged to. There wasn't time enough to wonder about her, though, because the doctor spoke.

"There you are. You had us worried. How do you feel?" He handed her a cup. She took it suspiciously, until she realized it was only biogel. Which suddenly sounded wonderful. Her mouth felt dry and her throat rasped.

She took her time with slow swallows, giving herself a chance to assess the doctor. Olive-skinned Bennite with brown eyes. Cultured accent. Probably from a well-to-do family, though she'd never heard of a poor Bennite. Bennaris was one of the most prosperous members of the Planetary Alliance Cooperative. The doctor seemed reasonably athletic, in good physical condition as far as she could tell by looking. He was likely right-handed, given the scanner he held. She did not consider him a threat.

She ran her tongue over her lips, buying time before her reply. What could she say to these people? She had no idea who they were or what their agenda might be. She'd need to be careful.

"My head hurts a little. I'm confused. Not sure how I got here." Bewilderment was a good tactic. Unfortunately, she was also telling the truth.

The doctor nodded understandingly, while the blue-eyed woman's eyebrows pulled down with concern. She wasn't a nurse, so her purpose in this situation remained unclear. She didn't look like an official. Her features and coloring marked her as a Sarkavian. She had the white-blonde hair nearly all of her people had, though she'd fashionably tinted it a pale shade of pink. Her overalls and calloused hands marked her as a mechanic or engineer of some sort.

The doctor set the scanner down on a table and half-sat on a backless stool next to the techbed. "You got lucky. We almost didn't get you back in time. A few more seconds and we'd have lost you, along with the shuttle."

"Shuttle?"

The doctor paused. "The shuttle you took out to inspect the station." When she didn't respond, he asked, "What's the last thing you remember?"

Her gaze flickered between the two of them. Her first priority was to avoid telling them too much. On the other hand, she couldn't think of anything to say. No memories came to mind.

"I don't know."

For the first time, the blue-eyed woman looked away from her, fixing her attention on the doctor. The anxiety in her expression and posture indicated a vested interest in the doctor's assessment.

The doctor didn't acknowledge the woman, though. His lips compressed slightly before he asked, "Do you know where you are?"

"An infirmary."

"Yes. You're in my infirmary. Do you know what station we're on?"

She shook her head.

"Do you recognize me?" he asked.

She strongly suspected that by this point, she should. "No."

He had gone still, his manner grave. "Do you know *your* name?"

She opened her mouth to answer, and nothing came out. No name rose from the quagmire of her brain. She closed her mouth.

"I see," he murmured. "Well!" His tone picked up, seeming more energetic. He squeezed the hand of the pink-haired woman, who now looked distraught. "I warned Wren here that the injury to the memory center of your brain might leave you with a few difficulties. It's very likely that, as your brain adjusts, your memories will return. At least some of them, anyway."

"How long should that take?" she asked. She continued to ignore "Wren" and focused entirely on the doctor, as he had the answers she needed.

He looked regretful. Not a good sign. "I'm afraid I can't say. There's no telling. A week. A month. Possibly longer." He paused. "There's also a small chance that your memory could be significantly impaired."

"Meaning I might not remember anything, ever?"

"It's possible."

The blue-eyed woman pressed a hand to her mouth.

"Who are you?" she finally asked the woman. The presence of this emotional person was not helping.

Stricken, the woman looked to the doctor.

"Ah, well. Let's start with you," he interjected. "Your name is Emé Fallon. Em to your friends, which means most of the people here on Dragonfire Station. You're the security chief and second in command." He gave her a moment to consider that, and when she nodded, he continued. "I am Dr. Brannin Brash, chief medical officer on Dragonfire."

She nodded again and he paused, putting his arm gently around the pink-haired woman. Supportively. Clearly, her feelings mattered to him. "And this is Wren Orritz. Your wife."

FEIGNING fatigue accomplished her first objective, which was getting Wren Orritz out of the infirmary. The woman's emotional state had begun to wear on her. Getting information was her only priority, and pussyfooting around a distraught wife's feelings was the last thing she needed.

Once the doctor had served a couple dozen platitudes to

Wren and insisted that rest was the very best thing for the patient, he finally guided her from the infirmary, gently but firmly.

Her eyes popped open and she sat up as soon as the infirmary doors closed behind Wren. She felt anything but tired. Adrenaline pulsed through her and she felt the need to run, move, to *do* something. She fought the urge and remained seated on the techbed. Instead, she took a slower visual tour of the infirmary. Large. Ideally equipped with all of the latest medical technology, as one would expect of a Planetary Alliance Cooperative station.

Hm. Interesting. She seemed to have a detailed understanding of PAC bases and installations, as well as military structure. As she thought along these lines, information bubbled up, populating her thoughts almost mechanically. She felt a streak of relief wash through her. Apparently, in some respects, her memory was just fine. She had something to build on, as soon as she got a handle on her situation.

For now, she needed to focus on her current, unfamiliar surroundings. The walls of the infirmary were lined with voicecom screens and removable infoboards, as well as various techbed accessories. At the far end of the infirmary she saw a large private area, which could be utilized as one bay or divided into individual private rooms. Two doctors and three nurses moved around the periphery of the infirmary, poking at screens and probably waiting impatiently for their patient appointments to resume. Dr. Brash would have to downgrade her official status before that could happen.

She herself sat in the forward portion of the infirmary. The emergency area. At least that corroborated the doctor's story of her having experienced a critical accident. It wasn't much for her to go on, but it was something.

"Emé Fallon." She tried the words out, rolling the vowels off her tongue, testing them to see if they felt familiar. They didn't.

She felt like she should have some visceral connection to her own name. "Emé. Em. I'm Emé." Nope. It didn't click.

"Fine," she said decisively, focusing instead on Brannin Brash. "I need information, Doctor."

He didn't seem surprised. If anything, his eyes conveyed understanding. "How can I help? And by the way, you've called me Brannin for quite some time, so you might as well continue." He kept his voice soft, so that his words would not be overheard by the others.

"Brannin, then. How long have I been the security chief of Dragonfire Station?"

"A year."

"What happened to the previous chief?"

"He requested a transfer to be closer to home."

"Who's the captain of the station?"

"Hesta Nevitt," he answered promptly. "It's her third year."

She turned sideways, letting her feet hang over the side of the techbed, then stood. Brannin didn't object, so she began to walk around to see how her body felt. "What's my physical condition?"

"Excellent, other than your memory and some light swelling around the area of your brain that was injured. You had a few broken bones, some small lacerations and lots of bruising, but we took care of all that."

She felt fine. Great, actually. Her body was strong, lean but muscular, and brimming with energy. Judging by Brannin and the other medical staff, she appeared to be of medium height for a human or a Bennite. But was she either one of those? The tan skin of her hands didn't offer any clues, as they could belong to someone from any number of worlds.

"I need to see my personnel file."

He nodded, as if he'd expected that. He motioned her over to a voicecom terminal, touched it several times, then pushed a low-backed stool over for her.

She sat and studied the file. Human. Female. Age twenty-eight. Born on Earth. Three-quarters Japanese, one-quarter unspecified. Meaning that whatever composed the final twenty-five percent, it was not enough of any one thing to bother with listing. She skimmed down the vital statistics of height, weight, and birth date before slowing at her service history. She'd entered the Planetary Alliance Cooperative's academy at age seventeen and gone straight into security training in officer training school. Dragonfire Station was her eighth duty station, which was a lot for someone her age.

After she'd gleaned all the information she could, she scrutinized the photo. She saw a woman who looked entirely Japanese. No visual evidence of that unspecified twenty-five percent. She had an oval face with longish black hair. Large brown eyes. Most importantly, she looked strong. Capable. The woman in the image wore a hard, closed look. She approved.

She started to turn away from the terminal, then touched the screen several times in succession to bring up the specs for Dragonfire Station. She studied its elongated shape, noted that it existed near the edge of a red nebula. She'd known that, she realized. The colorful gas cloud had spawned the station's name. Some dreamy PAC administrator must have thought that the nebula looked like what a fire-breathing dragon would exhale. To Em, it looked like a nebula. She didn't need fiction to make it more interesting.

When the publicly available all-access mechanical specs weren't detailed enough, she mentally reached for a way to discover more. Data populated her brain and she input several codes, allowing her to pull up the security details without hesitation. Ah, that was more like it. Weapons. Defenses. Onboard monitoring system. The important things.

The doctor quickly turned his back to the screen. "I'll just give everyone an early lunch and occupy myself with some work. No one else here has clearance for those files." She didn't spare him a glance as he marched away, but felt the room emptying behind her. She heard Dr. Brash muttering something to himself about core memories.

She quickly memorized the full measure of the station's composition, then followed up by researching the PAC itself, though she seemed to have an excellent working knowledge of the cooperative.

She then took a look at Dr. Brash's service record just for good measure. Finally, and with less confidence, she studied Wren Orritz's file.

She was a twenty-six-year-old Sarkavian mechanic. An engineer, but a very hands-on sort of engineer. Also a citizen of a PAC planet and an employee of a PAC station, but not a member of the PAC military. That meant that either Wren wasn't exceptional enough to be accepted into OTS, or she lacked enough ambition to apply. Em studied Wren's face. A bit sharp-featured, but attractive in an interesting way. Prettier than Em's own rather plain face, at least.

According to the file, Wren had a gift for anything with moving parts. She didn't even have a specialty, as mechanics normally did. The PAC had given her a superior rating for every category of mechanical work, from ship engines to space elevators. Exceptional indeed.

On Dragonfire, Wren primarily worked on station mechanics and incoming ships that needed repairs, but she seemed to frequently help out with many other things as well, of her own volition. A small notation indicated a hobby of repairing kitchen appliances in her spare time.

Was Em married to some sort of do-gooder grease monkey? She didn't *feel* married. But then she didn't feel like a lesbian either. Did that even feel like something? The doctor didn't do anything for her in spite of being a handsome man just a few years older than her, so she didn't feel particularly heterosexual, either. She imagined most women would be attracted to his dark good looks, and his kind brown eyes. She appreciated his smooth, accented voice, though, as it went up and down in the pleasing cadence unique to Bennites.

She liked Brannin Brash. She felt in her gut that she could trust the doctor, and at the moment, all she had was her gut.

When all her immediate questions had been answered, she twisted around on the stool to face outward, toward Brannin. "It seems I remember security protocols and how to access restricted information."

He turned from his console to look at her. "Yes, I noticed that. It's a good sign." He stepped across the room, stopping at the end of a techbed well outside her personal space.

"Is it?" she asked.

"Yes, a *very* good sign. It means that your actual memories weren't damaged. Not all of them, anyway. Think of your brain as a highly complex computer. You might not have information in your RAM, but you have files stored in the hard memory. When those files are accessed, you might be able to restore some of the programs and files that were in your RAM. It's a clumsy analogy, but I think it does the job."

She liked his metaphor, and it did seem to fit with her ability to pull information from her brain. She also liked how he presented information to her, upfront and without any touchy-feely prevarication. She had a feeling she was a hard-facts sort of person rather than a thoughts-and-feelings sort. Perhaps Brannin already knew that about her. He might very well know her better than she knew herself, at this point. She supposed she should feel comforted by that, but she felt a lot more caution than trust. Regardless of how well he might know her, Em's instincts urged her to proceed carefully.

"So how do I go about restoring all my programs?"

"That's where the metaphor breaks down," he explained, somewhat apologetically. "The brain is a living organ—almost its own organism, in fact. And each brain has its own idiosyncrasies. The damage your brain sustained is located in your memory center, but how that will affect you remains to be seen. Though your active memory seems to have gone on sabbatical, your core memories are clearly intact." He paused, his eyes going unfocused for a moment. Then he shook his head and continued. "I advise you to return to your regular life as much as possible and go through the motions. Familiar actions might restore those memories, just as using the voicecom did."

"So, what? Return to my quarters? Go back to work?" She had no mental image of her living space, or her job.

"Yes. As much as you're able."

"The captain won't have a problem with her security chief having a hole in her head?"

Brannin's nose wrinkled. "I'd hardly call it that. You remember enough about your job to pull up classified documents. If you can do that, I'm willing to wager you remember things like import-and-export laws and protocols."

At the suggestion, the information began populating in her mind. When Brannin arched his eyebrow at her, she nodded. Yep, she knew them, all right.

"And the required maintenance schedules for ships operating within the PAC zone," he added.

She nodded again.

"And how to handle an attack on the station."

Her mind blazed with defensive and offensive capabilities and tactics. So many thoughts sprang forth that she actively had to stuff them back into the recesses of her mind before she could answer. "Yeah."

Brannin smiled, looking very pleased with himself. "As I suspected. I'll talk to the captain. My recommendation, along with an agreement for you to work closely with your legate, Arin, ought to do the trick."

"Arin?" she asked warily.

Brannin made a dismissive gesture. "You'll like him. You

handpicked him as your second in command of the station's security."

"Fine. If the captain okays it, and you think going back to work is the best option, then I'll do that. What about my living situation?"

"You have crew quarters on Deck Five."

"With Wren, right?" She didn't like the idea of sharing space with a stranger. Especially one she was married to. According to the records, they'd been married six months ago, making them newlyweds.

"Of course." When he saw her distaste for the thought, he gave her an understanding smile. "Don't worry, Em. Wren is great. You're a very lucky woman."

Of their own design, her eyebrows raised in a way that felt both disdainful and satisfying. Yes, she liked disdain. It suited her.

The doctor spoke quickly. "I mean, she'll be understanding. She loves you very much and will do whatever she can to help."

She let the eyebrows ease back down. "Hm."

"I want to keep you under observation today, but if all remains as it is, you can go home tomorrow."

How could it be home when she didn't remember it? But all she said was, "If that's what it takes, I'll do it."

EM STUDIED Dragonfire Station with almost obsessive interest after her release from the infirmary the next day. She already understood the station's layout, thanks to the design schematics she'd scrutinized. Now, as she walked along the concourse toward the lift, she scrutinized the station's details. She memorized every decorative element, each area where people tended to congregate, and every face that traveled past her.

She'd already realized that she possessed a nearly eidetic

memory—what people used to call a "photographic memory." Perhaps that was an irony, given her loss of personal memories, but at least it would give her an advantage in getting her life back. Brannin had given her every test he could think of, and had determined that the only memories she seemed to lack were ones that involved her personal identity and experiences. The phenomenon seemed to fascinate the doctor, though he'd tried to dial his enthusiasm back every now and then, when he remembered himself.

The woman walking beside Em evoked as much familiarity as her surroundings did—exactly none. She pretended she didn't notice Wren's surreptitious glances or her obvious anxiety. Em sympathized with Wren, who had essentially lost her wife, only to have her mate replaced with a lookalike. Em's sympathy didn't alleviate her unease, though. Instead, she had only distrust and suspicion. She bristled with it as they rode the lift upward to the fifth deck.

Deck Five, which housed the crew quarters, was the highest of the decks, farthest from the docking bays far below. Only two things sat above Deck Five—the service bays that housed the majority of the systems that kept Dragonfire Station running, and the station's bridge, known as ops control.

Em appreciated the station's functional design, which made the most sensitive areas the hardest to access while also cushioning the habitat decks between other layers of the station that could be evacuated in the event of an emergency. A minimal "crisis" ops control was buried in the center of Deck Five, behind many layers of security. Em hated to think of the disaster that would necessitate using crisis ops.

Too soon, Em and Wren arrived at the one section on the station Em really didn't want to see. The placard next to the door indicated the quarters' designation. Five-eleven. Her home.

Wren smiled nervously and stepped toward the door, causing it to whisk open. When Em didn't enter, Wren walked into the room then turned, waiting for her with an expectant look.

Em suppressed a sigh, then entered. The doors efficiently swished shut behind her, sealing her in. Trapping her. She fought an urge to bolt. Instead, she walked slowly around the living room, noting a couch and a table with a voicecom display alongside a slim chair and a much more comfortable-looking reclining chair. An abstract painting hung on the wall, and the colors suggested that either she or Wren preferred warm, earthy tones. The living room seemed cozy, its low-slung furniture designed for use rather than style. Not that everything didn't look attractive—it did, in a relaxed, homey sort of way. There was a mix of Japanese and beachy Sarkavian elements that created a unique but relaxing ambiance.

Em supposed she and Wren had compromised on the room's décor, which seemed perfectly logical. At the far end of the quarters she saw a kitchenette, as well as a dining area with a small table with two chairs. She turned to look for the bedroom, but an image screen on a side table caught her attention.

She picked up the picture. She saw herself, wearing a gauzy pink and white dress with flowers in her hair, standing barefoot on a beach. She faced Wren, who wore a long, breezy blush-pink dress and a small hat with long ribbons. They appeared to be laughing as the wind carried the ribbons into twirly shapes. Joy clearly radiated from both of them.

"Our wedding." Wren sat on the couch, gesturing for Em to do the same.

She hesitated, then sat at the opposite end. "Six months ago, according to what I read."

A flicker of something showed in Wren's pale eyes, but Em couldn't discern what it meant. Loss, maybe? "Yes," Wren agreed. "It was a wonderful day. My whole family was there, at the beach temple on Sarkan. We kept it all very simple, very relaxed." Her mouth softened into a romantic smile.

"Have I always been a lesbian?"

Wren's lips parted in surprise, then she laughed softly. "I should have known you'd ask something like that." Her laugh was warm and for some reason made Em think of a thick, hearty stew. "I actually didn't know that word until you taught it to me. Sarkavians don't recognize sexuality as something that's governed by gender. But that suited you fine, because you said you'd never felt like you needed to pin yourself down to a particular type, either. Pansexual, some people call it." Wren's lips twisted with humor. "You were less enthused about my skepticism when it comes to monogamy. That's not a usual thing for Sarkavians, either."

Wren's laughter had brightened her features, and the glow remained, eclipsing her earlier sadness. Her body language had relaxed as well.

Until Wren had mentioned it, Em hadn't really considered the Sarkavian approach to sexuality, which consisted of unfettered, though tactful, indulgence. Sarkavians considered monogamy to be antiquated and limiting. "Right. I imagine that must have been quite a conversation."

Wren laughed. "You convinced me to give it a try. If I didn't like it, you said, if it didn't give me a greater sense of closeness, we could try it my way."

"How did that go?"

"Okay so far. I mean, we're still newlyweds." She made a small, tasteful shrug.

"I see." Em returned the picture to the table, then faced Wren. She didn't really want to delve into the details of their sex life, which meant it was time to move the conversation along to other topics. "So far, nothing is familiar to me. It's possible that I might not regain my memories. Brannin told me that my brain sustained an unusual degree of injury in comparison to the amount of damage done to my scalp and skull. I don't want to be harsh or unkind, but it's possible that you'll never get back the person you married."

Instead of looking upset, Wren cocked her head to one side and her eyes narrowed with sly amusement. "Now, I *did* expect you to say something like that." She seemed pleased about it too, for no reason that Em could fathom.

Wren reached behind her head and released the clasp that held her light-pink hair in a twist. She put the clasp in her pocket and ran her fingers over her scalp. "Ahh. That feels better. The only bad thing about being a mechanic is all the grease I get in my hair when I wear it down in the shop. You always say you like it up, but I think it makes me look like my mom." She stood. "Come to the bedroom."

Em froze. "I don't think…"

Wren laughed. "To complete the tour. Try to jog some memories, and all that."

Right. Fine. Stiffly, Em stood and followed her to the bedroom. A quick survey revealed a bed covered with a blue comforter. A starscape mosaic hung above the bed, which was flanked by a pair of nightstands. A wide closet and a doorway to the necessary stood at the far side.

She stepped closer and the door opened. The necessary had all the basics—shower, toilet, and sink—with only a few personal effects here and there to clutter it. Em barely spared those elements a glance. Her attention was focused on the rectangular mirror above the sink. She found herself in front of it, skimming her fingers through the black hair that hung just past her shoulders. She'd already found that she disliked the feel of it sliding over her shoulders and back. It felt untidy. Fussy.

She touched two fingers to her forehead, watching her own eyes in the mirror as she traced the contours of her cheekbone and chin before letting her hand fall to her side. She tilted her head, examining her face from different angles.

She was attractive enough, but unremarkable. Forgettable.

Good. She might not know the face in the mirror, but she knew she must have lived and breathed security protocols. They ran through her mind constantly, spurred by whatever her situation and surroundings happened to be. Having a face that people wouldn't particularly remember was in her favor if she wanted to go about her business unnoticed.

"Have I always worn my hair so long?" She turned away from the mirror and stepped back into the bedroom. The door to the necessary closed behind her.

Wren's forehead creased. "Yes, for as long as I've known you, anyway. Why? Don't you like it?"

"I don't."

Wren nibbled her lip, looking thoughtful. "Well, we can always get it cut to something you like better."

"I think I'd like that." She sat on the edge of the bed, running her hand over the blanket, measuring its cottony texture against her palm. She looked up at Wren. "I'm sorry, but nothing here seems familiar."

Wren's gaze didn't waver. "Don't be sorry. It isn't your fault." When Em started to speak again, Wren cut her off. "And now I bet you're going to say that since you don't know me, you don't feel comfortable sleeping in a bed with me."

Her surprise must have shown, because Wren chuckled. "I may seem like a stranger to you, but you're still the same Em to me. All your gestures. The thoughts I see on your face. You don't have to worry about offending me. I know you, how you think. Just be real with me, and I'll be real with you."

Em didn't know whether to find that comforting or disturbing.

"I'll sleep on the couch tonight." Em stood and smoothed the nondescript infirmary-patient pants she still wore.

"Like Prelin, you will. You just had a brain injury. You'll sleep in the bed. I'll take the couch." Wren folded her arms over her chest.

"You're taller than I am." Wren stood about a forehead taller than Em. "Makes more sense for me to take the couch. Besides, it's your home. I don't want to put you out of your own bed."

"*It's your bed too, Em.*" Wren's voice didn't rise, but she enunciated each word like precision strikes.

Em opened her mouth, then closed it. Some battles weren't worth fighting. "Very well then. I'll take the bed." She frowned, displeased by the exchange, even though she felt relieved by the idea of having the bedroom. It was more defensible than the couch and she knew she'd sleep better there.

Wren's pale eyes gleamed with satisfaction. "Good then. Glad that's settled. Now, are you ready for dinner? I made your favorite. Bennite stew and Sarkavian biscuits. My mom's recipe."

"Dinner sounds good."

Wren led the way to the small table Em had noted earlier, and gestured for her to sit. "Go ahead. I'll just make up a couple plates."

She felt like she should help rather than sit and be served, but guessed that the suggestion would only provoke another spat. So she sat. Wren's efforts created soft clattering and clinking sounds. Finally, she transferred bowls, cups, and a plate of biscuits to the table before sitting down.

"Smells great," Em said, breathing in the rich, meaty aroma of the stew.

Wren smiled and bit into a biscuit.

They ate quietly, with little conversation. Em appreciated that. She made short work of her stew and neglected to notice how many biscuits she went through.

"That was delicious. Thank you. I can see why it's my favorite." She folded her napkin and set it on the table.

"I'm glad you enjoyed it." Wren sipped from her water glass. "My mom always makes biscuits when she knows we're going to visit. She enjoys spoiling you."

She didn't know what to say to that. She'd have to study up on

Wren's family later. The bedroom had a voicecom terminal built into the wall and there'd been a display on the nightstand as well. Maybe after she retired for the evening she could do some investigating.

"It must be nice for you to work on Dragonfire, given how close we are to Sarkan. I imagine you visit quite often." It seemed like the right thing to say. Personal. Em felt somewhat surreal, attempting dinner conversation with a wife she didn't know, as part of a life she didn't remember.

"Yes. Dragonfire isn't the fanciest station, but being so close to home is lovely. I'd like it here even if it were far away, though. Being a trade hub, we see a big variety of visitors. You never know when someone's going to show up with a load of hungry cats, or some outdated technology I've never seen. There's always an adventure around the corner." Wren popped the last of her biscuit into her mouth and chewed slowly.

"No doubt that keeps me busy securing everyone's safety," Em surmised.

"Your attention to detail has earned you respect here." Wren laughed, covering her mouth with her hand. "As well as a few disgruntled adversaries intent on some not-so-legal enterprises."

"Sounds like there's a story or two there," Em said.

"More than that." Wren's eyes twinkled. "I'll fill you in on them if you don't end up remembering them on your own. It would be fun, telling you your own stories." She rose and began clearing the table with relaxed, graceful movements.

"Can I help?" Em stood.

"Not tonight. Why don't you go have a shower? Change into some of your own clothes. Left side of the closet is yours."

That sounded good, actually. She didn't care for the plain pants and shirt. "All right. I'll be back in a bit."

"Take your time," Wren called from the kitchenette, her back to Em. She'd relaxed tremendously through the course of the evening, apparently because Em's personality hadn't changed at all.

In the necessary, Em peeled off her clothes and stuffed them into the wall-unit processor. She turned on the shower at a medium heat setting and stepped in. *Brr.* She quickly dialed up higher heat. She saw two cakes of soap. She sniffed the pink one and found it floral, perfumey. *No.* The green one smelled of sandalwood and nutmeg. *Yes.* That one must be hers.

She grabbed a scrub-sponge from the shelf and worked it over her shoulders, down her arms, and over her breasts, studying all of these parts that belonged to her. She traced the small, swirling tattoo inked over her abs to the left of her navel. It looked vaguely like the outline of a clover leaf, but in looping swirls, all in a flat black color. Other than that, she had no particularly noteworthy features. No scars or birthmarks to be found.

She took her time, enjoying the steam that clouded the air. Finally, she shut off the water and dried off, slapping the air-evac panel. The mirror immediately cleared and the humidity disappeared.

On a left-handed shelf in the closet, she found a soft pair of low-rise pants and a matching top. She slipped into them and worked at toweling off her hair as she returned to the living room.

"Better?" Wren asked from the couch, setting an infoboard on the side table.

"Yes. Thank you." She made an irritated sound, scrubbing at her hair with the towel. "This stuff is like cold, wet snakes attached to my head. Ugh. Why do I have it?"

"Here. Let me." Wren reversed positions with her, standing behind Em, rubbing the moisture-wicking towel over her hair in quick, practiced movements. After a few moments she stepped back. "There."

Em put both hands on her head, feeling the hair, now only slightly damp. "Thank you." She pushed it all back behind her shoulders. "I think I'll get it cut tomorrow."

"Seems like you'll be happier that way," Wren agreed. She walked around the couch and sat on the other end, giving Em plenty of space. She let out a long sigh. "So."

Em met her gaze. "So."

"Are you doing okay? Really? I can't imagine what this is like for you."

Em considered. "I think so. But I don't really know what all I've lost. I imagine things must be harder for you."

Wren's lips quirked in a not-quite smile. "It's not my favorite. But at the same time, I got lucky. You're here, breathing. Alive and healthy. I'll take that, however it comes, over the other any day."

Em saw wisdom in Wren's eyes. She knew Em might never remember. She knew their marriage might effectively be over. But she wasn't complaining. Wasn't crying. She was glad for what she still had. Em respected that, and it further improved her opinion of Wren.

Wren's expression changed, showing satisfaction. She'd watched Em's face and followed her thoughts, Em was certain. Wren's eyes were knowing, in a smug sort of way. Almost challenging.

Em might just grow to like this wife of hers.

―――

EM LIKED RUNNING. Wren had suggested that she go for her customary morning workout before her duty shift. Her body clearly knew what it was doing. She'd immediately fallen into an easy rhythm, and she enjoyed seeing her surroundings stream by as her muscles propelled her forward. Running felt remarkably good—easily the most enjoyable thing she could recall having done. Ever.

She even enjoyed the feeling of sweat soaking into her shirt and pants. Somehow, the damp sensation felt like proof of her hard work and her determination to be strong. After twenty-five circuits around the track, she slowed to a brisk walk to cool her body down. She didn't know how far she typically ran, but five kilometers seemed like a good amount.

As her heart rate gradually slowed, she took the time to better study the gymnasium. It had space for a variety of physical activities. She saw a ring for sparring which piqued her particular interest. She felt an urge to get in there and start throwing some punches. Maybe tomorrow, if she could find a sparring partner. Wait. Head injury. Yeah, she'd have to check with the doctor about that.

The far wall had a climbing installation, which she also found enticing. Clustered in the center of the gym sat a wide array of cardiovascular and weight-training equipment. Em knew that there were separate rooms for target practice and pegball alongside this main complex. She looked forward to trying everything out. But she had a job to get to.

Brannin had suggested that she leap right into her normal daily routine. She saw no reason not to take his advice, so she'd spent the remainder of the previous evening quizzing Wren about what Em's days typically consisted of. The woman had been helpful and forthcoming, and Em believed she could trust the information. Wren had even supplied details about her working relationships with various colleagues. That would prove helpful, since Em had no intention of letting on that she'd lost her memory. Brannin and a few key healthcare personnel knew, but they were bound by confidentiality. The doctor had certainly already briefed Captain Nevitt of the situation, but it wouldn't be in her best interest to advertise Em's memory loss either. You didn't go around telling wolves that the chickens might not be as well guarded as they should be.

How the captain would decide to handle the situation, though, Em had no idea. Perhaps Nevitt would choose to put her legate, Arin Triss, in charge for the time being. But that would certainly put them all in an awkward situation. All Em could do was wait for the captain's determination.

She took the stairs down from the track. PAC safety and accessibility standards required there to be a lift down from any elevated walkway, but that one probably didn't get much use. Who would want to admit that they couldn't take the stairs after a good run?

She grabbed her bag and headed to the showers. She nodded to two people who glanced up as she walked by, but kept moving to avoid any chance of conversation. She saw a lean, muscular guy on his way to the climbing wall, and her previous question about whether she felt attracted to men was answered. She did. She just had very high, somewhat particular standards, apparently.

Once in the women's facility, she showered quickly, then toweled off. As she stepped into the pants of her PAC officer's uniform, she traced the pattern of the tattoo on her stomach with her forefinger. Wren had told her that she'd gotten the tattoo on the day she'd graduated from officer training school. According to the story, she and a group of her close friends had all gotten tattoos.

She tucked her undershirt into her pants then shrugged into the jacket and zipped it up. Fastening her belt around her hips, she double-checked her weapon and comport to ensure they were secure. She ran her fingers through her newly short hair and studied her reflection. The blue-gray uniform fit nicely, and the fabric felt like it would be sturdy while allowing a great deal of movement. The bars on her shoulder indicated her rank as a commander, as well as her position on the station as security chief. She felt inordinately pleased about her new hairstyle. Mostly because she was relieved to be liberated from its previous length. Partly because it felt like a small rebellion to re-envision herself. Kind of like sticking it to the old Em, whoever that person had been.

Now her hair parted on the side, with the left side sheared short. The length elongated gradually toward the right side, with the longest point in the front right at chin length. She liked her new, much edgier look. The person in the mirror felt like someone she could be. Most importantly, her hair stayed out of her way now, rather than constantly moving around.

After drying her hair and finger combing it into place with a dab of oil, she grabbed the straps of her bag and headed back up to Deck Five to drop it in her quarters. After that brief detour, she returned to the lift and headed to ops control.

EM WONDERED if she should be nervous. She wasn't. Perhaps that was a failing, or perhaps it was exactly what made her successful as a security officer. Either way, her only concern when the lift doors opened was seeing if Dragonfire's ops control jogged any memories. She peered through the widening crack, staring at the bridge.

Nope. Not a wisp of familiarity. She had no recollection of ever being in this large room, though she did recognize the PAC esthetic, all smooth lines and angles, sleek surfaces, and a lack of excess. All of the materials used in ops control were the highest quality, and the contoured, padded seats surely offered comfort. But ornamentation and extras weren't built in. This was a high-tech military station, not a luxury-stay outpost.

Em recognized the various command stations by their configurations, and she knew their functions as well. She saw station control on the left side, the captain's post in the center, and the security and science stations in the back. She scanned the view provided by the starport, which stretched across the entire bulkhead of the station, giving them a panoramic look at the universe beyond Dragonfire.

The previous night, she'd studied the ops crew, which allowed her to identify the engineer at station control, as well as the astrophysicist at the science station. She certainly recognized the regal captain, who stood and turned to fix Em with a hard look as Em executed the proper PAC bow for a superior officer.

"So you're back to work. Brannin told me to expect that." Rather than seeming impressed, the captain seemed resigned. She returned the bow, less deeply, according to protocol.

Captain Hesta Nevitt was tall and statuesque. Her skin and eyes were very dark brown, and she wore her thick black hair in short, textured twists. Her high cheekbones framed a thin-bridged nose that grew broader down to its tip. Her looks and bearing made Em think of ancient royalty. Certainly, her aloof expression heightened the resemblance.

"Yes," Em answered. "The doctor thought returning to work would be the best thing for me."

"So he insisted," the captain muttered, almost too low for Em to hear. "Your condition remains the same?" Nevitt's tone suggested skepticism. Maybe she planned to remove Em from active duty, after all. She might be right to do so, in spite of the doctor's assurances of her mental competence. Em wasn't sure she'd take the doctor's word for it, if she were the captain.

"Yes."

Nevitt frowned. "Carry on, then. But if you put my station in danger, I'll launch you out the nearest airlock."

It seemed Nevitt had faith in the doctor's opinion, after all. "Yes, Captain." Em gave the proper bow, then turned to her right and sat at the security station, scanning the current readings and reports.

She hadn't expected any tenderness from her captain. Wren had told her about her difficult relationship with Nevitt. The woman was on the fast track in the PAC, destined to join the inner circles of admiralty one day. She'd been leading Dragonfire for two years when her previous security chief took an assignment closer to home. Nevitt should have been allowed to choose the former chief's successor, but instead, Em had been foisted upon her at the insistence of Admiral Krazinski. Nevitt had spent the last year taking her displeasure out on Em. Wren had assured her that, in spite of the captain's dislike for Em and her apparent lack of a social life, Nevitt did an excellent job for Dragonfire. Em could only hope that meant the captain would refrain from pushing her too hard while she tried to regain her footing.

She spent the next twenty minutes ascertaining the station's well-being and noting the day's arrivals and departures. Once that was done, she found herself at a loss. What did she normally do to use the time during her duty shift? Wren had not been able to provide many details.

Em went to stand in front of the captain with her hands behind her back. "Captain, all decks have reported in, well and accounted for. One minor injury was reported outside Docking Bay Five. A visiting Kanaran tripped and twisted an ankle but the doctor has taken care of the situation. We have three trade ships and one private vessel departing today, and four trade ships scheduled to arrive."

Nevitt glanced at her. "Understood, Fallon. Dismissed."

Em bowed and wasted no time in leaving ops control. It had a nice view, but not nice enough to compensate for the captain's animosity.

Back down the lift she went. She considered checking in personally to the security office on each deck, but didn't know if that was her usual practice. Instead, on Deck Four she disembarked, strode the short distance down the concourse, then stopped at her office. She input her handprint, retina scan, and the code that changed daily, based on an algorithmic cypher that only she knew. She felt almost surprised when the door whisked open. It seemed odd for her brain to know things that she didn't realize it knew. What else might be in there?

She stepped in and locked the door behind her. She didn't

want any surprises. Actually, she probably always locked it behind her.

She liked the room. When she'd stepped in, it had automatically activated daylight illumination. The creamy yellow walls gave the room a bright, alert feeling. The space had an uncluttered modern Japanese design, as did almost all of the official areas of the station. She wondered if the décor had been her choice, or if it just happened to suit her taste remarkably well. Either was possible, since the PAC had a tendency to lean toward Japanese esthetics, possibly because the first PAC base had been stationed in Tokyo.

She had a comfortable-looking brown couch, a desk with a chair, and two additional chairs facing the desk. A painting of Dragonfire hung on the wall opposite the desk, showing the station sedately floating in its fiery nebula. Em immediately liked the artwork, which she supposed wasn't a surprise. The other walls remained bare, and had no portholes. No staring out into space for her.

She walked behind the desk and sat. The voicecom display dominated the surface. Two infoboards sat to the left of the display. She reached for them and found that she had a general board, which was a portable, lower-powered voicecom display, as well as a separate menuboard of all the station's eateries. Infoboards didn't offer enough processing power to do major work, but they were incredibly convenient for smaller tasks.

She set the boards on the desk, then pushed her seat just far enough back that she could give the deck plate a good push with both feet, sending her chair spinning in slow circles.

It felt good to be alone. Truly alone. The night before, she'd had the bedroom to herself, but she'd been constantly aware of Wren's presence on the other side of the wall. Now, she felt like she could just think. Except she didn't quite know *what* to think. Was this her life now? Accepting that she was whatever other people told her she was? Doing a complex job that she seemed to completely understand, while she didn't even know her own favorite color? Brannin and Captain Nevitt must have a lot of faith in her, at least professionally, to let her go about her business with a gaping hole in her memory. Which perhaps said more of Nevitt's estimation of Em than her twitchy disdain did. Or did it?

Maybe they were all holding their breath, hoping that at any moment, everything would come flooding back to her. Perhaps circumstances would change if that didn't happen. Nevitt might have enough reason to finally oust her from her position as chief.

Or what if things weren't what she thought they were? What if someone was manipulating her? Using her for some purpose? But she didn't know what anyone could stand to gain. Maybe she had information someone needed, and he or she was just biding time. Or maybe she'd had information someone hadn't wanted her to know, and her accident in the shuttle hadn't been so accidental after all. If that was the case, her memory loss might just be the only thing keeping her alive. *That* was a perplexing possibility.

She wished she knew for sure who she could trust. Even Wren might have a reason to want her dead. At the moment, the only person Em felt she could trust was the doctor. If he'd wanted her dead, she'd already be dead and no one would be the wiser. Nonetheless, she'd have to tread carefully with Brannin. Regardless of his kindness toward her, he was a PAC officer, and would follow PAC regulations even if they stood to endanger her. That was his job, and she didn't blame him for it.

The sound of bamboo wind chimes had her slamming her feet to the floor to stop her slow rotation and sitting up straight. The sound wasn't a standard door alert, so she'd clearly customized it. Interesting.

She checked the security camera and saw her legate standing there with an ambassador of somewhere or other. The ambassador wore elaborate white robes that swept the deck plate as he waited. Deck Four housed dignitaries of all types. Ambassadors, religious and government leaders, and higher-ranking PAC officers. Anyone who had political reasons to need better security and privacy than the average visitor. Deck Four also contained meeting rooms and dining halls so that Dragonfire could host in-person briefings or exchanges between dignitaries, if necessary. The station wasn't well-equipped for entertaining high-ranking officials, though, and most events like conferences or trade negotiations took place on Blackthorn station or planetside somewhere.

Since Dragonfire didn't need an entire deck just for dignitaries, the rest of the space had been sectioned off for security. That allowed Em to have her office there, along with the security team training rooms. Convenient to have such a quiet, relatively unpopulated deck for such activities.

The convenience was tempered by inevitable dignitary drop-ins, though. Like the man on the other side of the door.

"Open doors and permit entrance," she told her security system.

When the doors parted, Legate Arin Triss escorted the man into the room and indicated one of the chairs. He waited until the ambassador sat, then seated himself.

"What can I do for you?" Em asked from across the desk after nodding politely at the ambassador.

Arin said, "Ambassador Kovitz is from the Barony Coalition. He has an item of particular value, and he wishes to have it stored here."

"The vault in your quarters is not secure enough?" she asked. The Barony Coalition was a group of five farming planets on the edge of the PAC zone. They provided a great deal of the foodstuffs used in the sector, and they traded with non-PAC entities in unregulated space as well. Barony ambassadors were treated well, everywhere they went. No one wanted to be regarded poorly by the Coalition.

"I'm sure it is," Kovitz answered smoothly. "But the item in question is rare and exquisitely valuable. A gift, you see, in some particularly tricky trade negotiations." The man was human, midforties, and handsome in a distinguished sort of way. No doubt he was quite successful in his job as ambassador. He had the pleasant and easy manner of a diplomat. Or a salesperson.

"I don't want to invade your privacy, but any item stored in the security office must be catalogued with its exact value and size, along with images to be stored in the database. For verification purposes. Also, your handprint and retina scan will be necessary for both drop-off and pickup."

"Of course," Kovitz agreed. He removed a small wooden box from a bag on his shoulder and laid it on the desk. "This is eighty-four-point-four-two grams of linnea root." He opened the box and turned it around for her inspection.

She saw three small brown lumps that looked anything but valuable. "Very good. And what is linnea root?"

"A fungus, technically. The tiniest amount will transform a tasty dish into a feat of culinary wonder."

"So it's like a truffle?" she asked.

"An excellent analogy, in that linnea is so rare, and only grows wild under specific conditions. But in terms of quality and value, truffles and linnea are as much alike as a spoon and a class-four Kiramoto luxury cruiser. There's just no comparison."

"I see." She picked up her infoboard and began to enter the item into classified inventory. Then she retrieved a scanner from her desk and recorded precise measurements, weight, and images of the linnea root. She also ran a thorough diagnostic, ensuring that the item posed no threat to the station in terms of pathogens, explosives, radioactive isotopes, or the like. Scanners at the docking bay should have caught such things, but following protocol ensured that an attack on the security office was virtually impossible.

"Eighty-four-point-four-two grams, just as you said," she

noted approvingly. The ambassador seemed to take this as praise, and gave her a charming smile. Which was fine. The last thing she needed was a disgruntled ambassador.

She took Kovitz's security data, then said, "Your item is logged in. I've assigned it number nine-nine-eight-eight-Tango-Charlie-six-five-three-seven. I will send that number to the voicecom in your quarters. When you wish to collect your item, you must give at least twelve hours of notice, and come to this office in person, unless you wish to designate a proxy at this time."

"No, not necessary." Kovitz rose and made a slight bow. "I can tell you now that I will collect it at noon, the day after tomorrow, when I meet with my trade partner. I look forward to seeing you then."

Em and Arin stood as well and returned the small bow. "Please let us know if there's anything else we can do for you, Ambassador," Em said.

"Thank you for your help, Chief Fallon," Kovitz returned, just as politely. "I can always count on Dragonfire for the best security."

So that was why he chose Dragonfire over Blackthorn, she mused as Arin escorted the man out. The ambassador and his guest would certainly have enjoyed better entertainments on the other station. *Interesting.*

Arin returned to his seat and grinned at her. "All in a day's work, huh?"

"If that's the toughest issue that comes up today, we can call it a win," she agreed.

She studied her legate. Arin was thirty-two, though his boyish grin made him look like he was in his midtwenties. As an Atalan he had particularly smooth, tanned skin and facial symmetry and bone structure that made him remarkably attractive. He wore his light-brown hair short, and his eyes were a startlingly intense shade of bright blue. His height gave him an advantage when it came to security work, and his difficult background on Atalus probably had given him the fighting skills that had qualified him for the PAC officer training school. No doubt the OTS selection board had found the civil war on Arin's homeworld a boon to its security program. Atalans lucky enough to escape were highly motivated to make a successful new life for themselves and their loved ones.

She wondered how much she could trust Arin. She'd chosen her legate personally, of course. That meant she must have faith in his skills and his trustworthiness. Since the security staff of a ship or station had its own hierarchy separate from the overall command structure, and members had to rely on one another for survival, he would be more loyal to her than to anyone else on Dragonfire. Unless he had ulterior motives. As her second, he would have been in the ideal position to make her shuttle accident look like an accident. But if that were the case, who would he have been working for? Or might he have been motivated by a desire to take over her job?

Either he was her man, no questions asked, and she could trust him implicitly, or he had some plan she needed to uncover. Whichever it was, her best course of action would be to draw him in. Keep him close.

She smiled at him conspiratorially. "How've you been holding up, Arin? No doubt the past couple days have been rough on you." With her briefly out of commission, he'd have been constantly on call or on duty.

The crispness melted away from his posture, and he relaxed into the chair. Now they were talking as comrades. "I'm doing okay. You picked a busy time to take a time out. The Emerson delegation had a big shipment of grain, and you know how tedious they can be. Always nitpicking and looking for some advantage. So that kept me on my toes. And we had a Briveen ship dock, too. Only two of them, and only for a day, but—" he made a guttural sound of frustration, "—the rituals! Just saying hello and goodbye are a ten-minute ordeal."

Em laughed. It took her by surprise because she hadn't heard her own laughter yet. She was no fan of the Briveen's exacting social rituals, either. "I'm kind of glad I got to miss that," she admitted.

Arin snorted, but he wore a reluctant smirk. "How are you doing, then? Nevitt told me your memory..."

Ah, of course he already knew. Just as well, as it saved her the trouble of explaining.

She shook her head. "Still gone. I know things about life. How to make blistercakes for breakfast, how to use the clothes processor. I know everything about the station. Specs, protocols, distance to Sarkan. I memorize information almost as soon as I see it, so clearly my memory is usually excellent. Not eidetic, but I don't forget much of anything. But as far as who I am?" She shrugged. "I know what my personnel records told me. Otherwise, I'm stuck with what others tell me. It's like the part of my brain that held all the parts of who I am and what I've done somehow managed to be the only part that got damaged."

He made a sympathetic noise. "That must be rough. I can't imagine."

"Hopefully it will come back. Brannin said my brain may find a way to rewire itself, more or less, and regain its ability to access those memories."

"Yeah, we can hope." He fell silent, then he grinned. "Otherwise, you'll never remember that you owe me a thousand cubics."

"Hah!" A thousand cubics was far more than one person would loan another in any normal circumstances. When it formed, the PAC had a hard time standardizing money, but in time, all allies agreed to base currency on the thing they all valued equally—fuel. Everyone needed orellium to power their ships, and cubic units of the mineral had proved to be the ideal measure.

"Damn. Should have gone for two hundred. I got greedy." Arin affected a look of chagrin.

"I wouldn't have believed you then, either. Actually, my instincts tell me not to trust you at all."

He laughed. "You seem like the same Em to me, memories or not. Except for the hair. I like the change. What did Wren think?"

"She seemed to like it." Thinking of her wife, Em pressed her lips together.

"Sore subject. Sorry." Now Arin looked *truly* chagrined.

"No. Not exactly. I just don't know what to make of being married to someone I don't remember. She seems great, though, as far as I can tell."

"She is. Everyone loves Wren. We always joke that Wren could make a space station out of a stick and a ball of wire."

"Mm," she murmured.

"Anyway, I was headed back to my quarters when the ambassador nabbed me. I need to get back for some food and some sleep."

"Right." He'd been on the night shift, since she had the day shift. "I'll see you later, then."

"Let me know if you need anything, okay? Really. Anything."

"Thanks, Arin." She sensed nothing but sincerity. She watched him leave her office, thinking he might be someone she could really trust. As long as he hadn't tried to kill her.

SECURING the linnea root in the priyanomine vault was almost an event all in itself. It took her ten minutes to get through the combination of identity and code checks, waiting each time for a predetermined duration. Priyanomine had a black, glassy appearance similar to obsidian's, but its remarkable durability, light weight, and nonconductivity made it the ideal material for a safekeeping device. Priyanomine could endure extremely high temperatures, as well as low- to midlevel explosions.

With the root secured, Em spent the next hour reviewing her

work logs. She'd recorded detailed information about every duty shift for every day she'd been on the station. She began with the most recent one and worked her way backward. The logs were only accessible from within her office, which she found interesting. She paid particular attention to the weeks leading up to her shuttle accident but was disappointed to find nothing noteworthy. She'd need to organize all of the events into a database so she could analyze them more quantitatively.

That would have to wait. Her logbook indicated that she was due on the outer concourse of Deck One for a daily tour. Deck One, the lowest on the station, housed Dragonfire's shops and eateries on its outer concourse. This large area of abundant commerce was commonly called the boardwalk. Guest quarters were located on the interior of the inner concourse.

She felt confident about visiting the area without letting on that, for her, it would be her first visit. She wondered, though, why she afforded that level of personal attention to the area. Surely, any one of her eighty-seven staff members could handle the task, just as they were handling the day's arrivals and departures. Deck One even had its own security office, which always had a full complement of officers on duty. Besides, security feeds would show her most everything. She had no real reason to go down there.

Yet she chose to walk the concourse with her own two legs. Clearly, the ritual was less about monitoring and more about something else. Showing her presence? Visiting the people entrusted to her care face-to-face? Interesting. Perhaps that spoke to her role here. Not just as security, but as a member of the community.

After securing her office, she rode the lift down. Her logs had not indicated which direction she usually went, so she stepped off the lift and followed the concourse to the right. Not knowing why she was there, she strolled slowly, hands behind her back, trying to look official yet relaxed. She received some nods and smiles of acknowledgement, but for the most part people ignored her as they scurried about. She saw luggage-laden travelers struggle in from Docking Bay Two and make their way down one of the bisecting hallways—which were arranged like wagon-wheel spokes on each circular deck of the station—toward the guest quarters.

A pair of giggling young children brushed against her as they ran down the boardwalk, jostling one another. A harried young father hurried to catch up to them, giving her an apologetic smile. She returned the smile and wished them a pleasant stay. Did she normally do that? It felt natural, and she decided to let those instincts guide her. If anyone reacted strangely, she'd re-evaluate that tactic.

She smelled food. Rich, meaty aromas wafted her way long before she came into view of the Bennite restaurant. A sign outside the door promised a meal that would make her feel her very best. The claim must be an honest one. Bennite cuisine was known for its hearty, restorative properties. Not surprising, since the entire planet of Bennaris was devoted to healthcare. According to the arrival and departure logs, Dragonfire hosted a steady stream of Bennite hospi-ships that traveled from planet to planet, delivering medical supplies and care.

Em enjoyed a deep lungful of enticing, savory aroma, and she made a mental note to return at lunchtime, or at least have an order delivered to her office. Her records had indicated that she ate the Bennite restaurant's food as often as not. The next establishment was a tea parlor, no doubt offering a multitude of hot beverages and pastries. She passed several clothing and supply stores, a pub, and more restaurants before she even got halfway around the concourse. She noticed an unoccupied bench across from Docking Bay Four, and took a seat to observe, checking her comport for the time.

Though many people carried personal infoboards, few carried portable voicecoms, known as comports. Conducting electronic conversations in public was considered offensively rude, unless it was time-sensitive official business. All of her security staff wore comports on their belts, along with their registered weapons. Command officers and medical staff also wore them. Very few others ever did, given the social taboo. Voicecom terminals and displays were hardly difficult to come by on a PAC station.

Em kept her eye on a cargo bay. Right on schedule, the bay doors opened and three Rescan traders stepped out, accompanied by one of her security officers. He was young and low-ranking, but wore a serious, steely expression. Em resisted a smile. No doubt the officer was determined to ensure that the traders got up to no mischief on his watch. Rescans had a reputation for a particularly cutthroat business acumen, and were often the ones that people turned to when they needed to procure goods without too many questions being asked. Oh, they certainly did their share of legitimate trade, and they were as likely to be good people as those from any other planet. But if a security chief wasn't careful, she'd soon find her station flooded with contraband and stolen goods. Not only from Rescans, but from any traders willing to take big risks for big rewards.

The steely-eyed young officer nodded at her as he passed, on his way to show the traders to their quarters. And let them know that he'd be watching them, no doubt. She chuckled to herself once they'd gone by.

Feeling lighter, she stood, only to turn when she heard a voice call, "There you are!"

She couldn't identify the man. His high-quality utilitarian pants and shirt marked him as a merchant of some sort, most likely. He was Rescan, which put her on her guard despite his friendly smile. She had nothing against Rescans per se, but their shrewd business dealings and frequently not-quite-legal methods of acquiring merchandise stood in diametric opposition to her own purposes. She had no idea if this particular Rescan was one she could trust, or not.

The Rescans simply had a different way of looking at trade than the PAC did. They weren't much for regulations, and adopted a widely laissez-faire approach to life in general. It was always wise to double- and triple-check the provenance of any items acquired from Rescan traders. Provided everything had been verified, they could pull off some amazing feats of procurement. The PAC frequently dealt with them. But carefully.

This particular fellow seemed relaxed and genuine. She stood where she was, letting him approach. Nothing about him raised her suspicion.

"Glad to see you back. We all missed seeing you the last couple days," he said.

Em judged him to be middle-aged, with average looks and physical condition. Rescans looked mostly like humans, though they had a thicker, more rugged build. Their fashions tended to be much more elaborate, though the person in front of her showed no evidence of that. He was simply dressed and groomed. His long, light-brown hair was pulled back into a low ponytail, and he regarded her warmly.

"Thank you." She waited for him to say more.

"You seem none the worse for wear, so I assume you're back to your regular self?" His blue-gray eyes seemed to convey genuine concern.

"Yes, Dr. Brash took excellent care of me. I'm good as new."

"Excellent. Any idea what caused the accident?"

Was this idle curiosity or did he have a reason to want to know? "Still under investigation, but it appears to be a simple malfunction."

In fact, the mechanical team, led by Wren, had come to no conclusions so far. But it was a safe story to circulate for the time being.

"A shame. Good thing it wasn't worse though," the man said.

"Yes," she agreed.

"Do you have a minute? Or were you off to somewhere specific?"

Em paused. Based on the question and his familiar attitude, it seemed she had some sort of relationship with him. Better to play along and figure it out. "I'm in no particular hurry."

He brightened, and the earnestness in his expression made her feel that perhaps he'd been someone that she'd trusted to some degree. There was something about him, an expectation of familiarity that suggested she'd had a friendly relationship with him.

"Glad to hear it. I have something I've been saving for you." He hitched his head back toward the way she'd come and began walking. She followed. "It came in with a shipment from the Briveen. Tools. Knives, laser cutters, and the like. But for some reason, someone had tossed this item in as well. Someone who had no idea what it was." He chortled. "You'd be amazed by the things that come to me by mistake."

He led her into a tidy storefront. Inside, the well-lit shop displayed a wide variety of curiosities and collector's items. Artwork hung from the walls and stood on shelves and pillars. The kinds of things that a person bought individually, rather than as part of a large shipment. Apparently this man handled both types of trade.

He gestured for her to sit at a small table, then moved behind the counter. He bent down, stood, and returned carrying a small, nondescript box. He sat down across from her. Opening the box, he reached in, then offered the contents to her.

"Ahh." She gently took the knife from his hand, admiring the masterfully forged little blade and the engraved handle. "An ancient Briveen protector's knife." Such knives had been custom-made and presented to a member of the protector caste once he or she came of age. Normally they were passed down generation to generation in a family as an heirloom. It was rare to find them for sale.

She fitted the first three fingers of her hand into the widely spaced holes. It made for a remarkably awkward hold. The Briveen were born with three long fingers on each hand, but after adolescence they had their short, weak arms removed and replaced with cybernetic limbs. As the only people in charted space that had evolved from reptiles, the Briveen had always been a particularly fascinating people to Em. Though adopting cybernetic limbs had catapulted their world forward in technology and standing, they maintained their caste system and a great many ancient rituals.

"You like it," the man observed, clearly pleased.

"It's wonderful," she agreed. Normally she wouldn't praise something she hoped to acquire, but there was no denying the magnificence of the piece.

"I paid for it in bulk. Breaking it out by unit, plus your ten-percent markup, makes it five hundred and fifty cubics."

Suspicion stole over her. It was a ridiculous price. "It's worth ten times that. Maybe more." She set the knife carefully into the box. If he was offering a bribe of some sort, she'd been mistaken about him. Maybe she shouldn't start trusting her instincts just yet after all.

He shrugged. "Just my standard discount for you. I'm not going to lie and say it cost me more than it did."

He always sold to her at a paltry ten-percent markup? Was she involved in some under-the-table trade? She stood and stalked to the front of the counter, needing to do something with her sudden surge of energy.

"Why sell to me so cheaply?" There was no way to know but to ask.

He seemed puzzled. "I had to catalog it into my inventory. I know you'll see that inventory report. If you saw that item and realized I hadn't offered it to you, your feelings might have been hurt."

Her feelings? For Prelin's sake, why would a Rescan trader give a flying flare about her feelings?

He interrupted her thoughts. "Are you okay? Should I call the doctor?"

She took a breath and smiled. "I'm fine, thanks. Just a little of the dizziness the doctor said I might have for a few days. It's passed." Better he think her not-quite-recovered than suspect anything close to the truth.

"Would you like some tea?" he offered.

"No, but thank you. Another time. I should get back to my rounds."

"Ah." He nodded. "Of course. Shall I have the knife delivered to your quarters?"

"I'll pick it up after my shift, and transfer the cubics then, if that's okay."

"Of course." He stood and placed the box on the countertop, gesturing for her to lead the way out of his shop.

At the doorway, she gave him a tiny bow. A slight dip of the head and shoulders, really. He was outside of the PAC hierarchy, but bowing still made for a polite sign of respect. He returned the gesture, but slightly more deeply. "It's kind of you to give me such a bargain on so beautiful an artifact." She figured a little flattery couldn't hurt.

He waved away her sentiment. "It's nothing. As I've told you before, since you've been on the station I haven't been robbed once. And you made sure that dreadful woman who attacked my accounts paid for it in kind. It's more than worth it for me to give you incentive to remain on Dragonfire, rather than moving on to another post."

Ahh. That made her feel much better. His generosity did, in fact, have a self-serving purpose, despite being completely above-board. She trusted self-interest a lot more than simple kindness. "I hope all the merchants on Deck One feel as safe as you do."

"Oh, they do, without a doubt. Everyone appreciates your personal attention. Well. Except for the ones that were bad news, but you already chased all of those out of here." He smiled at her knowingly, and she returned the smile as if she understood the reference.

"Let me know if there's anything you need." She made a note to find out his name as soon as she got back to her office.

"You bet, Chief. And let me know if there's anything *you* need." He walked back into his shop, chuckling at his joke.

THE WORKDAY PASSED QUICKLY. After collecting her new knife, Em rode the lift up to Deck Five. With the box tucked under her arm, she contemplated the day's activities. She'd discovered, with some surprise, that she could function just fine as security chief without her memory. Brannin had been correct, after all. Her instincts had proven reliable time after time, and she decided that if she leaned on them, no one should suspect she'd lost her memory.

The Rescan trader's name was Cabot Layne. It sounded like the name of a street, but it suited him somehow. His record wasn't spotless, but no trader had an immaculate record. Most importantly, it looked like he ran a clean operation on Dragonfire. Numerous people had even filed reports about how helpful he'd been. He seemed an interesting character.

Em discovered that Wren had not yet returned home, which gave her a moment of relief. She didn't know quite how to handle coming home to a spouse, and didn't think it was cowardly to be glad to avoid it for one day. The best way to handle a dicey situation was not to be in one, after all.

Once inside their quarters, Em went straight to the closet and removed a heavy gray case. She'd found it the night before, and had enjoyed perusing the contents. She set it on the bed and sat next to it. A simple handprint unlocked it, and she opened the lid. Four rows of hinged trays folded out into one single layer of weaponry. She removed the Briveen knife from the plain box and wiped it down with a cloth before placing it into an empty slot. It looked quite nice between the medieval hunting dagger from Earth and the Bennite gentleman's pocket knife. She admired the collection for a couple of minutes, then folded the trays in so that they were once again stacked. After securing the case in the closet, she considered her next move.

Dinner seemed like a reasonable course of action, but did she cook? Only one way to find out. She went to the kitchenette and opened the cooler. She saw packets of meats, vegetables, and fruits, stacked neatly according to type and date. A few ready-made meal packets lay on the shelf below. She rolled out the third drawer and found it stocked with sauces and condiments, as well as some beverage additives.

She closed the cooler and opened the pantry door. She recognized all the fresh fruits and vegetables inside, as well as the dry goods like sugar and flour. An impressive collection of spices sat to one side. But did she ever use any of them? None of the ingredients called "Cook me" to her. Maybe she didn't cook. Or maybe she needed to start doing it for her brain to make the connections. Fine. What to try?

She aimed for low-hanging fruit. Or pasta with cream sauce, as the ready-made packet said. She put the packet into the heat exchange, which recognized the label and made a soft click as it began the appropriate cooking cycle. In less than a minute, the heat-ex clicked again, and she pulled out the hot packet.

Okay. Now what? She opened another door and found dishes. She unsealed the packet and emptied the steaming pasta and sauce into a serving bowl. But it looked awfully plain, lying there. Just some noodles. They needed protein.

She grabbed a packet of chicken and opened it onto a cutting board. After chopping it into bite-sized pieces, she set the heat-ex for "grill." While the chicken cooked, she sliced an onion and added it to a bowl with some butter. After the meat came out, smelling delicious, she set the heat-ex to sauté and waited on the onion. She added the chicken and onions to the pasta, stirring it all with a spoon, and felt pleased with herself. The aroma was wonderful, and her stomach growled. Maybe she hadn't truly cooked, depending on one's definition of the word, but she'd managed to put together a meal.

With the dinner in the heat-ex to keep it hot until Wren got home, Em set the table with napkins, water, and chopsticks. Did Wren like something else to drink when she got home? Maybe some Sarkavian wine? She'd noted a few bottles of it. But so far she'd only seen Wren drink water, so she decided to stick with that.

The knife slipped off the wet cutting board and started to fall off the counter. She caught it and noticed that it wasn't badly balanced, for a kitchen knife. She hefted it in her hand, measuring its quality in a way she hadn't before. Quite good, actually. She turned from the counter, shifting her grip so that she held the knife by the blade. She took two steps and snapped her arm forward. The knife flew across the space and embedded itself half an inch into the wall. Hm. Interesting.

She retrieved the knife, returned to her previous position, and threw again, aiming for the same spot. She pulled the knife from the wall and examined the marks. Only about three millimeters apart.

She threw again, aiming for the space between the two marks. Perfect. She walked back to the kitchen with the knife in her hands, considering. She could throw a knife with the best of them. Literally. At any interplanetary contest, she'd be sure to place, if not win. But knife-throwing skills were not listed in her personnel file. They absolutely should be. Hm.

She wondered if she had other skills not listed in her file. She'd start investigating that tomorrow. Actually, it sounded fun. A thrill of enthusiasm buzzed in her abdomen. Discovering herself on her own, rather than being told by a computer or some other person, sounded like an exciting change.

The doors opened and Wren stepped into the quarters. She smiled at Em. "You cooked. It smells really good. Chicken?" She shrugged out of a greasy lab coat and turned it so that she held it by the clean inner side.

"Chicken and pasta."

Wren's smile broadened. "The ready-made doctor at work, huh? Nice." She started toward the necessary.

"Ready-made doctor?" Em busied herself with washing up the cutting board and knives.

"Nickname. You were always good at doctoring prepared packets into something much better. I'm glad to see you at it. Especially today." Wren smiled cheekily. "I'm starved."

"I don't cook from scratch?" Em asked.

Wren paused in the doorway to the bedroom, looking over her shoulder. "Not often. I mean, you can, but you like starting off with something. You always said it gave you more ideas than raw ingredients."

Wren's gaze caught on the mark on the wall and she turned back around to face Em. "Knife practice?"

"Uh. Yeah. It just seemed..." She trailed off, not knowing how to explain.

Wren laughed. "I just repaired the wall from last time the other day. Seriously, we need to put up a board for you to throw at. Every time I suggest it, you promise it won't happen again. Then it does." She shook her head with amusement. "I'll just get cleaned up. Should only take me a few minutes."

Five minutes later they sat at the table. Wren had changed into lounge clothes, but Em still wore her uniform. She didn't see a reason to change, though she'd removed her belt and secured her weapon. She felt perfectly comfortable. She did sense that she should make conversation, though, so she decided to ask about Wren's day. Seemed like a safe subject.

"How was work?" She spread a napkin over her lap.

"Busy. Had to refit a personal cruiser that had burned hard all the way here from the Terran system. They made it in three weeks and fried their engines in the process. Three weeks! Crazy, even for a high-end cruiser like theirs. I have no idea what they were in such a hurry for, but it was definitely a very *expensive* hurry."

Em wondered if she knew much about mechanics. She cast her thoughts toward engines and repairs, but failed to pull up much beyond schematics and basics. Nope. Engineering and mechanics were clearly not her thing. No talking shop about Wren's work, then.

Wren dabbed her mouth with a napkin. "What about your day? Everything go okay? Or maybe it didn't, and that was why you were throwing knives in our home?" She sent Em a teasing look.

"It was fine. Met Cabot Layne. And Arin. Several of my staff. Nevitt was just as you described." She pinched a piece of pasta between her chopsticks.

"Did anything seem familiar?"

Still chewing, Em shook her head. She swallowed. "I remember skills. My job. Knife throwing." She smirked. "But nothing about myself, or my relationships with people."

"Nothing at all?" Wren made a valiant attempt to cover her disappointment, but failed.

"No. I'm sorry."

Wren smiled brightly. "We'll figure it out. Don't worry." She took a hearty bite of her dinner.

Em appreciated Wren's optimism. She could tell that Wren wanted to be supportive and not add to Em's worries with her own feelings. Em wondered if she should start to trust Wren.

Maybe share her discoveries, such as the aberrant knife skills. Wren could be a big help in sorting things out. But Em wasn't sure yet. She needed to wait a little longer.

She didn't know what else to say, so she took a bite of pasta and chicken. The creamy sauce slid over her tongue with the perfect texture and flavor. Maybe that was why she preferred to start with packets. She couldn't imagine being able to do better on her own.

After dinner, Wren helped clean up. It felt almost companionable. Almost comfortable. Em imagined her life might have been quite nice before her knock on the head. She felt bad for Wren. It had to be hard on her, but she didn't let on. She seemed brave and stalwart, qualities which Em admired. It made sense to her that she wouldn't pick a fussy, fragile mate.

"So what did you think of Cabot?" Wren asked when they'd retired to the couch.

"I liked him. Which surprised me. He wasn't what I expected." Em told her about the knife she'd bought.

"Ahh, another for the collection. You'll need a second case soon." Wren's smile was fond and indulgent. "I've always thought we should have Cabot over for dinner. But you always say it would blur the line too much between personal and professional."

"Hm." That would have been her exact response if Wren had asked. "I suppose we could always meet him somewhere for dinner. Being out in public wouldn't cross the line."

"That sounds perfect. We'll have to do that. I've always liked Cabot. And he has the best stories."

That made Em wonder. "What do we usually do with our off-duty time? For recreation, or whatever."

Wren picked up a throw pillow and hugged it to her chest, fiddling absently with the short fringe along the side. "You don't do a lot of recreation. Not enough, anyway. You work long hours, and love exercise. You seem to really enjoy pushing your body to exhaustion. I've never understood it. Your devotion to target practice and sparring seems almost freakish sometimes." Wren grinned to soften her words. "But when I can get you to just relax, we like walking the concourse and visiting with other people. We have Arin and others over for dinner, and they invite us in return. We play card games like two-ten-jack. We go to almost all of the traveling entertainments and exhibits. But then most people here do."

Wren fell silent, her eyes unfocused and thinking. "Oh! Whenever we get a couple days off together we go to Sarkan. Visit my family, hit the beaches. You love the beach. Especially if there are water sports involved. Though sometimes we go inland to the countryside and just enjoy the sunshine and fresh air."

It did sound nice. Em felt perfectly at ease on the station, but real sunshine and breezes particularly appealed to her.

"What about my family?" Em asked. "I didn't see any listed in my file."

Wren's face saddened, which looked odd on her. "You don't have any, other than some cousins you're not close with. There was an earthquake, and they were hiking…"

"I see." It seemed a shame that she didn't have family, but she did have in-laws, so maybe she'd made herself a new family.

"I'm sorry." Wren's pale blue eyes seemed to wash out even more.

Em shrugged. "Can't miss what I don't remember."

"That might be even sadder. Especially if you never get your memories back. I can remind you of all the things we've done together. But if you lose your memories of your family, they will just be gone, like they never existed."

Put that way, it did seem pretty terrible. Em frowned. Which was worse? Missing what you had, or not knowing that you ever had it? She wasn't sure.

Wren broke into her thoughts. "You must be tired. Why don't you go shower and change?"

It was an obvious subject-changer, but Em didn't point it out. Wren was trying to help. "Sure. That sounds good."

She stood and Wren tilted her head to one side, studying her. "I'm getting used to your new hairstyle already. I think it actually suits you really well."

"Thanks. I do too."

Which was odd, since she didn't even know who she was.

2

Em exhaled slowly, taking stock of the training room. After she'd done her usual check-ins and reports, she'd locked herself into one of her designated areas on Deck Four for security drills. So far, she'd found she had superior reflexes, exceptional strength for body size, and beyond-superior skills in targeting. She already knew she could run for both speed and distance, having tested her endurance earlier that morning. She also knew she had extraordinary knife-throwing skills. The throwing target in the training room had proven just how sharp her ability was. Exceptional. More than.

All of these abilities were underreported in her personnel file. It was possible that she might have improved in one or two areas and her record had not yet been updated to reflect that, but this systematic downgrading of her skills was something else. But what?

Either she had misled the PAC about what she could really do, or someone was trying to hide her expertise. Since no PAC officer would do less than their best, she needed to figure out who would want to make her appear less exceptional. Oh, her records set her in the upper echelons of security officers, and her work history was spotless, but her true skills would mark her as a standout.

So why make her appear to be less than she was? And had she participated in this subterfuge, or was she the victim of it?

She paced the wide room, shaking out her arms and legs. She needed a sparring partner. Based on the drills she'd run herself through, she expected she could kick some serious ass. But she needed to spar against someone with significant skill, and she'd need to make sure that person wouldn't talk about it. So sparring would have to wait until she knew whom she could trust.

She picked up a towel and wiped a light sheen of sweat from her face and neck. She was tempted to do more target practice with her stinger. She'd found she enjoyed it. It was like a game, almost. Both her service weapon and the larger-yield training rifles had felt remarkably comfortable to hold.

Set to target-practice settings, the simulated bursts wouldn't hurt anyone, but allowed officers to keep their skills honed. The holster-worn stinger, a requisite part of a security officer's uniform, was a particularly lovely bit of technology. Heavy for its small size, it fit her hand like it belonged there.

Most often, a stinger's directed electrical charge was used to incapacitate rather than harm. The PAC had strict protocols about how much force was appropriate in a given situation. With a subtle adjustment, though, a stinger's output became a lethal charge, capable of stopping any living creature's heart. The stinger also had an energy-generator mode, in the event of emergencies. A remarkably clever design, to fit so many useful features in one small package.

She felt better having thoroughly run herself through stinger targeting drills. The day before, she'd been certain she could use her weapon expertly, but had felt somewhat disconnected from it. Now, as she rested her hand on the holster just in front of her hip, it felt like it belonged with her. She added three knives to the belt, for later. This, too, made her feel better. More complete, as well as more prepared. The weight of the belt felt right, anchoring her into her place in life.

She returned the heavier-firepower rifle to its place and secured it before leaving the room, logging out as she went. She required all of her training rooms to keep tabs on who had used them and for how long. Not only was it good for accountability, but she could see which of her staff were stepping up and which were slacking off. She approved of her own exactingness, as if judging another individual entirely. In a way, she felt like she and the earlier version of herself *were*, in fact, different people. She hadn't yet figured out how to merge that duality into a single identity.

Back in her office, she sat at her desk and opened her personnel files again. This time she went all the way back to OTS, digging into her academic and athletic performance class by class. The more she dug, the more intrigued she became. She had always come in second or third in her classes. Never first, and never fourth. During her four years of officer training school, she stayed in the top of the pack for her class, but never took any titles. Not even for knife-throwing.

She pushed back from her desk and ran her fingers over the short side of her hair. She'd developed a habit of that. She liked the soft, bristly feeling. The tactile sensation helped her get out of her head sometimes.

It was just that the more she found out, the more lost she felt. Every answer prompted more questions. What she really needed was someone she could trust. Someone she could work with. Nevitt was not an option. The woman clearly didn't like her and might be the person behind all this. Wren and Arin were the next-best candidates. Arin could be very helpful, while Wren had less pull at the station, and no PAC access. She was a contractor, not an officer, which limited her usefulness. But although a legate security chief had plenty of reason for loyalty, a wife had even more. So Em was stuck between utility and fealty. She shook her head. No, her choice was clear.

———

"Hey, Em. You wanted to see me?" Wren still wore her work coveralls, with her pink hair up in a tight twist. The doors of Em's security office whisked shut behind her.

Em stood from her seat at the desk. "Yes. Thanks for coming. I'm sure you're ready to relax and have dinner, but I need your help."

"I'll do whatever I can."

Em gestured to the couch, and seated herself after Wren sat. "Last night when you saw I'd been throwing a knife, you weren't surprised. I'm curious if you know how good I am at throwing."

Wren folded her hands over her knees. "Yes, I've seen you practice. Even make trick shots. You're amazing."

"See that mark on the wall?" She gestured to the spot she'd made. She pulled the three knives from her belt as she rose from the couch, whipping them at the wall in quick succession.

Thwack, thwack, thwack. The knives nested tightly together, embedded side by side into the wall. Perfectly aligned, perfectly spaced. If she'd thrown the second or third the slightest bit off, it would have glanced off one of the others and clattered to the floor. Not a trick shot, by any means, but the sign of a master. "Can you go get those?" Em asked.

Wren shrugged, walked to the wall, and pulled the knives free. She seemed curious but unsurprised as she handed the knives to Em and returned to her seat.

"So you knew I could do that?"

"Yes," Wren answered, looking increasingly puzzled.

"Did you know that my service record rates my knife throwing far below what I can actually do?"

Wren's lips parted. "Um, no. Why would your record be wrong?"

"Exactly." Clearly, she'd trusted Wren enough to expose her abilities. Which meant that either Em hadn't been in on the downgrading of her skills, or she'd had faith in Wren. With few options left to her in the pursuit of the truth, she decided to embrace her apparent confidence in her wife.

Em leaned forward. "The reason I wanted to talk to you here is that I'm certain no one can hear us. I'll need to start sweeping our quarters to make sure no one's listening whenever we've been out. Anyway, the problem I'm coming up against is that my entire service record seems to be engineered to put me among the upper echelon of officers, but not make me a superstar. I've run myself through various tests, and my ratings are all significantly higher than what's listed. It's a systematic deception, and definitely not a mistake."

Wren's eyebrows pulled together. "Why underrate you?" Then she sat up straighter. "You don't think this is related to your accident, do you?"

Smart woman. Em liked how quickly Wren had put the facts together. "I don't know. But it seems highly suspicious."

"Okay." Wren rubbed the tips of her index fingers together absently as she mentally worked through it. "So what do we do?"

"I need to know who I can trust. Ideally, an officer who knew me before the accident. For as far back as possible. Trouble is, I have no idea who that would be."

Realization lit Wren's features, making the corners of her mouth lift. "You decided to trust me."

"Yes. It seems I trusted you before, so it made you the best candidate."

Wren's smile dimmed slightly, but she nodded. "Right. Well, there's Arin. He's always been honest to a fault and I know you trusted him before."

"I considered him. He'd be an ideal ally, but since he stands to gain in the event of my death, it gives him plenty of motive."

"No." Wren's answer was immediate. "Not Arin. He's too honorable. After what he grew up with, I know he'd never hurt an innocent person. The war on Atalus still haunts him, you know. He just wants to keep people safe."

"What if I'm not, in fact, an innocent person? I might have a very shady background. Arin might have found out about it."

Wren rolled her eyes. "That's a line of reasoning you can just skip. There's no way you're involved in something nefarious."

Em wasn't convinced of that, but it was good to know that Wren felt certain.

"Arin would know if I've been downplaying my abilities. If I've been performing at a lower level than I'm capable of, that means I was in on the deception. That might be the place to start."

Wren started to say something then paused, seeming to change her mind. "That seems reasonable. Can I do anything to help?"

"Actually, yes. Could you invite him to have dinner with us tonight? Maybe down on Deck One? Someplace we've gone before, to give an appearance of life as usual to anyone who happens to be watching."

"Putting it that way creeps me out a little, but sure. Anything else?"

Em's eyes tracked to the damage the knives had made. "Do you think you could repair that wall without anyone knowing about it?"

Wren brightened. "You bet. If you want to bring me back here after dinner I can get it patched up in no time."

Em stood. "Thank you. I'm...it's good to have someone I can trust."

Wren rose to her feet, too. "I'm really glad you decided to trust me."

She turned away from the intimacy in Wren's expression,

walking behind her desk and sitting. "I'll just finish up here, and then I'll meet you in our quarters to change for dinner. Hopefully Arin hasn't eaten yet."

"I doubt it. He's a late-night kind of guy when he's on day shift. Mostly, we need to hope he doesn't have a date. There aren't too many single men on Dragonfire, so your legate rarely eats alone."

Hm. Well, that was useful to know.

ARIN PROVED to be surprisingly good company. Em and Wren enjoyed dinner with him at a cross-cultural fusion restaurant, then went to the Tea Leaf afterward. Em was surprised to find a Bennite fermented nut milk tea on the menuboard, and promptly ordered one due to how odd it sounded. Not only did it taste delicious in an oddly earthy way, it had reputed brain health benefits, including improved memory. Em considered making it her new favorite drink.

Wren laughed at her when she ordered a second cup. Apparently it was already a favorite. Well, at least that was another point in favor of trusting her instincts.

They kept the conversation light, but every so often Em found an opportunity to ask Arin a question that she hoped would give some insight into his character. He was easygoing, quick to laugh, and modest. Whenever she tried to direct him into talking about his accomplishments, he downplayed them. He'd graduated first in his class at OTS and his file had a commendation from none other than Admiral Ito, the oldest officer of the PAC military. Em wondered how he'd earned that, but when she asked, Arin seemed embarrassed. Wren changed the subject.

The three of them got a great many hellos and smiles of acknowledgement throughout the evening. It seemed they were all well liked, which Em supposed was a good thing.

Em studied the dregs of her tea while Wren told Arin about a tricky manifold coupling she'd wrangled with that day. Em only half listened, thinking about the old soothsayers who pretended to predict the future by the sediment left behind from someone's tea. Em had no tendencies toward superstition. All she saw were wet bits of leaves and a cup that needed cleaning.

"Finally I got the cover back on and it was good as new," Wren said with a chipper lilt to her voice.

Arin chuckled. "I think I would have given up long before and just ordered a new one."

"That's why you're security and I'm a mechanic," she replied. "Only the truly exceptional can work in *my* shop."

Em smiled vaguely when they glanced at her to include her in the conversation. She remained unconvinced about Arin's loyalty. They'd accomplished nothing but a pleasant evening, and that sure wasn't going to fill the blank space in her head.

She tipped her cup back onto the saucer and picked up the menuboard, putting the drinks on her account. "Arin, would you mind coming to our quarters? I'd like to talk to you about something in a quieter spot."

"Yeah, you bet. It *is* pretty noisy here." He pushed back from the table and stood, and she and Wren followed him out of the parlor.

UP ON DECK FIVE, they sat in the small, cozy living area that already seemed homey to Em. She'd made sure to do a security sweep in the quarters, ensuring their privacy from any recording devices. She'd repeat that practice regularly, and show Wren how to do it as well.

As she filled glasses with water in the kitchenette and carried them to Arin and Wren, she thought about how to start the conversation. The other two sat in the living area, she on the couch and he on Em's favorite chair. Arin was saying something that Em couldn't quite hear. Something about a recent date, from the sound of it.

As soon as Em sat next to Wren, Arin took the initiative. "I know what you want to talk about, and I don't blame you. I'm sorry the investigation is taking so long, but I've been trying to track down some details. Right now, I still can't tell you precisely what happened to your shuttle. I'm getting close, though."

"What do you know?" Em asked.

Arin nudged his water glass with his forefinger, then sank back into the chair with a sigh. His hands rested at his sides and his knees and feet were wide in a casual posture. Em saw no tension in him at all, only mild frustration.

"The accident happened because of a malfunctioning coil pack in an auxiliary generator. As you know, when a shuttle is in operation, the failsafe sends test pulses to the auxiliary systems periodically, to ensure proper functioning. One of those test pulses overloaded the coil pack, causing a circuit board to blow. Unfortunately it happened to be the particular circuit board that controlled navigation, and it caused the shuttle to ram itself into the station while the inertial dampeners were fluctuating. If you'd been farther out in space, the system would have had time to right itself. Cracking into Dragonfire like that was some damn bad luck."

Wren's expression had sharpened. This was her area of expertise, after all. "Why did the coil pack fail? That only happens when there's a factory defect or the coil pack has far exceeded its use life. And there's no way any part of any of Dragonfire's ships has gone out of spec. I personally make sure my team keeps those birds in factory-issued shape."

Arin nodded. "That's what I found out. So I've been tracking down that shipment of coil packs. Or trying to. It was easy to get the lot number from the shuttle's maintenance files, but I've had a hard time getting the shipment details. The manufacturing company was in the middle of a merger, and both companies have claimed that the other was the one responsible. I don't care about that, but it's all about the liability to them. So far I haven't been able to figure out that shipment's path from manufacture to the shuttle."

Wren huffed out an annoyed sound. "I want another look at that shuttle, and the coil pack."

Arin's gaze bounced from Wren to Em. "It's a bit tricky. I'm leading the investigation to avoid any conflict of interest. Normally you're the first person I'd ask about this kind of thing but I didn't want to put either of you in an awkward position."

Em would rather have someone she knew to be on her side squinting at the mechanics of the event. "I'll sign off on it. I trust Wren."

Arin nodded and leaned forward to sip his water. He'd probably expected that, but Wren had frozen in place with her gaze fixed on Em. She looked...touched. Yes, that's what it was. Wren reached over and wrapped her hand around Em's, giving it a gentle squeeze before letting go.

Double points for her, then. Not only had she gained an insider in the investigation, she'd managed to please her wife. Em gave Wren a sly smirk, and Wren's expression shifted to barely repressed glee.

"Should I leave you two alone?" Arin hadn't missed the byplay between them. Good thing, too, since he was her legate and she expected him to be able to pick up on things like that.

She shook her head and Wren laughed. "Just a sort of inside joke," Wren assured him.

Close enough. Arin didn't need to know how reserved she'd been with Wren up to this point.

"Anyway," Em said, steering the conversation back, "have you decided on your finding? Does it seem purely accidental?"

Arin's face smoothed out, businesslike again. "I haven't turned up anything that suggests sabotage. I haven't conclusively ruled it out, but it does seem like simply a malfunctioning piece of equipment." He fell silent, studying her. "You suspect otherwise, don't you? Why?"

Well, hell, he could read her, even when she was trying to be inscrutable. She hadn't anticipated that. He must know her very well indeed. "Probably just paranoia, given the state of my memory," she hedged.

"That would make sense, but I feel like there's more to it."

He had good instincts, too. She might have chosen her legate too well. But then, if he'd had some part in engineering the crash, he'd have reason to suspect that she would consider foul play. How could she test his loyalty?

"The truth is, without my memories, I'm just not entirely sure who I can and can't trust." She held her palms upward and spread her fingers in a gesture of earnestness.

He rubbed his hand over his cheek, looking thoughtful. "Yeah, I can't imagine what that's like. What can I do to help?"

"You seem to know me well. Who did I have questions about before the accident?" In other words, whom might she have suspected to be up to something?

His gaze floated upward toward the ceiling. "Nevitt's hostility toward you never completely added up. You understood her initial reaction to your appointment as security chief, but after you proved yourself, you expected her to thaw out." He paused, apparently plumbing the depths of his memory. "There are several traders who come here on a regular basis that you have us watch extra hard. There are a couple officers you keep an eye on because of incidents in their past, but it's nothing to do with you personally." He shrugged, out of answers.

This was getting her nowhere. He was too good at his job for her to get at his intentions with anything but a full frontal assault. She decided to go with the element of surprise. She stood, and with a quick motion, grabbed the three knives from her belt, throwing them in quick succession at the wall.

Arin stood slowly, his mouth slightly open. Wren watched with interest.

"Go check those out," Em told him.

Arin walked over, seeing the tight formation of the knives. He reached out and pulled them free with a hard yank, then handed them back to her.

"Did you know I could do that?" Em asked.

"I've never seen you throw that fast, or quite that close together, but yeah, I know you're good."

"Better than my record indicates," she clarified.

Arin showed no surprise. "Yeah."

Relief washed over her. If he knew that, then she must have known she could trust him. Thank goodness for her knife throwing. Now she had two allies.

She could work with that.

―――

"Report." Captain Nevitt eyed Em with the look of distaste she'd become accustomed to.

Em ran through the morning security briefing. The usual rundown of the day's scheduled comings and goings, along with some petty misbehavior during the night shift. Her staff had handled it all perfectly.

Nevitt acknowledged the report with a lift of her chin. Instead of dismissing Em as she'd expected, the captain said, "I need to see you in my annex." Without waiting for a reply, Nevitt stood and strode across ops to the doorway at one side. The door opened and Em followed her into the captain's annex.

When the door closed behind them, Nevitt sat and indicated that Em should do the same. From behind her desk, the captain studied Em, not quite frowning, but almost.

The small room was decorated sedately in shades of burgundy and charcoal. The standard-issue desk and chairs ate up most of the space. The only other noteworthy features were a low shelf filled with infoboards and a window that was more than a porthole and less than a starport.

Nevitt spoke abruptly. "Any improvement with your memory?"

"No. So far I haven't remembered anything about myself. Everything not directly associated with my identity is completely intact, but I'm sure Brannin already told you that."

"Yes. He also said that your condition could prove to be permanent." Nevitt's expression gave nothing away.

Em acknowledged the fact with a small nod. "I have an appointment to see him this afternoon."

"During your shift?" Nevitt's tone sharpened.

"Doctor's orders. He said it was the only time he could manage it." The chief medical officer had the authority to countermand the captain's orders, when he judged that health matters trumped all else. Besides the doctor, Em was the only other person on the station who could countermand a captain's order. In the case of a security crisis, Em could take full control of the station. Which was precisely why a captain preferred to select his or her own security chief.

Nevitt narrowed her eyes, staring at Em for long moments that would be uncomfortable for most people. Finally, she spoke again. "I've been informed that a Briveen ship is on its way to Dragonfire. They're experiencing a malfunction in their navigation system."

"I'll add the arrival to the schedule and assign an officer as their liaison."

"I want you to handle that personally. One of the Briveen is a high-ranking official and I want to be sure that they feel they've been properly received."

Oh, scrap. Em kept her expression neutral, but dealing with a Briveen group was as appealing as driving a nail through her hand. It wasn't that she didn't like the Briveen. But the most basic thing, such as saying hello, became a ritual that took at least ten minutes, and often longer, depending on which ones were necessary. Oh, and *woe* to the officer who did not perform the ritual properly. That would require an atonement and apology ritual.

Em simply nodded in compliance because there was nothing else she could do.

"Good. I'll send you their ETA and the ship's registry. It will be up to you to organize the repairs." For once, Nevitt's expression softened. She didn't quite smirk, as she was too regal for that. But she knew exactly what she was demanding of Em, and how unpleasant it would be.

Em kept her tone brisk and professional. "Excellent. Thank you. Is there anything else I can do for you?" She wasn't about to let Nevitt think she'd scored one on her.

"No, that's all. The doctor will update me if he discovers anything I should know about during your appointment." She paused. A normal captain would inquire about Em's general well-being. "Dismissed."

Em stood and bowed, and Nevitt returned the gesture from a seated position. A tiny slight, but not technically impolite, by PAC standards.

On the way to her office, Em bristled. Nevitt must really hate her to stick her with a Briveen official during a time that was presumably already difficult for her. What was the point of all that animosity? It wasn't like Em had appointed herself to Dragonfire. An admiral had done that, for no reason Em had been able to discern thus far. Nevitt's pique should have been directed toward the admiral, but she couldn't risk that. Instead, she clearly enjoyed complicating Em's life.

Fine. It would be boring and tedious, but Em would do her job flawlessly. Once in her office, she updated the schedule with the Briveen ship's details and requested Arin's assistance for the arrival. Having the top two security officers greet them would certainly look good, and if they liked Arin, she might be able to excuse herself from a ritual or two. She smirked. The benefits of authority worked in a downward trajectory, and being the second most senior officer had its perks.

She raked her fingers through her hair, shrugging off the interaction with Nevitt. Fortunately, her duties ensured that she only crossed paths with the captain once or twice per day. Now she could get down to work.

First, she ran through her mechanical checks, ensuring the proper performance of all sensors and security subroutines. Then she went through her non-urgent messages. She liked the feeling of efficiency as she worked through her morning work ritual. The thought made her pause, wondering if the Briveen got a similar feeling from their customs. It was something to think about. Later. When she didn't have work to do. She was booked up for today.

She made her boardwalk rounds early, adjusting for the arrival of the Briveen. She nodded hello and exchanged pleasantries with the shopkeeps and maintenance workers who kept an eye out for her on the boardwalk. She peeked into Cabot Layne's shop but he was busy showing some sort of instrument to a customer. He gave her a wave though, before she moved on.

"Hey, Chief." An adolescent Atalan girl grinned at her. She was twelve or thirteen, and all elbows, knees, and teeth. Em smiled, recognizing the awkwardness of the age. In spite of her gangliness, the girl had enviably smooth, naturally tan skin and huge violet eyes, as well as a crop of long brown curls. Atalan genetics had a lot to recommend them. Whenever the girl burst out of her awkward cocoon, she would be stunning.

Em didn't recall her own awkward adolescence, though she was sure she'd had one. For once, her memory loss didn't seem like such a terrible thing.

"Hey, sport," Em answered playfully, going with her instinct.

The girl rolled her eyes, but her smile didn't dim. "That's the worst one yet. What age do I have to be before you'll just call me by my name?"

"Fifty-two."

The girl rolled her eyes again, giggling.

"Tell you what," Em said in an I'll-make-you-a-deal sort of way. "Get top marks in all your subjects this term and I'll think about it."

The girl pouted thoughtfully. "I earned seconds and thirds last term. I could probably get some firsts if I studied extra. I don't know about *all* firsts though."

"I'll sweeten the deal," Em offered. "Get top marks this term and I'll give you a student internship in security." Could she do that? Did that exist on Dragonfire? What the hell. She was the chief, so she'd make it exist, if it didn't already. Maybe the girl wouldn't be at all interested, anyway.

But the girl's jaw dropped. "Seriously? Would you teach me to fight?" Her eyes glowed with excitement.

"I would teach you self-defense, as well as some methods to subdue, if your parents agreed to the internship."

"Oh, they would!" The girl bounced, hopping around in an ecstatic circle. "I'm sure of it!"

Her antics caught the attention of a boy about the same age, who approached them. "What's up, Nix? Is there a sale on holovids?" He nodded to Em. "Hey, Chief. Cool hair."

Em nodded back. "Thanks, Ratboy." She froze, horrified. Prelin's ass, what kind of thing was that to say? Who called a kid Ratboy? But the boy laughed and flashed two fingers, which Em interpreted as the latest way of saying something akin to "cool."

Huh. She got along with kids and they liked it when she called them names. That was certainly interesting. She'd have to ask Wren about that later. And do some studying up on the children of the station. Kids would be a lot harder to fool than adults. They didn't respect the same boundaries and demanded more.

"You should add some color to it," Nix suggested. "Like some bright blue and purple. That would look really good on you."

Actually, Em liked that idea. "I'll have to think about it. Maybe I will. For now, I need to finish my rounds. Stay out of trouble, all right?"

They laughed and both flashed her the hand sign. She considered returning the gesture, but thought better of it. She gave them a wave instead. No sense in making herself look like an old person trying to be young and trendy. She might lose her credibility with these kids.

She felt oddly chuffed about her encounter with the teens. For some reason, it pleased her that youth on the station knew and liked her. That must mean she was doing a good job. They saw her as someone to like and look up to, rather than fear and avoid. She felt really good about that. She made a mental note to check into creating a program for kids, if there wasn't one already. She hadn't come across anything like that so far, so she suspected there wasn't. Getting kids involved in their community could only be a good thing, and they could learn some useful skills as well.

AFTER ROUNDS she had a quick lunch in her office and got herself to Docking Bay Three. Arin stood beside her, looking solemn. Once the four Briveen disembarked, the elaborate bows, gestures, and pro forma responses ensued.

Nothing about the greeting ritual was that terrible, really. It was just so *long*. And exacting. The Briveen official, Honorable First Son Gretch of the House Arkrid, seemed pleasant enough. The other Briveen, of lesser castes, remained quiet behind him. She and Arin gave them all a brief tour of the parts of Deck One that they'd be using during their stay, since they'd declined to visit their quarters on Deck Four just yet. It turned out that Gretch had been on Dragonfire before, but the others hadn't.

After the tour, they took their leave of the Briveen outside the restaurant that catered to their people. Their flaring nostrils indicated their rapture at the scent of mandren meat—a delicacy from Briv that few offworlders could tolerate.

As the only PAC species descended from reptiles, the Briveen were unique compared to what they called the "simian" species, which included humans, Bennites, Sarkavians, and everyone else descended from primates. None of the species in question considered it a derogatory phrase, and in fact, many had adopted it into their own vernacular.

The somewhat dragonlike people had an acute sense of smell, far superior to that of any other sapient species. They had fewer facial muscles, which resulted in a much smaller range of facial expressions, so they'd evolved to communicate with one another by emitting scents that corresponded to emotions. Most of them were pleasant enough, but a few of the more passionate aromas were ones a wise simian avoided. A weaker sense of smell and a lack of many offworlding Briveen meant that few non-Briveen learned to interpret the smell communication properly anyway.

After the goodbye ritual, which Gretch graciously shortened to a mere ten minutes of gestures, bows, and statements, Em and Arin went to her office.

In the lift, Arin let out a long sigh. "Glad that's done. I've always found the Briveen perfectly cordial, but it's draining to be around them."

"The rituals can be tough," Em agreed. "And if you get something wrong, there's the teeth clicking." The sound could mean disapproval, frustration, or irritation, but never meant anything good. The Briveen took their rituals *very* seriously.

"Well, yeah, that. But also the way they look."

"Really? I think they're lovely. Their scales come in such brilliant colors, and most of them have that two-tone color shift. That bothers you?"

He shifted from one foot to the other. "Not really. It's their eyes. They don't, you know, blink a lot. Makes me feel like they're staring. Like they disapprove of me."

Em laughed. "I guess. I never thought about it that way. I like looking at them. Their faces are…I don't know, almost majestic. Stoic."

Arin shrugged. "Maybe it's their lack of expression that unnerves me. I mean, I know it's just how they are, and I don't hold it against them…" He trailed off, looking embarrassed.

"Yeah, I get it. We're used to people who smile or frown or glare. They don't do much of that. But imagine how much harder it was back before the PAC had ironed out an official pidgin language. We have it pretty easy, comparatively."

"Yeah, we do." He bit his lip. "I didn't mean that I dislike the Briveen or anything. I do like their scales," he added sheepishly. "And they have awesome cybernetic arms. I especially like it when they don't match their scale color and just go with metal. That always looks wildly impressive." His words came in a rush of explanation.

"Relax. I know you're not racist. I think if you spent more time with people from Briv, you'd become more accustomed to their uniqueness." Her lips twisted into a slow grin. "So to help you out with that, I'll let you be their primary contact."

He sighed, smiling ruefully. "I walked into that. Fine. You need time for your info gathering, anyway."

She sent him a warning glance. She hadn't secured the lift, and it could have a monitoring device. He nodded his understanding.

"They should be fine for now. Their meals take a while, with the giving of thanks ritual and all. The mechanical team has already started on their shuttle. It's an off-the-line cruiser class, so that should be an easy fix. In the meantime, I want to do a little sparring in the training room."

"Sparring?" He clearly hadn't expected her to say that.

"Make sure I'm up to par, after the accident and all." She sent him another meaningful glance.

"Right. Sure. If you're certain you're up to it."

She absolutely was. But she only said, "I'm sure."

———

"Again." Em stood sideways, ready for anything.

Arin didn't move to strike her this time, but to trap her. A better strategy, since she'd evaded or rebuffed every one of his attacks. She was extremely strong for a woman her size, but he was stronger.

She slipped away, refusing to give him a shoulder, an elbow, a wrist to grab. He went for her feet, forcing her to the ground. Again, a better strategy than going toe-to-toe with her, where she could evade any of his attempts to strike.

She resisted the urge to throw a punch, which would give him the grip he needed to grapple her and force her to submission. She kept herself in check until she saw her opportunity, grabbing his elbow, extending his arm, and twisting herself around onto her back. She started cranking his arm back at the joint, letting physics do the work that pure muscle power couldn't.

Arin smacked the floor and she released him. They both got to their feet, breathing hard.

"Are we done?" Arin asked, taking a swig from his water bottle. Em considered him from an esthetic standpoint. Not only did he have a handsome face, he had broad shoulders, a slim waist, and lots of muscle. For her purposes, he was a well-built fighting machine, but from a more objective perspective, it was no wonder he was one of the most eligible singles on the station.

"I think so." She grabbed a towel and wiped her forehead. They'd been at it for nearly an hour. There'd been no doubt from the start that though he was an excellent hand-to-hand fighter, she outmatched him in every skill set. She compensated for her inferior strength by using his own strength against him. She could anticipate moves before he made them, based on his posture and balance. Every time he tried to strike her, she'd latch on and force him down or off-balance. She used precision hits and obscure stress points. She had all the skills, and she knew how to fight dirty, too.

"The question is—" she tossed the towel to a bench that sat along the wall of the training room, "—have you seen me fight like this before?" Her blood sang with the glory of the fight. She felt nearly invincible.

"No. Not like this. You've beaten me before, but not every time. That means you were throwing matches, doesn't it?" He didn't seem offended, just bewildered.

"Seems like it. I have no idea why."

"What's your target accuracy?" he asked.

"Ninety-eight-point-three percent."

His lips puckered in a silent whistle. "Your record says ninety-two percent."

His was eighty-eight. An excellent rating. But nothing like hers.

"You should have been top of your class." He rolled his shoulders, stretching the muscles after the workout.

"Yep. But I wasn't. I was always right up there among the best, but never received the top scores. The question is why. Did I suddenly improve after school, or was I intentionally keeping my scores down?" She sat and adopted a yoga pose to stretch her back.

"How could you improve that much, so fast? And why would you sabotage your own grades?" He bent at the waist, stretching his legs.

"Rapid improvement wouldn't explain why my current records aren't accurate. I think there's some systematic effort to keep me from looking exceptional." She shifted into another pose, stretching her hips and thighs.

"For what purpose? You don't want to get too much responsibility? You don't want to overshadow someone else? You want to stay below the radar? What?"

She paused between poses. "That last one. Not wanting to stand out and get noticed too much. That seems to fit." She pursed her lips, running the idea through her mind. "Maybe I didn't want someone to find me? Someone from my past?"

Arin sat on the bench, leaning against the wall and stretching his legs out in front of him. "Maybe. But how would you find out who, and why, if that's the case? You don't have any family, do you?"

"No, not really." But maybe that wasn't as accidental as it had seemed. Had she been hiding from someone for decades? Someone who'd been after her family? "I'll have to look into it."

"Let me know if there's anything I can do to help."

"Thanks, Arin. I will. And thanks for..." She waved a hand from her to him, then around to indicate the space. "All this."

His face lit up. "You bet! It's good motivation for me to train harder." He stood. "I'm going to go to my quarters and shower, then put on a fresh uniform. I don't want to offend the Briveen with my sweat stink."

"Very thoughtful of you." She wasn't sweaty enough to need a shower, but she did have an appointment with Brannin to get to. She put their towels in the processor before locking the room up.

"Keep me posted on the Briveen," she said as they parted ways.

"You bet. And keep me posted on what you turn up."

"I will." With a sigh, she headed to the infirmary.

"Look up," Brannin Brash's soft, cultured voice instructed. Em looked up as he shined a light into her eyes.

"Now down." She cast her eyes to the floor.

"Left." He peered into her eyes intently. "Now right." He took a step back, slipping the tool he held into the pocket of his lab coat.

"See anything?" Em sat sideways on the techbed with her legs dangling over the edge. She'd been poked, prodded, scanned, and had offered up various fluids for inspection.

"A healthy young woman in her prime," Brannin confided, as though delivering bad news. He was pretty good at deadpan humor.

"Nothing to worry about?" she pressed. "Anything that indicates a change in my brain?"

Now he looked regretful. "The swelling in your brain has disappeared and you're the picture of health. But there's nothing to indicate any particular regenerating activity." He hurried on. "Not that that means anything. I can't *see* memories, or the actual mechanism that conveys them. Your past may yet return to you."

"What's the statistical likelihood? Surely you must know that."

His expression became guarded. "I don't like to talk about statistics in a case like this. There are too many variables that can affect the outcome. Your case is unique, given the specificity of the memory loss and the nature of your wound."

"Percentage." She set her jaw and gave him a steely look.

He sighed. "From a purely statistical standpoint, I'd assess the likelihood of memory return to be twenty-three percent."

"Twenty-three percent," she repeated.

"Yes. But as I said, your case is unique. Statistics don't always tell the whole story."

"Right." She slid off the techbed and reached for her belt, which Brannin had asked her to remove so that the stinger's energy pattern wouldn't affect her scan results. She felt better with its comfortable weight around her hips. "Anything else?"

He put his hand on her forearm. "I'd like you to speak with Gray."

Her brain clicked the information into place. "Grayith Barlow. Station psychiatrist and counselor." She hadn't met him in person yet but she'd committed all officers' names and faces to memory. She'd also begun working through the shopkeeps and the families of officers and shopkeeps. With a complement of seven hundred eighty-three people, it was taking Em time to memorize everyone. A couple more days and she should have it down.

"That's right."

"Why?" She didn't love the idea of talking to a psychiatrist. She wasn't about to spill all of her suspicions and activities, and tiptoeing around the things she didn't want to divulge would take effort.

"Well, first to ensure that you're handling recent events as well as you seem to be." When Em started to speak, he cut her off. "I know, you say you're fine. But I have a duty to the station to be sure of that. You're the chief of security, and we can't afford to have you going off on a mad rampage or something." His lips twitched, and was that a twinkle in his eye? It was, dammit. He really seemed to think he was very amusing.

"More importantly," he continued, cutting her off again, "he might have some ideas about prodding your memory. Associative therapy, perhaps, or even hypnosis."

The idea of hypnosis set off a huge red alarm in her mind. No way she'd let that happen. But maybe Grayith Barlow could be of help in some other way.

"All right," she agreed. "I'll see him. Once, at least. We'll see how that goes."

"It's a start. When I hear what he has to say, we can go from there. If it's necessary, I'll order you to regular sessions. This is something you need to take seriously." He stared her down, proving he had some iron underneath his charming bedside manner and dubious humor.

"Understood." She couldn't hold it against him. He was just doing his job, and she respected that.

"Good! Then you're free to go wrangle pickpockets and thwart conspiracies." The humor was back in his eyes again.

"You're an odd one, Doctor," she told him on her way to the doors, trying to figure him out.

He chuckled. "That's not the first time you've said that." He gave her a small bow, which she returned before taking her leave. Before she even made it to her office, her comport chirped. When she stepped off the lift, she had an appointment with Gray Barlow for the next day. Clearly, Brannin was not one to waste time. She wasn't surprised.

―――――

The Briveen ship had received its repairs. The official and his friends were ready to leave the station, having been on board Dragonfire barely long enough for an extended lunch and some shopping. At Arin's notification of their imminent departure, Em met them at the docking bay.

She bowed to the official with her arms raised, palms inward, in the proper Briveen fashion. "Honorable First Son Gretch of the House Arkrid, it has been our honor to serve as your hosts during your brief stay. Can we not tempt you to remain longer?" She took a single step back, then nodded once.

"Security Chief Emé Fallon, Legate Arin Triss, it is we who are honored by your aid and hospitality. House Arkrid hopes to repay your kindness one day, should you ever be in need. We must depart, as we have a schedule to keep and business to attend, but we shall well remember Dragonfire Station's esteem and respect."

Em smelled fresh-cut grass and lemons as the official and the others returned her bow, made several arm gestures, and bowed again. A hint of something sweet sneaked in, and a small shift in Gretch's facial muscles indicated amusement.

"And we'll remember the excellent mandren meat, too," he added.

Em chuckled. Gretch had deviated from the ritual with that statement, proving he had a sense of humor, and perhaps was not as devoted to the traditional ways as most Briveen. She continued the ritual though, taking a personal card from her belt and handing it to him. It listed her name, rank, position, and post, serving as a way to contact her in the future. He handed her his own card in kind.

"My respects to you, Honorable First Son Gretch of the House Arkrid. May the sun shine on your scales, and may your clutches be many," she intoned respectfully. Wishing a guy lots of kids seemed like a strange goodbye to her, but the Briveen took breeding seriously. In fact, only the breeding caste was permitted to reproduce, to ensure the genetic health of the species.

"My respects to you, Security Chief Emé Fallon, Legate Arin Triss. May your leave time be plentiful and your sector of space free of deadly asteroids."

She laughed outright that time. He'd changed the wording again. He made a snuffling laugh sound and, with a casual wave, boarded his cruiser.

The docking-bay door closed and locked, and the launch sequence began. That left only Em and Arin in the bay.

"That was unexpected," Arin remarked, grinning.

"Yup. I bet he'd be fun to know," she agreed.

"Chances are he'll be back here at some point."

"I'll put a flag on his name in the system, to make sure I hear about it. So where are you off to now?" she asked.

"Deck Two. A little minor vandalism. Either an accident or some kids, probably. We'll see. You?"

Good question. She'd done her rounds early, and the Briveen hadn't required as much of her time as she'd expected. "Back to my office. I'll check in with all departments and go from there."

"Let me know if anything comes up." A lift of his eyebrows communicated his double meaning.

"I will."

She took a long route back to her office, taking time to identify as many of the passing faces as she could. She tried to conjure memories of herself next to a certain shop or near that pylon to the left, as if her brain were a computer she could use to access a file that had been moved to another location. Her processor grinded away at it, but nothing turned up.

She wished she could dredge up just one shadowy memory. Something that would be proof that her entire past hadn't been erased forever. Anything to give her some hope. The idea of forging forward with no knowledge of what lay behind her made her feel as if she'd been trapped in a service conduit, with inadequate lighting. Unable to go back or to call for help.

There was no sense in belaboring it, though. She smoothed her hands down her uniform, brushing over her belt. Turning her thoughts away from her past, she switched mental gears. If she couldn't find her personal history through her own memories, she'd pull it up on the computer. Maybe some research would reveal whether someone had a grudge against her family. One way or another, she'd put the pieces together.

SURPRISINGLY, her personal records said little about her family. Her mother, Maria Lin, had been a personal accountant. Her father, Reg Fallon, had been a mechanical engineer. They'd lived their lives on Earth, moving from country-state to country-state every few years for Reg's work. They were nice-enough looking, but not remarkable. She didn't notice any resemblance to either of them, but since her own appearance was fairly unremarkable as well, she could see being their daughter. Their faces looked like those of complete strangers, though.

She'd had an older brother named Marco. He and their parents had been hiking through a national park that was full of craggy rock formations and sheer cliffs. A surprise earthquake had hit. Not a big one, but big enough. Their bodies were found at the bottom of a ravine. Only weeks later, Em had started OTS.

Her grandparents and aunts and uncles had all gradually died off since then. She had a couple cousins in Japan, and one in England. Apparently her people didn't care to leave Earth. Except for her.

That was the extent of her family history. Her personnel files said even less. She didn't seem to be the sentimental sort, either. She had some photos and a few mementos here and there from places she'd visited. Mostly stuff she'd done with Wren.

She owned nothing on Earth. After her parents had died, their assets had been liquidated and deposited into her accounts, which explained why she owned so many cubics. Everything she owned was here on Dragonfire, which meant she had no additional family records anywhere.

She let her head drop back and pushed her chair away from her desk, giving herself a good shove with her feet so she could spin in slow circles. Her final options were to dig through old voicecom files for any official records or unofficial mentions, and to track down those cousins. She'd rather not look for the cousins. There must be a reason she didn't have a relationship with them, and whatever that reason was, she didn't want to upset the balance by blundering around trying to find them. No, as tedious as it would be, she needed to plow through the records. At least for that, she could enlist Arin's help. She knew he'd be glad to do something.

Later. She was already ten minutes past her shift end. She needed to get home. She'd promised Wren she'd make dinner.

3

"That was delicious. Thank you." Wren stood and began clearing the dishes. When Em rose to help, she waved her off. "I'll get it. Why don't you change while I clean up? I thought we might watch a holo-vid tonight."

"A holo-vid?"

"One of your favorites." Wren didn't look up as she began washing the dishes. "I thought it might...you know."

Help jog her memory. Sure, why not give it a try? Anything was worth a shot. "Okay. I'll go take a shower, then."

"No rush," Wren called after her.

In the shower, Em traced the tattoo on her stomach. Doing so had become something of a ritual. She wondered about the people she'd attended school with. Had they known her real abilities, or had she not yet become exceptional? Maybe she should contact some of her better friends from her class in OTS. It never hurt to catch up with an old pal. Though if the pal wanted to reminisce about old times, Em might be at risk. She'd have to think that through before contacting anyone.

She took her time showering, letting the hot water work some of the tension out of her muscles. She was glad her quarters had a hydro-shower. They'd gone out of fashion for a while, due to the space they took. Sonic and chemical showers had become more popular, particularly on spacecraft, where room had to be carefully considered. But she had a hydro in her quarters, and had found she took great pleasure in the heat and the steam.

Feeling more relaxed afterward, she slipped on a soft shirt and pair of pants and toweled her hair in front of the mirror. She took a moment to study the face that was becoming increasingly familiar. With the new hairstyle, she certainly looked more distinctive. More like she expected to look. More edgy. Less fussy. At least, the longer hair had *felt* fussy.

"A good shower does wonders, doesn't it?" Wren had finished cleaning up and sat on the couch, fiddling with a holo-projector. She'd already changed into lounge clothes, and let her hair down. Em admired the shade of pale pink Wren wore, which complemented her eyes and fair skin nicely.

"Mm," she agreed as she joined Wren on the couch. "Much better."

"Tough day?"

"Busy," Em answered. "A lot to keep up with, because of the Briveen arrival. Plus doing my personal research." She'd already swept the quarters to ensure no one could be listening to their conversation, so she felt confident about speaking freely.

"Well, since I didn't have to actually see the Briveen, and the repair was so simple, it barely affected *my* day at all." Wren sent her a taunting look.

She pretended to scoff. "That's because your job is easy and mine is hard."

"Easy!" Wren affected an expression of outrage. "I'd like to see you crack open a nav system and repair it in thirty minutes flat." She lifted her chin and looked down at Em condescendingly. "It's not about being easy. It's about being damn good at what I do."

Em laughed and Wren joined her. It felt good to laugh together.

"I saw that the *Onari* will be docking here for a few days," Wren said.

"Yes. Some scheduled maintenance to keep it within regulations, as well as several acquisitions meetings." Em hadn't paid particular attention. A Bennite hospi-ship was nothing to worry about.

"That ought to be fun."

"Why? The maintenance doesn't look like anything out of the ordinary. Just the routine stuff for a ship that sees a lot of high-speed and long-distance travel."

"Not the ship," Wren corrected. "The crew. They're favorites around here. The *Onari* isn't like other hospi-ships. It's more… well, I don't want to say renegade. I guess I'd say independent."

"Why, what do they do?"

Wren pursed her lips thoughtfully. "They aren't corporate. They aren't supremely proper, and they're *not* driven by profit."

Okay, well, that did sound different.

Wren explained, "The captain and CMO, Dr. Jerin Remay, has organized her ship and crew to help the underprivileged. The crew works for way less than the going rate, sometimes for free, on those worlds. And they all have unique backgrounds."

"So I should be on the lookout for them?"

Wren laughed. "No, nothing like that. I mean they all have personal histories that made them want to do charitable work. They're great people, nobody to worry about. Jerin only recruits the best and the most trustworthy."

"How do they stay in operation?" The entire Bennite homeworld was organized around providing healthcare, making Bennites incredibly specialized. They were also known for being very cubic oriented. "I can't imagine a hospi-ship being allowed to lose money."

"That's true," Wren agreed. "Jerin has several sources of private funding, as do some of her crew. She also does a fair bit of pricy elective work. The ridiculous prices for that sort of thing helps fund the altruistic stuff."

"I see. Very commendable." Em wondered what the crew would be like.

"Yes. They tend to be very popular wherever they go. It doesn't hurt that she has some premiere scientists on board, either. For example, the cyberneticist is at the top of her field."

"I look forward to meeting them."

"Glad to hear you say that. Endra will be joining us for dinner tonight. Maybe some of her friends, too." Wren's eyes lit with enthusiasm.

"Endra? Sarkavian, I'm guessing from the name?"

"Yup. She's the *Onari*'s lead systems engineer. She and I have been friends since we were teenagers. You two have always gotten along great."

"Then I'm sure I'll like her." So far Em hadn't found a single thing that her knock on the head had changed about her likes and dislikes.

They fell into a companionable silence for several minutes. Em almost felt downright domestic, and she was surprised by how comfortable it was.

"So what's this holo-vid?" she asked.

"It's *Widow's Sword*. A woman's husband is killed in the line of duty, and she tracks down the killer, both for vengeance and to complete her husband's last case. She also teams up with a handsome mercenary with a heart of gold, and finds new love." Wren sighed dramatically. "Something for everyone."

It did sound good to Em, especially the murder and vengeance stuff. "Right after her husband dies? Sounds kind of cold."

"Nahh. It takes years. The killer's a powerful guy and she has to work a long time to get to him."

"Well, that sounds okay then. But now you've told me all about it. Are you sure we need to watch it?"

Wren leaned over and nudged her with an elbow. "We've watched it dozens of times. It's still good." She straightened, but didn't scoot away again. Em didn't mind. She'd begun to feel quite comfortable with Wren, who never pushed or asked anything of her.

"If you say so. Do we have movie snacks?"

Wren's eyes lit. "Yes! Actually." She jumped up, ran to the kitchenette, and ran back, all in just a few seconds. She dropped a paper sack tied with a green ribbon into Em's lap and kept another one for herself.

Em opened the sack to find an assortment of sugar dates, figs, and nuts. Sweet and salty, mixed together. Perfect. "Thanks."

"You bet," Wren answered around a mouthful of snack mix. She leaned forward and pressed a button, having already queued up the holo-projector.

A three-dimensional image snapped to life above the long, flat surface of the projector, with a black background behind it. A two-foot-tall woman began walking across the table, and Em snuggled back into the couch cushions, eager to enjoy the show. She felt Wren doing the same, and her right shoulder pressed against Wren's left. It felt...not quite domestic. More like cozy.

They spent the next two hours watching murder, mayhem, awesome fight scenes, and some touching romance. She hadn't been sure about that part of the story when Wren described it, but it turned out to be tastefully done. Not even a shred of histrionic angst, which suited Em perfectly. During the final scene, where the heroine and her new love end up together, Wren, probably unconsciously, had reached for Em's hand. It didn't feel as weird as she'd have expected, and the longer their hands remained clasped, the more natural it felt.

When the vid ended and the projection turned off, Wren sat up, gently tugging her hand away. She looked embarrassed and unsure. Em didn't want her to feel that way, but didn't know what to say.

"What did you think?" Wren asked in a chipper voice.

"I loved it. No wonder it's one of my favorites."

Wren smiled, looking satisfied. She didn't ask if it had prompted Em to recall anything. They both knew Em would have said so immediately. But Wren didn't look regretful. She seemed relaxed and happy. She looked very pretty, actually.

Em stood. "I suppose I should get to bed. I need to get a lot done before my appointment with Gray in the morning."

Wren nodded. "Plus you had a busy day." She stood and began arranging the couch for her to sleep on. Em felt a pang of guilt. Wren was still sleeping on the couch in her own home.

"Why don't—" The words stuck in her throat and she coughed. "Why don't you forget the couch?"

Wren froze, her eyes wide. Then understanding dawned and she looked hurt for a split second before nodding, not meeting Em's eyes. "If you're sure you're comfortable with me sleeping in there with you."

Oh. Damn. She thought I meant more than sleeping. Em felt bad about the misunderstanding, however fleeting. Wren's hurt look still stung, though it had only been there for a moment. Em felt a surge of protectiveness.

She stepped forward and put her arms around Wren, who hesitated, then hugged Em back fiercely. Wren pulled her upper body back enough to peer into Em's face. Em saw loss, fear, and desperate hope all twined around one another. And so much love.

Well, what the hell? She's my wife. Impetuously, Em put her hand on Wren's neck and pulled her in for a kiss. It didn't feel like any kiss she could recall, but it felt right.

Holding hands, they went to the bedroom together. No one would be sleeping on the couch anymore.

Em took her morning run, then did her morning report in ops control. Captain Nevitt's continuing disdain shouldn't bother her. It really shouldn't. But it irked her, just a bit. She'd worked for the woman for a year, given the station a reputation of excellent security, and even kept working after losing a significant part of her memory. What more did the captain want? There might be more to Nevitt's dislike of her, but Em hadn't been able to turn anything up.

Then she dutifully reported for her appointment with Grayith Barlow. Better to get it over with than to live in dread all day. She was glad for the early appointment time.

He answered the door to his office immediately and showed her to a cozy parlor. He gestured for her to take any seat she wanted. Her first instinct was to sit in the padded, straight-backed chair, but he might read more into that than she wanted. The couch seemed to indicate a greater level of comfort. She was taking too long to decide. She went with her original choice, stealing a look at his face to see if he was judging her for it. If he did, his expression didn't give it away.

Gray was human, but from the Zerellus colony. The Zerellians had left Earth hundreds of years ago and had experienced just enough genetic drift to count as a different grouping of humans. Their society also diverged from that of Earth-derived humans, of course, giving them a very different cultural identity. Gray had light-brown hair, tan skin, and brown eyes, as was typical for Zerellians. Em remembered from his record that he was thirty-seven, unmarried, and a bit of an adventurer. Overall, he had average looks, but his eyes were quite nice. They were probably an asset in his profession.

"So, Em, how have you been doing?" he asked.

She hated open-ended questions. They were non-questions, really. Just an invitation to talk. "All things considered, very well, I'd say."

"No lingering pain? Headaches? Nausea? Vertigo?"

Each time she shook her head. "None of that."

"Good. That leaves us with what's going on up here." He tapped the side of his head.

Another open-ended invitation to talk. Blah. "Also fine, I think. I've had to relearn myself and all, but it helps that I have people to help me."

"No post-traumatic stress from the crash?"

"I don't remember the crash. So no."

"Hm." He tapped a note on the infoboard on his lap. "Have you had any flickers of memory of your life before the accident?"

"No. Do you think I'll recover any of it, at this point?"

He sighed. "I'll be honest. The longer you go without recovering any memories, the less likely it becomes that you ever will."

"Isn't it strange that my memory loss is so specific?"

"No. Different types of memory are stored in different places. Your memories pertaining to yourself were in a particular spot, and that's the area that was damaged. It's a good possibility that those memories were effectively deleted from your brain."

A more pessimistic viewpoint than Brannin usually presented. Also, not what she wanted to hear. "Dr. Brash suggested you might have some therapies, like hypnosis, that could help." Not that she was convinced about trying hypnosis. She had too many secrets to keep, at this point, to allow for that.

"I don't think that would help. Hypnosis is more for repressed memories. We prod associations to try to unearth them. With you, we have none of those associations to prod." He steepled his fingers and pressed them to his lips, looking thoughtful. "I've been researching a new memory-retrieval therapy, but I'm not sure it's right for your situation. I've asked a few colleagues to see if they've heard of anything. There are always new things coming out. Maybe we'll find something."

"Sure." She was not optimistic about his "maybe."

"How are you handling your situation? Emotionally? It would

be normal to feel angry, confused, scared, or any other number of things."

"I'm just trying to find my way. Do the best I can with what I still have. I think I'm doing pretty well with it. I mean, I get a little frustrated now and then, but I'm glad I'm able to keep working and doing my normal things. The damage could have been a lot worse."

"Yes, it could have. Still, losing your identity has to be traumatic."

"Not as much as you'd think. I don't know what I've lost, so I can't mourn it." She shrugged.

He looked sad rather than reassured. "That does make sense. How is Wren handling it?"

Em hadn't expected him to ask that, though she should have. "She's great, actually. I've caught her looking sad or worried now and then, but I think she's convinced we still have a future together."

"But are you convinced?"

Em felt a spark of offense. She didn't like him questioning her relationship with Wren, even if it was his job. "Yes," she said, trying to keep annoyance out of her voice. "We're married. We plan to stay that way."

"I'm glad to hear that. Having her support will be a great help to you."

"Yes. It is." She felt irritated. She shouldn't. But she had a sudden urge for a sparring match. She fought to keep her expression neutral and her posture relaxed.

"I see. I'd like to talk to you and Wren together in a couple weeks. I'm not making it a medical order. Voluntary only. But I think it would benefit you both."

"I'll ask her."

He nodded. "I'll keep in touch with Dr. Brash and request another meeting with you if it seems warranted. Also, I want you to let me know if you have any issues. Irritability, inability to sleep, anything at all, okay? I'm here to help."

"I will. Thanks." She stood, grateful to have kept the appointment so short.

He walked her to the door, though it was only a few paces away. "I sense your reluctance, Chief, but you can trust me."

Did he mean that at face value, or was there more to it? She had to admit that she did feel more and more suspicious of everything around her, but she was hardly going to report that to him.

"Thank you, Dr. Barlow."

"Gray. You've always called me Gray."

She nodded and, after a quick bow, wasted no time in moving on with her day.

———

It took Em some time to shake off the irritation. Maybe it was her increasing closeness with Wren, or maybe she'd always been protective of her marriage. Either way, Gray's prodding had riled her.

The arrival of the *Onari* after lunch made her forget everything else. She descended to Deck One to greet the hospi-ship herself, only to find the concourse crowded. She had to push through to get into Docking Bay Five. Arin arrived a couple minutes after she did. Three more of her staff walked in just behind him.

"Hey." He grinned at Em. "Big turnout, huh?"

"Is it always like this?" She nodded toward the throng out on the concourse.

"More or less. Everyone loves Jerin and her crew."

"So I've heard. I'm starting to wonder if I should assign some light security near the quarters they'll be using. " She frowned, studying the crowd.

"I'm sure no one would cause any harm, but for privacy, it's not a bad idea. Usually, we handle that internally on a volunteer basis, but if you want to put it on the schedule, no one will mind."

"I'll do that," she decided. "I don't want the *Onari* crew to feel mobbed or exposed."

"Or be petitioned for free medical procedures everywhere they go," Arin added.

Scrap. That was a good point. "Right. Let's increase security throughout Deck One as well, for all public areas. Just to ensure everyone's ease of movement."

Arin nodded. "You got it, Chief." He grabbed his comport and tapped some quick orders into it, alerting the Deck One security office.

She felt an almost imperceptible shiver from the deck plates as the clamps grabbed onto the *Onari* and began the docking procedure. The ship looked as good in person as it did on the specs she'd studied earlier in the day. Bennites kept their hospi-ships in excellent condition, and updated with the newest technologies. The *Onari* was big for its crew size, but that was due to all the labs and patient quarters. Healthcare took up a lot of room.

Finally, the airlock opened and the crew began entering the station, all wearing standard Bennite hospi-ship uniforms with long sleeves and pants. Arin took the lead, greeting each person, though Em had memorized the names and faces beforehand. Trin, a Kanaran physical therapist. Brak, the Briveen cyberneticist she'd heard so much about. Em felt odd not greeting her in the Briveen way, but her record had emphatically noted that Brak did not wish to engage non-Briveen in the formal rituals. It was a relief, but still felt weird.

Next came Ben, a human nurse; Endra, the Sarkavian friend of Wren's; and finally Jerin Remay herself, the Bennite doctor, who served as the *Onari*'s captain and chief medical officer. Em was glad for the airlock scanners. Surely the crew of a hospi-ship encountered more than its share of disease. The bioscanners on the ship side of the airlock scanned each person leaving the vessel. If the scanners indicated any potentially contagious contaminant, containment shields would automatically appear and the person in question would not be permitted to board the station without proper precautions.

Em offered greetings and bows as appropriate to all of the *Onari* crew as they began to fill the bay, but her deepest bow went to the doctor, who honored Em with an even deeper bow.

"Thank you, Chief Fallon, for allowing us on board Dragonfire. Between you and me, it's our favorite PAC station." Dr. Remay's golden-tan skin and shiny black hair contrasted with her green eyes in a strikingly attractive way. There was a certain kindness in her eyes that reminded Em of Brannin, and she wondered if it was a Bennite thing, or perhaps just a doctor thing. Brannin definitely didn't wear a ruby nose stud, though. On Remay's dainty nose, it looked both elegant and feminine. Remay was thirty-five, though she had an ageless quality about her. Em imagined that the doctor would look much the same in fifteen or twenty years.

"We're pleased to have you here, Jerin." Fortunately, Wren had advised Em to use the first names of the *Onari* crew. "I'd have thought you all would prefer Blackthorn Station for its amazing starport."

"We do enjoy Blackthorn. But we always feel so welcome and well looked after here." She leaned forward as if to tell a secret. "And the mechanics and the shopping are always fantastic!"

They shared a laugh and Em sent the junior security officers to clear a path through the concourse. Those officers would return to greet the lower-ranking crew members, who continued to come through the airlock.

"Well, if anyone gets too friendly, be sure to let us know. We're increasing security to ensure your comfort."

"We appreciate that. I'm sure we'll be fine."

Arin's attention was riveted on the woman behind Jerin, a new crew member whom he hadn't greeted. He must not have looked up the crew before the ship's arrival, assuming he already knew everyone.

"And you're Kellis Mayvits? The new mechanical engineer?" Em asked.

The twenty-six-year-old stepped forward. "Yes. Pleased to meet you." She gave a deep bow, which Em and her staff returned.

By Atalan standards, the woman was average looking. Which meant by human standards, she was exceedingly lovely. Her golden skin reminded Em of sun-baked sand, and her turquoise eyes were startlingly vivid. A soft cap of tawny curls encircled her head and framed her face.

"Have you been on Dragonfire Station before?" Em asked.

"No. I haven't been too much of anywhere. I only recently escaped Atalus."

Ah. A refugee from the planet's civil war, then. She and Arin would have much in common. Indeed, her legate seemed almost spellbound. She gave him a subtle nudge with her elbow and he blinked, shaking it off.

"Let us know if there's anything we can help you with. In fact, Arin, why don't you show Kellis around after she's settled into her quarters?"

Arin nodded. "I'd be happy to."

Jerin caught Em's eye and the two shared a knowing look.

Em had a good feeling about this visit.

EM LEARNED a great deal during dinner. She and Wren joined Endra and Kellis at the soup shop, where they enjoyed a leisurely meal and lots of conversation. Em found it interesting to watch Wren with her old friend, who seemed deeply fond of her. Kellis conversed freely, showing intelligence and good humor. In fact, as a mechanical engineer, she turned out to have a great deal in common with Wren.

Em and Endra sat politely sipping their soup while Wren and Kellis prattled on about the latest plasma converter technology. Though Endra was an engineer too, she was the kind who worked with schematics and systems tests, not the kind who got her hands greasy.

Em tried to think of something to talk to Endra about while the other two conversed in rapturous technobabble. "So what was Wren like as a teenager?"

Endra grinned. She was tall and had the white-blonde hair of a Sarkavian. Her face was rounder than Wren's and in a classical sense, she'd be considered the pretty one of the pair. But Em thought Wren's deviation from the classical was exactly what made her attractive. Wren's face had character, and her smile always spoke of fun and generosity.

"Not much different than she is now." Endra stole a sly glance at her friend, ensuring that Wren was entirely preoccupied with microtuners and diagnostics. "She got good grades, stayed out of major trouble. Though she did have a naughty habit of reconfiguring people's tech when they weren't looking."

"Like how?"

"Oh, like a classmate being befuddled that his holo-vid projector would do nothing but emit whale sounds. That kind of thing." She snorted with laughter. "She always put things back the way they were supposed to be, though. She never caused any real harm. She just liked being a prankster."

Em could imagine that.

"She dated a lot, but casually, you know? Whenever someone got serious, she ended it. Though she had a knack for remaining friends with them. Never knew how she managed that," Endra admitted. "My relationships always ended on a fairly nuclear note. A scorched-earth policy, as you humans might say."

Em laughed. "What kind of person did she like?"

Endra scrunched her face up as she delved into her memories. "Confident ones. Ones who were sure of themselves. Ones that didn't create a lot of drama. The low-maintenance kind, I guess you'd say. A few more boys than girls, but there were just more boys to choose from in our area."

Well, that was certainly interesting. It seemed Wren had gotten over her predilection for low-maintenance people, or she sure wouldn't have gotten involved with Em. Security officers weren't known for their breezy transparency.

Endra pushed her empty bowl away. "I was glad when she married you. Well, not right at first. I told you before that I thought you two had moved way too fast. But after I saw you together, it made sense. I've never seen her happier." She picked up her glass of mead and tilted it at Em in a salute.

She liked Endra. Given her own impressions of the woman, along with Wren's long history—okay, plus a thorough background check, but that was just good security—Em thought she could trust her. She couldn't discuss anything of a sensitive nature in public, though, so she picked up her glass of wine and returned the salute.

Kellis noticed the gesture and seemed to realize she and Wren were not the only people at the table. Her cheeks reddened. "Oh, I'm so sorry. That was rude of me. I just don't often get to talk about... Well, never mind, you're bored enough already." She shook her head and laughed self-consciously.

Em made a dismissive gesture. "It's fine. Endra was just telling me all about Wren's past as a mechanical miscreant."

Wren shot a wide-eyed look at Endra. "Uh-oh, what did you say?"

"Nothing too incriminating," Endra drawled. "But if any of Em's infoboards start misbehaving, she'll surely blame it on you now." She snickered.

"You're supposed to guard my secrets, not share them!" Wren swatted her friend's shoulder lightly and laughed.

Endra grinned. "Well, I've decided I like your wife, so all bets are off, now." She gave Wren a fiendish look and they all chuckled.

"So Kellis," Em said, deciding to shift the conversation away from her and Wren. "My legate seemed pretty interested in you. What if I invited you two back to our quarters, and suggested that Arin drop by?" That would not only be a favor to Arin, but a benefit to herself. If he occupied Kellis, Em would have a chance to talk to Endra in private. Besides, Kellis had looked just as interested as Arin had.

"Oh. That...sounds nice, actually." Kellis nodded approvingly.

"I thought you might say that."

To Em's surprise, Kellis didn't blush, but grinned wolfishly. All four women laughed.

ARIN ARRIVED WITHIN MINUTES, and the five of them had a great time talking and laughing like old friends. Which they were, actually, with the exception of Kellis. But the newcomer fit right into the group. Em learned that Kellis had lost the use of her legs during the war on Atalus, but fate had twisted her way when the *Onari* had rescued her from a Rescan ship and repaired her spinal injury.

"Since then, I've made a point of keeping healthy with exercise," Kellis told them. "It seems like the best way to honor the gift that Jerin gave me."

"We have a great gym here, actually," Arin said. "Have you seen it?"

Kellis shook her head. "Not yet. I haven't had time to see all that much."

Arin did a self-deprecating eye roll. "Of course you haven't, you just arrived. I could show you."

"What, you mean now?"

Arin's eyebrows lifted and he cast an uncertain look around at the others in the room.

Em took pity on him. "Sure. Then you'd be familiar with it whenever you find time to use it."

Arin shot her a grateful look and the two made a quick departure. That left Em and Wren alone on the couch, with Endra in a chair opposite them.

"Something tells me Kellis will be spending all of her leave time on Dragonfire, whenever she can possibly manage it," Endra predicted.

"I'd say you're right." Wren looked pleased.

"Tell me about Kellis," Em said to Endra.

"Aw, you're worried about your friend. That's sweet. But don't worry. Kellis is as honest and genuine as they come. She got a second chance at life and she doesn't waste a moment of it with pettiness or negativity. Actually, she can be annoyingly upbeat some days." Endra smiled, as if a fond memory had occurred to her. "But Arin can trust her, and so can you."

That was more information than Em had expected, and it suited her perfectly. She caught Wren's eye, and Wren gave her a meaningful nod. She still had reservations about bringing Endra into her confidence, but Wren trusted Endra, and Em had faith in Wren.

"Actually, since you mention trust, there's something I want to tell you." It took surprisingly little time for Em to describe the accident and her memory loss. Funny how a person's whole life can be whittled down to a few sentences.

"Wow." Endra looked from Em to Wren and back again as she processed the state of affairs. "And people haven't noticed?"

"You didn't," Em pointed out. "I've done my homework, and Wren fills me in on things I can't uncover on the voicecom. The captain and Arin know about it, and the doctors of course, but that's about it."

"That must be so hard." Endra's sympathetic gaze veered to Wren, who lifted her chin resolutely.

"We're working through it," Wren said. "There's more though." She scooted closer and slid her palm over Em's, twining their fingers together. "Tell her. She might be able to help."

Em battled briefly between two instincts. Her gut reaction was to keep her mouth shut about sensitive information. But she wanted to prove her trust in her wife. Gaining an ally would be a very helpful side benefit as well, if it happened. It sure wouldn't hurt to have someone with strong ties to medical professionals on her side.

Em squeezed Wren's hand and spilled everything. Her suspicions, her abilities, even her new habit of sweeping their quarters every time she'd been away, just as she'd done earlier that evening.

"Prelin's underpants. Wow." Endra blinked slowly. "That's...a lot. How can I help?"

Wren gave Em's hand an I-told-you-so pat. "We don't know," Em admitted. "I'd hoped to come up with some clues by now, but so far I only have deduction and suspicion."

"Okay. So, let's set aside the thing where you aren't what you appear to be. If someone had sabotaged your shuttle, then who would have done that, and why?"

"My primary suspects were Arin, who might have wanted my position; Wren, who might have wanted a wife out of the way; and Captain Nevitt, who's always had a grudge against me. But I've eliminated Arin and Wren."

"Which leaves Nevitt," Endra mused. "She's always seemed a little proud to me, but I've never seen her be unprofessional. Granted, I don't know her well."

"I'm not sure anyone does," Wren put in. "You can't keep your comings and goings very quiet on a station like this, but no one's ever spotted her with a lover, or with any close friends. The woman is an island, and seems to be married to her career."

"Which might be why she took it so personally when she wasn't able to choose her own security chief," Em noted.

They all fell silent, considering that.

"There might be some grudge I'm not aware of, but I haven't been able to uncover any other suspects of note," she added.

"No outraged officials who felt they got a raw deal on the station? No angry traders who got cheated, or got caught at cheating and took it personally? No one you've refused to allow to dock who might want revenge?" Endra asked.

Em shook her head each time. "Nothing I can find on record, and my records are extensive and exacting. There are people I haven't granted trade privileges, and people I've busted for illegal or unethical acts. But mostly, it's part of the game to them. Sometimes they win, sometimes they lose. They don't take it too personally." She paused, then clarified, "They don't win on *my* station though."

Wren and Endra chuckled.

"I guess that leaves Nevitt to investigate, until and unless some other suspect turns up," Endra observed.

Em nodded. "I'm going to start digging through her communications logs. The official and the personal. And I'll look for hidden communications over the past several months. There are always some of those."

"Can you do that? Go through the captain's comms?" Wren asked.

"I'm investigating a possible attack on an officer. That gives me cause. It doesn't matter that I'm the officer in question, so long as I follow the protocol and the chain of command." Em had no doubts about her jurisdiction. Of course, if Nevitt found out what she was doing, things could get ugly fast. She'd just have to make sure Nevitt didn't find out.

"So...again, how can I help?" Endra's face had hardened with determination.

"Right now, just knowing that we have you on our side helps.

Honestly, I'm not sure there will be anything you can do. Maybe help me get access to medical treatment that isn't available here. I don't know. But since anyone we haven't specifically cleared of motive or wrongdoing is suspect, that leaves us surrounded by a lot of people we can't trust. We can use all the allies we can get." Em glanced at Wren, who nodded in agreement.

Endra chewed her lip thoughtfully. "I know you'll want to test it out for yourself, but I'm certain you can trust anyone on the *Onari*. We're all misfits who have found a place to belong, thanks to Jerin. I guess you could say we're fans of the underdog."

Em wanted to be sure of what Endra was saying. "So there's no one on the entire ship you'd have a doubt about trusting? Even with something serious and potentially dangerous?"

Endra squinted as she thought. "Not one."

It seemed too good to be true, and Em didn't trust things that seemed too good to be true. She'd only recruit allies when she was certain of them. But Endra had suspected that. Em liked her already.

After a long silence, Endra took a deep breath and said in a breezy tone, "So, what's it like being married to someone you don't know?"

Wren and Em shared a glance. They were only just figuring that out, but Wren seemed more and more familiar every day.

———

ON HER WAY UP to the running track the next morning, Em caught up to Brak, who was just about to begin her own run.

"Hello there," Brak greeted her. Her facial muscles pulled her lips into a small smile. "I see I'm not the only one starting the day with a run."

They didn't pause their climb up to the track, but fell in together. Em appreciated the opportunity to have someone to run with. Though as good a runner as she was, she suspected she'd have to work to keep up with Brak. Briveen had a sleek body type that Em admired, along with a powerfully strong lower body. Brak had a height advantage, as well.

Em had always found the Briveen a beautiful species. The iridescence of Brak's blue-green, scaly skin and fine-boned features appealed to her esthetically, though some people not accustomed to the Briveen found them a little frightening to look at. Em didn't understand that. Brak's work uniform had covered her arms and legs before, but now they were exposed by a short-sleeved shirt and shorts, and Em found them almost distractingly pretty. The slight shimmer of Brak's scales reminded her of gemstones.

"Starting my day with a good run makes me feel alive. Vigorous. Ready to tackle the day, you know?" As Em cleared the last step, she detected a faint scent of warm baked bread, the Briveen response for agreement.

Brak inclined her head but said nothing. She didn't need to. Em liked that about Brak's people. Sometimes Em thought other species talked way too much while communicating almost nothing.

By tacit agreement, they began a light warm-up jog together. The track was just wide enough to give two people room to comfortably run side by side. After a few laps Brak glanced at her questioningly.

"I'll follow your lead," she said in response. She caught a warm, musky scent. Respect mingled with just a little satisfaction. Em wondered if scent communication had been a curriculum requirement in OTS. She had no trouble at all translating the aromas into messages, which wasn't a common skill among simian species.

They picked up the pace and Em's heart rate began to increase. Another thing she appreciated about running was how it freed her mind. She could think about the workday to come, personal matters, or whatever else her brain presented to her.

She took the time to admire Brak's smooth gait. Briveen had a pelvic structure that made them much more efficient at both running and walking. Brak also had those wildly impressive cybernetic arms. Em couldn't imagine what it was like to grow up with a set of weak, undersized biological arms, only to have them surgically removed and replaced with cybernetic limbs as a rite of passage into adulthood. But they sure looked badass. Sleek, high-tech, and beautiful. Of course, as the top scientist in her field, Brak would always have the latest, bleeding-edge technology. Her arms had been covered in a scaly, blue-green synthetic skin to match the rest of her, but they could never be mistaken for biological. They proudly proclaimed their elegant, technological efficiency.

Em wondered how personal her relationship had been with Brak before. How well they'd known each other. Wren hadn't mentioned any particular friendship between them, but Em felt instinctively comfortable with her. Could it be some vestige of memory peeping through the quagmire of her mind? Or maybe it was just a product of her instincts, which had remained consistently reliable.

Brak ran hard for over an hour and when she finally slowed to a cooldown pace, Em was relieved. Every inch of her shirt and pants was damp with sweat. She made a mental note to increase the strenuousness of her daily workouts.

After they slowed to a walk, Em's heart rate began to return to normal.

"I'm impressed," Brak said as they walked down the stairs together. "Last time you didn't keep up as well."

Seriously? Out loud Em said, "Thanks."

"But then you're still the only non-Briveen I know who can run with me at all. It's a nice change. I still struggle sometimes on the *Onari* to interact with others."

That sounded like the continuation of a conversation they'd

had before. Which seemed to imply a greater familiarity between them.

"No improvement?" Em asked, as if she remembered their previous conversations.

Brak made a gentle snorting sound of equivocation as they stepped off the stairs. "A little. Kellis and I have become friends, and she's helped smooth the way for me socially."

"Wren and I had dinner with her and Endra last night. She seems very open and honest." She felt awkward for a moment, realizing she might have made a faux pas by mentioning that. Perhaps Brak would wonder why she hadn't been invited to dinner as well.

But Brak seemed unperturbed. She sidestepped slightly, allowing Em to enter the shower room first. Em gave her a tiny bow of thanks without slowing.

"More adventurous than you'd think, too, given her past," Brak continued. "And a good sense of humor. I think she takes it upon herself to try to make me laugh each day."

They headed to the showers. Em said, "I look forward to getting to know her better," before ducking into a stall.

As she showered, she wondered if it would be normal to invite Brak to dinner with her and Wren that night. Did they have that sort of relationship? Maybe that detail had slipped Wren's mind in her excitement to see Endra. Or maybe Em's friendship with Brak was something she'd kept private. But why would she? Whatever the answer was, the only way to find out would be to issue the invitation. So she did.

"I'd be honored." Brak bowed in a surprisingly formal, Briveen way. Maybe those little gestures slipped through from time to time.

After making plans, Em headed to ops to begin her workday, feeling invigorated.

When Em met with Arin in her office that morning, he was full of energy and enthusiasm.

"I'm guessing your date with Kellis went well," she observed dryly.

"I don't think you could call it a date. When I take a girl on a date, it doesn't involve a gymnasium or somebody's dirty running socks."

"Gross, someone did that again? Did you grab the socks?"

"Ew, no."

"I'll send the message to the janitorial crew. But next time you see something like that, bag the evidence immediately."

"You're going to do a DNA scan?" Arin seemed caught between amusement and disbelief.

"You bet I am. Nobody gets away with nasty littering on my station."

Arin laughed but she just looked at him. She meant it.

"All right," he agreed. "At least it would mean the end of finding someone's stinky biohazard socks."

She waved her hand to indicate a change in subject. "I'd like you to see to all of the arrivals and departures today. I'm going to start going through all of Nevitt's correspondence."

A pained expression crossed his face. "I guess we're in this pretty deep, huh?"

"If you want out, just let me know."

Arin shook his head.

"Good. It would have sucked a lot if you'd wanted out."

He put on a shrewd look. "One of these days, you're going to end up the head of something prestigious. Whenever you get there, I fully intend to ride your coattails into a life of distinguished service."

That got a guttural laugh out of her. Though she didn't discount what he'd said, she knew his primary motivation was his sense of duty and loyalty.

"I'll be sure to remember all of you little people when I'm

wildly powerful." She smirked. She doubted that would ever come to pass. She'd be happy enough remaining a security chief for the rest of her life, so long as it didn't come with any more threats to her life or losses of memory.

WHEN EM DID her rounds on Deck One, she found everyone in higher spirits than normal. Shopkeeps enjoyed booming business, and residents roamed the boardwalk in crowds much larger than usual. It took her twice as long to do her rounds because she was constantly stopping to talk to people. Along the way, she ran into several crew members from the *Onari*, including its captain, Jerin Remay.

"Chief, it's so good to see you. I'm on my way to meet with Brannin, but I do want to be sure to have a good visit with you before we leave." The doctor spoke in the same cultured, elegant way that Brannin did. Em always found Bennite accents so soothing. Jerin also shared Brannin's dark-skinned good looks, though of course in a feminine variety. Em wondered briefly about the possibility of a romantic connection between the two doctors. They had so much in common. It was certainly none of her business if they did, but she tried to be aware of the relationships going on around her, to help her do her job.

"I invited Brak to dinner tonight. Why don't you join us?" Em hoped Wren hadn't already made dinner plans. She needed to be sure to send her wife a message as soon as possible to prevent complications.

Jerin, as she'd insisted on being called, looked delighted. "I'd love to."

"I'll have to message you with the time, after I coordinate with Wren. I'm kind of springing this on her."

Jerin chuckled. "Of course. My schedule is wide open so just let me know."

After the doctor left, Em finished her tour of the boardwalk. She saw Cabot talking enthusiastically just outside the door of his shop with a young nurse's assistant. A Trallian. Cabot was trying to sell her something, no doubt. Em hoped the girl bargained for a good deal. She liked Trallians, she realized. They were a small-statured people, with thick brown skin, big eyes, and sweet smiles. Though, of course, she knew that appearances could always deceive. Maybe that was what she liked about the Trallians—that they had a built-in characteristic that might well prove to be misleading. It made them interesting.

———

ONCE BACK IN HER OFFICE, Em let Wren know about their impending dinner guests. Fortunately, Wren was delighted.

Em then opened up the communications files and resumed her slow slog through them. It was dreadfully dull work. But then, intelligence work usually was. Sure, moments of discovery were exciting, but they could only come after hours, and sometimes weeks, of tedious scrutiny. Very little security work actually involved fighting or intrigue. Mostly, it was an excruciating eye for detail while maintaining the ability for fighting and intrigue. Far less thrilling than most people probably imagined.

Poring through screen after screen of data, Em found that Nevitt didn't send many personal communications. Occasionally she sent voice-only or text-only messages, but Em couldn't find any video-feed messages or conversations that weren't work related. That didn't provide any clues, but it was a curiosity. All of Nevitt's official communications were completely by the book. Em cross-referenced every event and personnel issue and found nothing amiss.

She leaned back in her chair and rubbed her eyes. Hours had drifted by and she was nearing the end of her shift. She'd need to get home on time to start getting ready for dinner.

She still had the better part of an hour, though, so she began digging deeper. She applied message-recovery algorithms to search for deleted communications, as well as ones that might have been routed through non-communications servers to keep them off the record.

A short list of files was the reward for her efforts, but she quickly discarded most of them. That left her with three. One described plans for a janitorial worker's birthday. One had been sent from a Rescan cargo ship to Cabot, and she saved that to investigate the next day. The third turned out to be a recipe for blistercakes.

"Scrap." She rubbed her eyes again. They felt scratchy, like they were full of sand. She'd turned up nothing at all, for all her work.

She gave her chair a push and spun in slow circles. What now? Did a lack of evidence mean her accident had truly been an accident? Maybe she should stop looking. She'd settled into her life, and she liked it. There was no reason she couldn't be happy on Dragonfire.

Except for the mystery of the skills she shouldn't have. What about that?

She stuck her foot out, making the chair come to a drag-stop. What about her *own* private files? She'd never searched them for hidden messages. What if *she'd* been the one hiding something?

She applied a new set of algorithms to her private files, both the personal and the official ones. Her lips parted as her screen began to populate with recovered files. There were two dozen of them, dating from her arrival on the station to six months later.

Em tore through them, her heart racing. She read them all, then read them again. Finally, she closed all the files and sagged in her chair.

She'd been looking at everyone but herself. She pressed her palm to her eye socket, trying to reorganize everything in her mind. She'd thought she'd been solving a puzzle, when in fact, she hadn't even realized what the pieces looked like.

What would she tell Wren? She'd made a mistake, confiding in her. And Endra.

She was the one who'd been lying, all along. She'd been sent to Dragonfire to investigate Wren for smuggling. She was not who she'd thought she was, and sometime soon, someone was sure to show up and yank her back to where she was supposed to be.

EM WALKED alongside Jerin in the arboretum. After dinner, the doctor had suggested they walk off the heavy meal they'd enjoyed. Em could almost believe they were walking outdoors. The radiant heat of the lights approximated the warmth of the sun on her skin. The air smelled fresh and herbaceous.

The arboretum was the only room on the station that matched the gymnasium in size. Even the larger cargo bays, which could house commercial shuttles and small cruisers for maintenance, weren't this big. Designed to give the illusion of being planetside, it provided walking paths, benches, and even grassy areas for picnicking. It took a small cadre of horticulturists to tend it, but it also served as a learning lab for the youth on the station. Here among the leafy trees and reedy grasses, they could study horticulture, botany, entomology, and hydroponics.

Jerin paused to admire a purple-and-white flower the size of her head with long, feathery petals. "These were everywhere on Corvin VIII." She stroked a finger over a petal, watching the soft fronds float with the movement.

"That's part of the Barony Coalition, isn't it? At the edge of PAC space?" Em didn't know much about the planet, other than that it was a farming world.

"That's right. A non-PAC world. We were there about three weeks ago. They were having an outbreak of bovine flu. A nasty business." She stepped back from the flower and they continued down the path, some distance behind Wren and Brak.

"Were you able to get it under control?"

"Yes. It took us three weeks, but we quarantined the infected and treated them with aggressive antivirals. There were only five deaths, which happened before we arrived." She shook her head, regret clear on her face.

"That must be terribly hard, dealing with so many suffering people." Em peered up at a tall tree as they meandered by it. Apparently she'd never studied plants, because the names of the trees and flowers did not come to her.

"Unfortunately, viruses and bacteria are always mutating. When that happens and there isn't sufficient healthcare available locally, it can go very bad, very fast. If they can't afford to have a hospi-ship come, the death toll can rise quickly."

It sounded horrific to Em, but Jerin remained matter-of-fact. It was, no doubt, an all-too-common occurrence to her.

"Hopefully the PAC can establish accords with Corvin VIII that will help get them better access."

New PAC allies joined every year, but it was a slow process. A planet had to prove it was self-sustaining and could offer reciprocal benefits to other planets. It also had to prove a standard of ethical and humane policy.

Jerin seemed unconvinced. "That is always the hope. I'd like nothing more than to be put out of the humanitarian business because there's just no need for the *Onari*'s services."

"What would you do then?" Em asked.

Jerin slowed, then stopped as she reached to touch a branch of spiky needles. "Oh, probably the same thing I'm doing now. Except the *Onari* would become a fully research-oriented ship. We have some research and development going on already, like with Brak, but imagine if we could do it exclusively."

Maybe medicine would figure out how to prevent outbreaks

instead of rushing to battle them. Or maybe it could cure the diseases that so far no one had figured out.

Jerin broke into her thoughts. "What would you do?"

"What?"

"If you weren't in security."

Em drew a blank. "I don't know."

"Did you grow up dreaming of becoming a security officer?"

She had no idea. Em glanced around, ensuring no one was closer than Brak and Wren. "Did Brannin tell you about my recent accident?"

Jerin gave her a puzzled look. "No. Should he have?"

"Well, he never mentioned to me that he wanted to, or asked if he could." Though he could have asked Jerin theoretical questions without naming Em and still been in the clear with patient confidentiality.

"He wouldn't discuss a patient without permission. Brannin is as ethical as they come."

"I've heard the same about your crew," Em told her.

Jerin gave her a small bow of thanks, but remained quiet. Doctors seemed to have a knack for drawing out information with silence. It was a tactic Em admired and one she preferred for security purposes as well.

"Is there anyone on the *Onari* who specializes in neuroscience?"

Jerin gestured to a nearby bench, as she and Em had simply stalled out on the path. Wren and Brak had moved up out of sight.

Once seated, Jerin asked, "Do you mean cybernetic implants? Brak and I often work together to install the neural implants that control her cybernetics."

"No, I mean brain injury. Memory loss."

Jerin's brow furrowed. "Are you saying you've suffered memory loss?"

Em glanced around again. She felt squeamish about revealing

information, but she found herself with few options. Soon, people would be looking for her, and she needed to get her bearings before that happened. She nodded. "Only a select few know about it, though."

"Brak and I might be able to help. If we can't, perhaps Trin can."

"Isn't he a physical therapist?" Em couldn't exactly do aerobics with her brain to make it remember.

"Yes, but rehabilitation means more than just bones and muscles. Depending on the nature of the injury, cognitive therapy might be a possibility." Jerin sat up straighter, suddenly electric with purpose. "This isn't the place to talk about private matters, but I want to help however I can. Can we arrange an appointment for tomorrow?"

"Of course. Just let me know what time works for you."

Jerin touched the side of her nose where the ruby stud pierced it, thinking. "I'll check with Brak and Brannin, and send you the time in the morning."

"Brannin?"

"As your primary physician, he should be included. Unless there's a reason you don't want him to be?" Jerin's tone turned the statement into a question.

Em felt like she'd been letting too many people in on her secrets. Her instinct said she should involve as few as possible. But Brannin already knew about her memory loss. Why hadn't he suggested a consultation with Brak and Jerin? Her mind clouded again with suspicion.

"No, of course he should be," she said a beat too late.

Jerin pretended not to notice. "Good then. Should we go find Brak and Wren? I'm afraid they've left us far behind."

"I wouldn't be surprised to find them in a mech shop, with Wren asking Brak for advice on something metallic and greasy."

Jerin laughed. It was a pretty, musical sound.

"We'd better get to them, then, before we lose them

completely. Next thing we'd know, they'd have Kellis in there too and be up all night, engineering something that would take over the universe."

They both snorted with laughter as they strode quickly down the path.

DURING DINNER and the subsequent walk in the arboretum, Em had managed to keep her contact with Wren to a minimum. Back in their quarters, she was forced to confront her problem.

The previous night, Em had been perfectly at ease with Wren. Now she felt jumpy and nervous. She was certain Wren had known nothing of the investigation that had brought Em to Dragonfire. That meant Em had lied to Wren for the entirety of their relationship. Was their marriage even genuine? Maybe Em had married her for covert reasons.

Em had begun to think that her developing love for Wren had been old feelings seeping through. A vestigial memory of the past. But maybe her feelings for Wren were actually new. Possibly based on the assumption that she had felt that way previously. Had she talked herself into caring for Wren?

Oh, it was such a mess. She had enough on her hands without adding this. She managed to delay a conversation with Wren while she swept the quarters for monitoring devices, ensuring no low-pulse energy readings registered on the small scanner she now carried with her at all times. But once that was done and she'd put away her equipment, there was nothing left to do.

Wren sat on the couch while Em tucked the scanner back into her belt. It was a modified diagnostic tool, designed to seek out any electronics that had an open connection. A perfectly normal device for a security officer to have. Not so normal to use obsessively in her home and office, but her life could hardly be called typical.

"I had a great time," Wren said, stretching out and flipping her hair back so that it hung down behind the couch. "I'm glad you invited Brak. I hadn't gotten a chance to talk with her at length before, and it was great getting to know her better. She's positively brilliant. A fun sense of humor, too."

"Yes, I like her too." That, at least, she could say honestly.

"How's the search going on the communications files?" Wren propped her feet up on the edge of the table, resting her heels against an understated decorative curve. She tilted her head back and stared up at the ceiling rather than looking directly at Em.

"No luck. I got through all of Nevitt's files and didn't come up with anything." Her own files, of course, were a different matter altogether. And now she was back into lying territory. Scrap.

Wren made a soft sound of sympathy. "No wonder you seem down. What do we do now?"

Em wondered that herself. She couldn't just come out and tell Wren their marriage might be a lie. It would be too cruel to put her into the same limbo Em was living. But maintaining the charade, if that was what it was, might be even worse in the long run. Alternatively, she imagined one day telling Wren that she'd discovered her own possible duplicity and then chosen to keep Wren in the dark. Augh. It was an impossible situation.

"I have an appointment with Brak and Jerin tomorrow. Maybe they can help with my memory." She paced slowly around the quarters, avoiding sitting on the couch.

Wren sat up and looked directly at her. "Oh, do you think so?"

"No idea. But it's definitely worth trying."

Wren nodded enthusiastically.

"Wren, what if..." She trailed off, considering how to phrase it. "What if I never remember anything? How would you deal with being married to someone who isn't really who you thought you were marrying?"

Wren stood and closed the distance between them. "I'd deal with it fine, because it's you I'm married to either way. You're still the same you, regardless of whether you remember me or not. You haven't changed, even the slightest bit. Of course I want all of our shared memories back, but *my* real worry is that you might decide you don't want to be with me."

Wren caught Em's hand and twined their fingers together. She looked so vulnerable. Em fought the urge to pull away. She wanted to comfort Wren but didn't know if she had the right. She felt like a total asshole.

Instead, she said, "All I can say is that right now, the last thing I want to do is hurt you. I can't give you any promises about anything else."

Wren seemed reassured by that, and she pulled Em into a long hug before patting her on the shoulder. "You should go on to bed. I can tell you're exhausted."

"Sure. I'll just take a quick shower first."

Wren smiled. "I knew you would." She sent her a cheeky wink and picked up an infoboard. "I'll be in shortly."

Em watched Wren for a long moment, as she punched up a screen and peered at it intently, before turning toward the bedroom.

ON THE WAY to her morning run, Em received a call from Jerin about meeting. They agreed on an appointment that gave her just enough time to get in a good run, shower off, and then make her daily report to Captain Nevitt. Em wondered if Nevitt ever took days off work. Every PAC officer was entitled to two days off every weekly rotation, unless an emergency or operational necessity precluded it. Em's own schedule showed that she usually took her days off one at a time, except when she had plans to visit Sarkan with Wren. Nevitt, though, seemed to live solely for her job.

In the infirmary, Brak, Brannin, and Jerin awaited her. Brannin guided them to one of the private rooms in the back, to ensure that none of the other doctors or nurses were aware of her situation.

"Am I late?" She checked the chronometer on her comport.

"No, right on time," Brannin answered cheerfully. "I just wanted a chance to discuss the details of your injury with them beforehand." He paused, then added, "I'm delighted you decided to ask for a consult."

"Actually, I wondered why you didn't suggest it."

Brannin stepped up to the controls of a techbed. "I know how you feel about your privacy, and I knew that you'd be perfectly aware of the *Onari*'s arrival. I left it up to you to decide."

Well. That made sense, actually. Try as she might, she couldn't make anything more nefarious out of Brannin's intentions, and her suspicion slid away.

"Your injury is quite intriguing," Jerin observed. "I've never seen one quite like it. And the specificity of the memory loss seems to be indicative of something."

"I appreciate you and Brak agreeing to take a look. I know this is supposed to be essentially a shore leave for you."

Brak made a graceful waving gesture and Em's eyes were drawn to the sleekness of her arm. "We're glad to help a friend. In fact, just try to keep us from it."

They all smiled at her, and for a moment, Em felt a sense of... well, camaraderie, sort of. Some type of familiarity and fondness, anyway. It struck her almost like a blow, yet felt so good it was like something she'd forgotten to miss.

"I..." She fought to find words for the sudden gratitude she felt. Not just for their efforts on her behalf but for the sensation that people cared about her. "Thank you." That hardly conveyed it, but it was the best she could do.

Brannin gestured toward the techbed. "We'd like to start with a full work-up of your current health."

After an entire half hour of scanning, shifting, breathing, and basically just lying there like a lump, they finally let her sit up.

Brannin was the first to speak. "Physically, you're the same as you were the last time I examined you. Remarkably healthy. There are only the smallest indications of previous trauma to your brain. Some people might even miss it, if they weren't looking for it."

"But none of the doctors in this room," Jerin cut in with dry humor. She stepped closer to the techbed and examined an image, then shook her head. "I'm as puzzled as Brannin. The trauma to your skin and skull was relatively minor. The brain injury you experienced is not something you would typically see from such a wound. We see much more damage inside than outside, and there's an epicenter of damage surrounded by undamaged tissue. Very strange."

"What would usually cause something like the injury I had?" Em asked.

The three doctors exchanged a professional look of contemplation. "A localized trauma of great force. Say, getting struck in the head by a very small object at a high rate of speed," Brannin explained.

"Like something flew across the shuttle and hit me in the head?"

Jerin nodded. "Yes, exactly like that. As if something had exploded or burst, sending a small object right at you. But something like that would have caused more external damage than you had. Possibly even a cracked skull."

"What if the external injury prompted an aneurysm or something like that?"

Brak shook her head. "That would have been easy to diagnose. That didn't happen. Though the pattern of the damage is roughly similar. Intact tissue surrounding trauma."

Em frowned. They didn't seem to have a solid answer for her as to the nature of her injury. Not what she'd hoped to hear, but even if they couldn't explain exactly how she'd lost her memory, maybe they could help restore it. "Are there any treatments that might help me remember what I've forgotten?"

Again, the three exchanged a look. Em was getting tired of that. It didn't seem to bode well for her.

Brak's expression remained cool and professional, not giving away any of her thoughts. "I could try stimulating your nerve-fiber tracks in the area. It would be similar to the process of getting the brain ready to accept a neural implant. If that were successful, we might be able to stimulate some regrowth of the area that was damaged."

Brannin's lips twisted into a slight grimace. "There's a risk there, though. I'm not sure I'd recommend that."

"Why? What's the risk?" Em was comfortable with a degree of risk, but not if it meant a potential accidental lobotomy or something.

"First off, it would be very painful. Brain matter doesn't register pain like other parts of the body, but a growth stimulator forces the body to self-replicate cells at a tremendous rate. It's an inherently painful process. We could help with that a little, but we can't give you anesthetics that would make you sleepy or cloud your perceptions. We'd need you awake," Brannin explained, looking regretful.

"I can handle pain." She didn't relish the idea, but she wasn't afraid of it either. Not if it meant reclaiming her life.

"There's another issue," Jerin said. She seemed slightly less reluctant than Brannin, but more sympathetic than Brak. The three of them together sure were an interesting team. Perhaps it was best that most of the time, patients were treated by only one doctor.

Jerin continued, "It's possible that we might sensitize your pain receptors, causing chronic headaches. These could be mild or serious. Migraine headaches are possible, and they can be completely debilitating, making it impossible to stand, eat, or open your eyes."

Oh, great. Couldn't she just be at risk of death or something? "What are the odds of that?"

"About fifteen percent," Brak said.

At least they were low odds. "Okay. Anything else I should know?"

Brannin looked conflicted. "If you were going to try this procedure—and I'm not sure I'd recommend doing so—the sooner, the better. The more time you give your neural pathways to atrophy, the less likely they can be restored to functionality."

That wasn't really a problem for Em. She wasn't the sort of person who dithered over a decision, waffling this way and that. She'd make her choice and live with it.

Brannin frowned. "Working with Grayith and giving your brain more time to rewire itself would be a much safer option. You're physically healthy, in the prime of your life. You've been moving forward quite well, doing your job, socializing. I don't like risking that with a somewhat experimental procedure. Gray might be able to help you discover some of your memories with hypnotherapy."

Em looked to Jerin and Brak. "So this is experimental? You don't normally do this?"

Jerin answered, "No. But your memory loss is not a typical injury. I admit that Brak and I are of a different school than Brannin. We push boundaries. Flying around out there, trying to see to an entire sector of the sick and dying, we've learned to take calculated risks. To operate at the edge of medical science's abilities." Her eyes cut to Brannin. "But he's your doctor, and knows you better than we do. You need to do what's right for you, but objectively, I'd say you should weigh his opinion more heavily than you do ours. He's a brilliant doctor, and rarely loses a patient."

Jerin and Brak must have a much higher fatality rate. That unspoken truth rang in the air.

"In your opinion, is the hypnotherapy as likely to help me as the surgery? Before, Gray didn't think it was even an option," Em kept her eyes locked on Jerin.

"He was under the impression that the nature of your injury was different than it is, so hypnotherapy *is* an option. But no, I don't think it's as likely to help." Jerin's response came without hesitation.

"Then I want the surgery," Em surprised herself by saying. She hadn't realized she'd already made the choice, but the certainty on Jerin's face, and on Brak's, convinced her. Em needed to know who she really was. Who she'd been. She'd take the risk.

"Don't you want to talk it over with Wren first?" Brannin asked.

Scrap. She was a terrible wife. In more ways than one. She sighed. "Yeah, I probably should."

Jerin reached out and gave her hand a squeeze. "We'd want you to take a couple days to think it over, anyway. The *Onari* has five more days here before we disembark, so you have time."

"Right." Em flipped her legs over the side of the techbed and stood. "I should get back to work, then. Thank you, doctors, for your expertise."

She gave them a moderately deep bow to convey her appreciation and respect. As she straightened, she impulsively reached for Brannin's hand. His eyes sparked with surprise. "Thank you for looking out for me. It's good to know that someone is." She dropped his hand and left the infirmary quickly.

It was early for her to do her Deck One rounds, but she had the urge to move, to keep herself busy. She didn't want to be alone with her thoughts. So she took a leisurely stroll around the boardwalk.

Walking along, she felt more grounded. More like she belonged. The fragrance of food drifted past her. The excited conversation and laughter created a comforting hum. She liked the commotion of the boardwalk. The bursting vitality of daily activity. The intersecting of so many lives.

She nodded and waved at those who greeted her, stopping to exchange pleasantries here and there. It wasn't until she went past Cabot Layne's shop that she got pulled off course. Arin, standing with Kellis, had noticed Em from the doorway and waved her inside.

"Hey, Chief," he said. "You're early today."

"Yeah. I needed to stretch my legs."

Kellis smiled at her. She and Arin made a very attractive pair, standing together. "Cabot was just about to show us some artwork. I'd love your opinion, if you have the time."

"Oh. I'm not an art expert, but sure, I can give an uneducated opinion as well as the next guy."

Kellis chuckled, and Cabot cut in. "Bah, expert or not, Em has a great eye for craftsmanship." He gestured for them to come in from the doorway and turned to lead them to one side of his shop.

"Along this wall we have paintings, mosaics, and some three-dimensional wall art. On that side—" he gestured to the opposite wall, which housed shelves and pedestals, "—you'll find free-standing pieces. Any idea what sort of thing you're looking for?"

"Not really." Kellis looked down at the floor, suddenly seeming self-conscious. "I'd just like to personalize my quarters. I've had them six months now, and my rooms are as plain as they were the day I moved in."

"Ah." Cabot didn't need to say more. They all knew how little refugees from Atalan started out with. "Well, hopefully you'll find something you like. Any idea what styles you prefer? Ancient art? Modern? Atalan-inspired? Industrial?"

Kellis shook her head with good humor. "No idea whatsoever."

Cabot made a thoughtful humming noise. He pointed to a

gold-framed nature scene. "This is an impressionist-style painting of a pond on Earth. Popular among collectors of ancient art. What do you think of that?"

"It's...interesting," Kellis hedged. "I think I'd prefer something less..."

"Old," Cabot finished for her. "I'm not a fan of that style either, personally. Don't worry, my dear, I won't be offended by your opinion. Art is a very subjective thing."

Kellis relaxed a little, giving Cabot a grateful smile. Em wondered where the woman's reserve had come from. When she'd met Kellis before, she'd seemed outgoing and earnest. Was she uncomfortable shopping? Or perhaps her discomfort came from spending money on nonessentials. Refugees sometimes had difficulty with that.

"I kind of like that one." Kellis pointed to a textured painting of a brilliant blue quasar.

"Ah. Postmodernist Briveen artwork. It's considered edgy and flamboyant even today," Cabot explained.

"I like the brightness and the subject matter, but it's a little big for my quarters." Kellis scanned the other artwork on the wall, then walked to the opposite side of the shop. Arin stayed right with her, Em noted with interest.

"Oh." Kellis stood in front of a pedestal that held a brown ball that represented a planet. Atalus. She touched the metal tip of the display with her index finger, looking sad. Arin put his arm around her and they stood, looking at their homeworld.

"That's a globe. More of an antiquity than art. People used them like maps, before electricity. That one there is almost a thousand years old."

Kellis turned away from it, causing Arin's arm to fall to his side. "I don't think antiquities are my thing." She seemed to regain her confidence, and her chin lifted almost defiantly.

She moved to a crystalline sphere composed of twisting, intertwining swirls of a smooth, clear material that shifted from one color to the next. "I like this."

"That's a Sarkavian rainbow fetish," Em said.

"A fetish?" Kellis laughed. "That's a funny thing to call it."

"Ancient Sarkavians worshipped the sun and rain, and rainbows were the children of the two. They remain a very popular symbol, even in pop culture. Most houses have a fetish or two."

"How much?" Kellis asked. Cabot named a low price and she looked surprised. "Is that all?"

Cabot shrugged. "It's a modern reproduction, and very common."

"I'll take it." Kellis beamed at Arin. "And I have enough cubics for a second piece as well, provided it's not too valuable."

Cabot pursed his lips. "You know, I think I might have just the thing. One moment." He swept away, exiting the shop's showroom through a doorway behind the sales counter.

"Thanks for coming," Kellis said, smiling at Arin and Em. "It's nice to have friends to shop with. Yesterday, I did some clothes shopping with Brak. There are some crazy styles these days! Everything from way too many layers to not nearly enough to cover my skin."

"We see some of everything here," Arin said. "There are days I have to really work to keep my face blank when people walk off their ships." He snorted with laughter, apparently remembering something outlandish.

"I like all the variety on the boardwalk," Kellis protested. "It makes it seem like there's some big party going on, but no one was told how to dress."

Em liked that fanciful description. Before she could say so, Cabot returned, carrying a porthole-sized picture. He turned it around for Kellis to see with a flourish.

"Oh," Kellis breathed.

Em hadn't seen the picture before. It was a painting, rendered with photographic realism. It depicted Dragonfire Station, hanging in space at a slight angle, with the nebula blazing behind it. A small ship had docked on the lower section of the station, colloquially known as the stem, where larger ships usually docked. Three other ships hovered in space, approaching.

"I just got this in yesterday," Cabot said.

"I love it," Kellis said.

Em did too. "Who painted it? I don't see a signature."

Cabot's face went all sneaky-like. "The artist wishes to remain anonymous, but I don't mind saying that it's someone who lives here on the station."

"How much is it?" Arin asked.

"Three hundred cubics," Cabot answered.

Kellis wrinkled her nose. "That wipes me out financially, but I want it. It's beautiful."

Cabot smiled, looking extremely self-satisfied. "I knew you'd like it."

Out of nowhere, he produced an infoboard, punched in commands, and then presented it to Kellis. She input her credentials and took ownership of her new artwork.

She didn't seem to mind being a few hundred cubics poorer.

"I'll have these delivered to your quarters, if you like," Cabot offered.

"No, I'd like to take them with me." Kellis picked up the fetish.

"I can carry the picture if you like," Arin offered.

"Thanks." Kellis flashed him a grin.

"It was a pleasure doing business with you." Cabot gave his new customer a deep bow.

"Likewise. I'll stop by next time I'm on Dragonfire." Kellis returned the bow.

"Be careful," Em warned. "Once he knows your taste, he'll save things for you, and you can forever say goodbye to your bank account."

Kellis and Arin laughed, as did Cabot.

"No worries," Kellis said. "I'm careful about keeping my

savings in order. I only spent my discretionary budget. It's not like there's much to buy on the *Onari*."

Em was glad to hear that Kellis was being so responsible. No doubt it took great restraint to maintain a savings account when she had very few personal belongings and a universe of shopping opportunities.

The two Atalans took their leave, which left Em alone with Cabot.

"Any new knives?" she asked.

"Not yet. I'm always on the lookout."

"Have you had a lot of business, with the *Onari* docking?" She wondered how much he made in a year. He seemed to live a very modest life, so far as she could tell.

"A moderate uptick. Nothing to hasten my retirement."

"How much money would convince you to retire?" she wondered.

"Ah, you got me. I enjoy my work too much to ever retire, no matter how many cubics someone offered me. My love for business isn't really about the money anymore." He gave her a mock-severe look. "Don't tell anyone I said that, though. Bargaining is the fun part."

"You didn't bargain with Kellis. Or me."

His eyebrows raised. "Of course not. That's for the others."

"What others?"

His eyebrows crawled all the way up to his hairline. "The ones who aren't family. Really, Chief, it's like you don't know me at all today."

"Just checking, Cabot." She gave him a wide smile and his features smoothed.

"I'll let you know if I get anything new in for you," he promised.

"Be sure you do," she teased, and he winked at her.

She finished the rest of her rounds with a smile.

On her way up to her office, her comport alerted her to an incoming message. It was Brak. Since Em was alone on the lift, she took the call, though she doubted it was an emergency.

"I need to see you right away," Brak said without preamble.

"I'm just headed to my office. I'll send you a temporary passcode to get on Deck Four."

"I'll be right there." The line closed.

Odd. Em wondered if Brak had some bad news about her health. Why else would she want to see her immediately?

Once in her office, Em paced restlessly. It seemed to take forever for Brak to get there. Finally, the soft, hollow sound of dried bamboo pieces knocking together indicated her arrival. Em signaled the doors to open and Brak entered.

Em immediately smelled anise and smoke. Worry and suspicion.

"What is it, Brak?" Em faced her in the middle of her office.

"I hope I'm wrong. I hope I'm being paranoid. But I think I know what happened to you."

Em's heart seemed to freeze in her chest, then began thudding hard, as if to make up for lost time. She found herself sitting on the couch, with Brak sitting across from her, without remembering moving there.

She noticed her hands nervously twining around each other, so she pinned them, palms together, between her knees.

Brak clacked her teeth in agitation. "This room is secure?"

"Of course. I sweep my office for devices every time I return to it. My quarters too, actually."

"A wise precaution. If what I suspect is true, you might be in some serious trouble."

Em didn't find that idea as foreboding as she probably should have. Just the idea of having her crack at figuring out all of the recent events was enough to shove concerns for her safety to the background. "Tell me."

"About six months ago, Admiral Krazinski contacted me about doing some private research for them. That's not unusual. The PAC often has particular functions they require from cybernetics, and pay me well to engineer them. The research has also been helpful to advancing the field, so it's been a mutually beneficial relationship. The unusual thing about the request was that they wanted me to do something I found morally wrong. Implants that weren't simply therapeutic. They wanted me to adapt the neural implants I use for cybernetic controls for another purpose. Memory augmentation."

The idea of memory augmentation took her breath. Most of the PAC's treaties with coalition members and nonmembers alike included a total ban on developing brain augmentation technology. What Brak was saying seemed impossible. What Krazinski had asked for could directly cause the destruction of the PAC. And all-out war.

When she could keep her voice even, Em asked, "What did you say to the admiral?"

"I said *no*. Of course I said no. The admiral threatened that he'd have someone else develop it instead, but I'd hoped no cyberneticist with the necessary skills would be willing to do it. Artificial augmentation of the brain has always been taboo. Not only would it eventually create a necessity for people to undergo brain surgery to level the playing field enough to compete in life, it would never be a safe procedure. No matter how perfect the technology component, brains are too dissimilar from one another to achieve reliable results. The risk for brain damage would be too high."

"Could he have been testing you? Making sure you *wouldn't* do that kind of research?"

"The thought occurred to me afterward," Brak admitted. "But at the time, I fully believed it. And now, I have reason to believe that Krazinski eventually did find a willing scientist."

Em didn't need Brak to paint a picture for her. "You think I had one of those implants."

Brak hesitated, then tilted her head in affirmation. "The injury to your brain looks exactly like I'd expect a botched attempt at installing one to look."

"And it would explain why the external injury didn't match the internal one. And why my memory was affected." Em smelled the warm-baked-bread scent of agreement.

That left Em with a lot of questions. "Why the secrecy? Shouldn't Brannin know, since he's my doctor?"

"If I'm right, whatever was done to your head was classified. Which makes your head classified. Which makes *you* classified."

Em processed that. "Okay, so that means you have classified clearance, then. How's that possible when you're not even a PAC officer?"

"My services were wanted badly enough to make it happen. Believe me, I've certified a great many documents that ensure my compliance with all security protocols. But only one project I ever worked on was actually top-secret classified. This neural implant thing was something entirely different. I had to go through hoops for higher-than-top-secret clearance that don't even appear on any official record. And that was just to *talk* about it."

"There's no such thing as higher than top secret." Every first-year cadet at OTS knew that only a privileged few ever received top-secret clearance. Admirals, captains involved with key diplomacy, and high-ranking security officers. Not someone like Em. Not yet, anyway.

But when all alternatives are exhausted, the only possibility remaining must be correct. "Blackout. You're talking about Blackout."

The much-fabled, greatly feared and revered, often considered merely mythical covert special ops division of the PAC. People didn't even speak of it in public. Just in case naming the boogeyman made him come to life.

Em felt a sensation pooling around her calves and rising up to her knees. She didn't know if it was dread or excitement. Possibly both. "You're saying Blackout wanted you to create this neural implant for them. Which makes me—"

"A BlackOp," Brak finished.

"A BlackOp," Em repeated, trying the word out. Well, it would explain things. Her injury, her memory loss, and her underreported skills. Her investigation into Wren, as well. Blackout would have placed Em on Dragonfire, which was why Captain Nevitt had not been permitted to select her own chief of security. "Damn."

It all made sense. She stood and began pacing the room. Brak sat discreetly on the couch while Em thought it all through.

Em tried to come up with an alternate explanation, but no, it all fit too well. It had to be true. Once she accepted that as a fact, her mind flooded with yet more questions. What did Nevitt know? What was the implant intended to do? How and when had it been installed? What was the true nature of her accident? Who was she really? Was she endangering everyone on the station just by being there? Underneath it all, she kept wondering how Wren fit into the puzzle.

"I don't even know where to start," she admitted.

"It's true, then," Brak said.

Em stopped pacing and faced Brak from behind her desk. "It makes too much sense not to be. But where does that leave me? I need to come up with a strategy to figure out what happened without putting anyone in danger."

Brak inclined her head slightly. The light in the office shined over her blue-green skin, and its iridescence seemed like a color shift as she moved. "We'll need to plan carefully."

Em blinked. "We? You're no BlackOp. You need to stay as far away from this as you can."

Brak's eyes narrowed and her chin came up. "This is about my science. My science is my life. I'm not going to let anyone get away with what they've done. I may not have your officer training but believe me, Briveen do not grow up without learning intensive battle skills." Her lips twitched with the hint of a smirk. "No matter what caste you're born into."

Which made Em wonder about Brak's caste, but it would have been rude to ask.

"All right. I can't say I'm sorry to have a comrade in all this. First, we need to decide on our first objective."

4

While Brak was still in her office, Em received an emergency call. A fight had broken out on the boardwalk. Two different trading factions had crossed paths and words, then fists, had been exchanged.

By the time Em arrived on the scene, her staff had already gotten the situation under control, but it was her job to decide the consequences for those involved.

Two humans and a Rescan sat in the Deck One security office, looking hostile but only mildly battered. A black eye here, a split lip there. A minor skirmish, then, but Em didn't tolerate that kind of rubbish on her station. She wouldn't let foolish behavior like this put her wards in danger. Because she considered the safety of every single person on the station to be her own personal responsibility. She had a history of being exacting, and she intended to live up to that.

She remained standing, frowning at the two human miscreants as a couple of her middle-ranking staff gave her the details. She hadn't directly worked with the pair since her accident, and found them both to be effective and professional.

"My problem is that you two have a previous altercation on

your record here at Dragonfire, as well as one at Blackthorn. Who knows what you get up to on stations and planets not run by the PAC." Under Em's scrutiny, they both dropped their gazes to the floor.

They all knew that she could hurt their livelihoods. Without docking privileges on Dragonfire, they'd be at a significant disadvantage for trading. But considering that none of their documented offenses had caused major injury or harmed a resident of the station, she could afford a measure of leniency. A last chance, of sorts.

"You two will be locked out of Dragonfire for six months. Keep your record clean during that time and I'll reinstate your docking privileges. If you don't, your lockout will be much longer. Perhaps permanent."

The men exchanged a pained expression, but didn't meet her gaze.

"Also," she added, "once you do regain your privileges, you'll be on your last chance. Another incident like today's and you can forget about ever docking at Dragonfire again. Understand?" She pinned each one with a look.

"Yes, Chief," one said, while the other nodded.

"My staff will escort you to your ship and you will depart immediately." Em nodded to the three security staffers standing by the door. They snapped into action, ushering the two out.

"And you. Arlen Stinth." She focused on the Rescan. "Care to tell me your version, now that they're gone?"

The woman shifted in her seat. "I was just enjoying a cup of tea on the food court, doing some people watching. Those two sat at my table uninvited and attempted to flirt with me. When I stood to leave..." She trailed off, her shoulders tensing.

Oh, hell no. If they had sexually harassed the woman, Em would change her decision on their lockout.

"They insulted my ship," Arlen said, her tanned cheeks turning dusky. She sat up straight and fixed Em with a steady look. "No one insults my ship. It might not be pretty, but it's as solid and spaceworthy as anything else that docks here. I don't cut corners on my maintenance. I keep my crew safe."

The angry steel seeped out of Em's spine and she fought a smile. Arlen had picked the fight, and based on an insult to her ship rather than to her person. "Yes, your record is spotless, both for mechanical checks and your activities on Dragonfire."

Arlen nodded. Other than puffiness at the corner of her mouth, she seemed to be in good physical condition.

"Do you need medical attention?" Em asked.

Arlen's tongue probed the corner of her mouth. "I don't think so. They barely touched me."

Em allowed herself a grin. "Good job, then."

Arlen let out a light, surprised laugh.

"I'll note the incident on your record, but you're free to go about your business. Those two should have just let you leave when you wanted to. However, don't make a habit of this sort of thing. I really don't appreciate fistfights on my boardwalk."

Arlen ducked her head. "Of course. My apologies." She stood. "Thank you, Chief." On her way out, she gave Em a deep bow of respect. A little unusual, given that she wasn't a PAC officer, but the gesture had seeped into some well-mannered people. Em returned the bow.

Since she was already on Deck One, she did her rounds. She ran into Nix and the girl's friend Robert, whom she'd called Ratboy the first time she'd encountered him, just after her shuttle accident.

The way the adolescents teased and bumped into one another, Em wondered if they were on the verge of their first romance. Thirteen years old seemed about the right age. The thought made Em smile.

She wondered about her own first romance. Surely there had been one. Without a family to tell her about it, she might never know. She hoped she hadn't done anything foolish. But then, that was a defining characteristic of a first romance, wasn't it? Foolishness, and a good measure of awkwardness. She'd probably been as sappy as any other adolescent girl.

Cabot came out of his shop to invite her in for a cup of tea, but she had to decline. She had a ship of PAC ambassadors to greet. He kept her company, though, as she strolled back across the boardwalk toward Cargo Bay Six.

"Lot of ships today," he remarked.

"Yes. A few had to dock on the stem section and ride the lift up to Deck One. Good thing they didn't need maintenance. The crew's already maxed out. Hopefully we don't get any emergencies in."

He inclined his head in agreement. "Business is always good when a hospi-ship is docked. They attract the kind of folks that have money to spend. I wouldn't mind a bit if the *Onari* made Dragonfire into a home base."

"You and a lot of people, I'm sure."

"Your legate seemed quite taken with the Atalan engineer," Cabot observed.

"I feel like you're making some sort of point, or asking a question, maybe." She squinted at him.

He held his hands out palms up, all innocence. "Not at all. Just making small talk."

"Uh-huh."

He smiled benignly. "The more ties the *Onari* has to Dragonfire, the better."

"Well, I'm not going to marry my legate off just to improve your sales figures."

Cabot chuckled. "He does seem happy though. Maybe even enough to think about breaking some hearts and settling down."

Em made a noncommittal sound. Arin's relationship status was his own business. She didn't even like dealing with her own.

"I guess this is where I head back to my shop." Cabot stopped walking several meters short of the cargo bay. "It's been a pleasure, as always."

They exchanged bows and Em entered the bay to greet the ambassadors. Since they were only minor government officials for various planets, she expected a routine, low-maintenance exchange. Thank goodness. She had a distinct overabundance of tricky ventures in her life already.

EM WAS at her desk making out the duty roster for the next week when her voicecom display alerted her to an incoming call. A glance at the chronometer told her that she had only ten minutes left on her shift.

Em answered the call. Wren appeared on the screen, looking harried. She explained that she'd be working late due to a malfunctioning structural integrity field on a ship that had to depart the next day. She wouldn't be home until very late.

Em felt relieved. Then she felt guilty about her relief. She just didn't feel comfortable with Wren. What did her marriage even mean? Blackout had installed her on Dragonfire to investigate Wren for smuggling, but instead, Em had married her? Had that been a personal choice, or an executive order?

Ugh. She pressed the flats of her palms against her closed eyes until colors bloomed.

She pushed all of that away from her mind and pulled up Dragonfire's external security feeds. Once she'd assured the station's continued well-being, she focused on her investigation.

Brak had opened Em's mind to possibilities she hadn't known she should consider. After their conversation about her injury and Blackout, Em had decided she needed to start looking in places that only a covert operative would know to look. If she was a BlackOp, then she knew that those places existed, and how to find them. Theoretically. Just like she hadn't known she could throw knives until she did it, maybe just looking for clandestine affairs would get her to that jump-off point where her knowledge would kick in.

She just needed to make it happen, somehow.

Okay, brain, she thought. *I know you can do this.*

She sat at the voicecom display, hand poised. "I need to dig for clandestine communications, Blackout style," she said aloud. "Crazy secure, hidden stuff. Beyond OTS stuff. Beyond security school stuff. Using methods that no one outside of Blackout would ever…"

Something opened up in her mind and she touched the screen. In increasingly quick procession, she flipped through images, drilling directly into the subspace receiver. Once there, she programmed a temporary ghost relay directly into the code and entered ridiculously long strings of alphanumerics.

It felt almost too easy. Like she'd flipped a switch and suddenly, what she'd needed now rested literally in her fingertips. Though she didn't find exactly what she'd hoped for.

She understood what she'd constructed. A two-way communications relay. She could open it, and she could close it. Basically, she would have built and dismantled it anytime she needed to send a heavily coded message. It wasn't the database she'd wanted to find, but of course that had been foolish to hope for. You can't keep a secret by documenting it. Blackout wouldn't leave repositories of information for people to find. Although… that made her wonder about her own messages, the ones that had clued her in to her investigation of Wren. Why hadn't she destroyed those? Had she intentionally left some proof behind?

Hmm, but what to do now. She rapped her palms against the desk as she thought. Sending a message was almost sure to go wrong, with her lack of memory. She needed to *receive* a message. Before her injury she would have been checking this frequency daily for messages, she realized. Fortunately, there were no missives waiting for her, which would have served as a warning beacon to anyone on the other end that something had gone wrong with her.

On the other hand, that left her nothing to work with. She'd have to wait for a message and hope she hadn't been tasked with periodic status reports by whomever she answered to.

While she waited for Blackout to contact her and give her an opening, she needed information. The information that, hopefully, could be dug out of her brain by some clever doctors.

THE NEXT DAY WAS HECTIC, for both Em and Wren. They didn't even eat dinner together, which gave Em more guilty relief to add to her list of ways she was a bad wife. Instead, Em broached the subject of the surgery during the brief intersection in their schedules immediately preceding sleep.

Tired as she was after two days of nearly nonstop work, Wren roused the energy to put up a lively but fair debate. In the end, she respected Em's decision with a calm concern that made Em proud. Then her pride caused anxiety to zap through her like a stinger blast. She threw herself into the shower so Wren didn't have a chance to notice her change of mood.

The steam from the hot water comforted her, as if the wispy haze could conceal her worries and secrets. Regardless of what her feelings for Wren had been before her injury, Em felt strongly about Wren now. She didn't want to find out that the previous version of herself had only been fulfilling her duties as a BlackOp by marrying Wren. The idea made her want to go back and kick her own ass, if it were true.

Resolution hardened in her gut, blotting out her anxiety. Whatever her original purpose for marrying Wren had been, Em wouldn't let anything harm her, and she wouldn't leave her. If Blackout tried to interfere with that decision, then Em would turn Blackout upside down and obliterate any obstacles in her way. Yep. That seemed fair.

Decision made, she slapped the water control and toweled off quickly, feeling much cleaner.

When she slid between the blankets, Wren was already lying on her side, with her pink hair tumbled across the pillow and her pale eyes watching Em. Wren loved her, and rather than feeling uncomfortable as she had at first, Em realized she returned the feeling.

Maybe it didn't make sense, and maybe it was even wrong, but Em didn't give a damn. The connection between them was all she knew of that was truly real, and for the moment, it was all that mattered.

Em closed the space between them, reaching for her wife.

―――――

"Comfortable?" Brannin asked. He'd cleared the infirmary for the procedure, ensuring that only he, Brak, Jerin, and Em would be present.

"No. I'm lying on a techbed, waiting for you to dig into my brain." If anything was going to make Em uncomfortable, surely brain surgery would be it.

"Try to relax." Jerin's voice came from behind her, where she couldn't see. With Em's head and neck secured, she couldn't turn. Nor should she, since they were mapping her brain to prepare for cutting into it. Em was trying to be stoic, but her stomach felt like it was full of acid.

"Right. I'll just enjoy the time off work." Em wiggled her toes. At least she still had domain over those. She stared up at the ceiling, hoping she wasn't making a mistake. An existence of perpetual migraines wouldn't be much of a life.

Brannin's fingers slid between hers. He had strong, steady hands. Warm. Comforting. "Don't worry, Chief. Brak's the best at what she does, and she and Jerin make a great team. I'm going to stay right here and let you know what's happening as we go along."

"Thanks, Doc." She cut her eyes to the side to get a look at him, sitting on a stool alongside the techbed.

She felt a light pressure on her head.

"They're removing a small portion of your hair at the entry point to ensure precision. But they'll regrow that afterward and you'll never know the difference," Brannin told her. She was glad he was the one talking to her. He had a lovely voice.

"That's a relief. You know my looks are my top priority."

Brannin and Jerin both chuckled.

A few long moments later, the pressure stopped and Jerin said, "Now I'm going to administer a mild anesthetic to the incision area. I'm afraid we can't do anything for the pain of the regrowth."

"I understand."

Brannin's other hand came up, sandwiching both of hers between his. It must be go time.

"They're going to make the incision in your scalp, then put a tiny puncture in your skull to reach the brain tissue," Brannin said.

"I probably would have been happy living my entire life without ever having someone say that to me," she answered.

He patted her hand. She lay there, waiting for the pain to start.

"Okay. They're about to begin. I'm going to let go now, and activate the restraints, but I'll be right here beside you the whole time."

She looked at him from the corner of her eye. "Are the restraints necessary?"

"Yes. We can't risk having you move." Brannin tapped the techbed controls and she felt an invisible pressure immobilize her. Essentially, restraints were a small-scale force field. Undamaging but unyielding. She could blink and speak and breathe, but that was about it.

Brak's voice reached her ears. "This will take five to ten minutes. Hang in there, and remember, it *will* end."

She meant well. She certainly didn't mean to scare the scrap out of Em. She gritted her teeth. "Let's get to it."

The pain sliced into her head almost immediately. Like a lightning bolt burning into her brain. She clamped her lips together and focused her entire being on not making a sound. She shrank herself down to just that, just silence. Just enduring.

Time stretched. Became endless. Until suddenly the pain stopped. Poof, just like that. Like an infoboard turning off. She opened her eyes and the universe coalesced around her. She took a breath.

Brannin stood over her. "How are you?"

She tried to put a hand to her brow, but her body was immobilized. "Still breathing." She licked her lips. "How did we do?"

"It went well." Brak's voice drifted to her ears. "The tissue was healthy and responsive. We're going to heal up your incision and then we'll just have to wait and see."

When Brannin offered his hand to help her stand up from the table, it all felt oddly anticlimactic to her.

"That's it?" she asked. It seemed odd that they'd just let her walk right out. She felt almost disappointed that Brannin didn't want to keep her in the infirmary, running a constant stream of tests on her.

"That's it," he confirmed. "I want you to take it easy today though. You can go to work if you want, but no strenuous activity. No banging your head into anything."

"I'll have to cancel my afternoon bash-my-head-against-the-wall session. Pity." She rolled her shoulders. She felt a little tired, but otherwise not too bad.

Brannin just smirked. Brak and Jerin joined him, facing her. Em made eye contact with Brak, but the Briveen looked consummately professional. Em would have to try to talk to her privately later to see if she had discovered anything while poking about in her gray matter.

Brannin brought a cup of biogel and handed it to her. "Before you go."

"Why do I need this?" She peered at the colorless liquid.

"A cup of biogel never hurts. Actually, I'd prescribe one a day for everyone on the station if I thought they'd listen."

"They wouldn't," Em assured him. Jerin laughed. Em shrugged and downed the cup. Other than an almost antiseptic tang, it had no flavor. It wasn't exactly unpleasant, but not many people would down a cup of that without a doctor staring at them. She set the cup on the techbed. "I guess I'm off to work, then."

Brak advised, "Take it easy, like Brannin said. And try to get to bed early. You're bound to be very tired by day's end. Check in if you have any head pain whatsoever. Or blurred vision, dizziness, or confusion. Anything unusual."

"Right." She still felt strange about going to work right after brain surgery, but whatever. She felt strange about a lot of things these days.

EM STRODE from the lift to her office, only to falter when she saw Wren sitting in front of the office door. Wren's pinched face angled upward, searching Em for signs of damage.

"Ah, Love." Em sat right there, in the hallway, and pulled Wren into her arms. "I'm sorry."

Wren wrapped her in a nearly crushing hug, surprising Em with a strength she hadn't realized her wife had. She held Wren close, letting her burrow into her neck. For a moment. Then Wren pushed her back and glared.

"You did that all wrong!"

"You're right. I'm sorry." Em had no excuses. She'd been focused on her own concerns, and while protecting Wren ranked high among them, she hadn't accurately anticipated how upset Wren would be.

"I should have been there. I'm your wife, dammit!" A tear leaked out of the corner of Wren's eye and she dashed it away angrily.

"Not for the surgery," Em disagreed gently. "None of us wanted you to see that, including the doctors. But I should have had you there, so you could come in right after. I messed it up."

"You messed it up *big*. Don't even think about trying something like that again. I don't care what the doctors say. I can dismantle any bloody doorway on this station. Got it?" Wren's voice rose as she talked, ending in a shout.

"I got it. Message received. I'm sorry." She reached for Wren again, both of them still on the floor outside her office. Em didn't even care if someone happened by and saw. All that mattered was erasing the hurt and fear from Wren's face.

Wren leaned against her, breathing in harsh bursts. Em rubbed her back in slow circles. When she felt Wren's heartbeat slow, she stood and tugged Wren up to her feet. "Let's go sit on the couch."

She did her security sweep as quickly as she could, then sat next to Wren.

"Are you okay? Your brain's not even more messed up, is it?" Wren walked an interesting line between concerned and insulting.

"I feel fine so far. We just wait and see now."

Wren huffed out an annoyed breath. "That's all we do anymore. Wait. Hope. I want to..." She held out her hands, opening and closing them as if grasping for something. "*Do something. Have some sort of effect on what's happening to us.*"

"Yeah. I get that. I feel the same way." Em wanted a target, a task, something tangible that she could focus on and get done. She was tired of being in this passive position of not knowing. She could at least stop being a bad wife. She had that much in her power. She didn't know how Wren would react to the truth, though, or if telling her might put her in more danger. Em might regret it later, but she was sick of waiting around and letting unknown forces shape her life. At the least, she could take control of her personal life. For better or for worse.

"About what's happening to us," Em began. "There's more to it, and I hate keeping it from you."

She spilled it all out, in rapid fire. Blackout. Her suspicions about the accident. The signal relay she would build and dismantle twice a day, hoping for some hint of what to do next. And her investigation of Wren. Maybe it was the wrong decision, and maybe it would put them both in danger. But Em could only work with what she had and she didn't want to lie to Wren anymore.

Wren sat, back straight, as she took it all in. Her pale skin had lost its rosy glow and her mouth had set in a tight line. She blinked slowly as she processed it all.

"Is our marriage real?" she finally asked.

"As far as I'm concerned, yes. Absolutely. I love you. I don't know how it all started, but I hope to Prelin that it was always as real as it is right now."

Wren didn't react. "And you have no idea why you were sent to investigate me? Doesn't seem like I could do anything to warrant Blackout's attention."

"No. Just that there were concerns of smuggling."

"I see." She stood, and Em did the same. Wren's eyes didn't quite meet hers, and Em wondered if she'd made a terrible mistake. "I'm going to go. I need time to think about all this."

"Okay. I..." No, she wouldn't repeat herself. She'd already declared her feelings. The rest was up to Wren. "Okay."

She resisted the urge to touch Wren as she walked out the

door, knowing it wasn't wanted. After the door swished closed, she walked to her desk and sat.

She'd thought brain surgery would be the most painful part of her day. She'd been wrong.

EM'S MIND wasn't on her work. She ran through the routine checks and protocols just fine, but her thoughts kept returning to Wren. There just wasn't enough going on to keep her fully occupied.

She pushed away from her desk. She *had* just endured brain surgery. Surely that was a decent excuse for missing half a day of work. She'd remain on call, just in case anything significant happened. As she engaged the security on her office, her only problem was what to do with the next several hours.

She considered having Arin meet her in the gym for sparring. As long as she ruled out any head shots, she wouldn't be in danger, and physical activity seemed the perfect antidote to mental disarray. Plus, with luck, it would help her get to sleep that night. But as proficient as Arin was, he was nowhere near her combat level. She had to pull her punches too much to spar with him.

An idea occurred to her and she pulled out her comport.

Twenty minutes later, she stood in the sparring ring with her guard up, strafing around the most formidable opponent Dragonfire had to offer at the moment.

Brak let out a sighing growl, as if deeply satisfied. At least that was how Em interpreted it. A young sysops lieutenant in Em's peripheral vision twitched and turned around to look at Brak with anxious eyes.

Em made a snorty sound of amusement, and Brak's head tilted in a way that said she also found it funny.

"You're sure you're up to this?" the Briveen asked, adjusting her position each time Em sidestepped.

"If there were a good reason why I shouldn't be, you'd have said so already." She felt perfectly fine, physically. Brak had already told her that she hadn't found anything unexpected in Em's brain.

"We're both going to be in trouble with Brannin," Brak warned.

Em grinned, feinting as if she were going to hit Brak, but quickly dodging to the left instead, looking for an opening. "Oh, I have no doubt of that. But I find I like your flying-by-the-seat-of-your-pants approach. I think we have a lot in common."

Brak's chin came up and her head angled slightly. "My pants? Are these not typical sparring gear?" She didn't drop her guard or her gaze. Smart woman.

Em snorted out a laugh. "It's an old expression. It means making choices as you go along. Taking risks by not planning ahead."

Brak pressed forward, forcing Em to step back. Brak definitely had the advantage in both size and strength. She topped Em's height by a good six inches, and her naturally muscular lower body would make her kicks a force to reckon with. Plus, she had those arms. Those magnificent cybernetic arms that made Em almost a little envious.

Brak moved in with surprising speed and threw a punch at Em's chest. Years of training clicked into place and instead of blocking the blow, Em dodged it and pivoted so she could use her entire body to follow through on Brak's own momentum, pulling her off-balance.

That was exactly the opening she needed. Careful to stay out of the reach of those arms, Em launched a volley of punches at Brak's chest and stomach. If she were really fighting, she'd go for the throat. A Briveen's throat was her most vulnerable area. The scaly skin was thinnest there, and vital arteries and veins lay just beneath it.

Though her attention stayed focused on Brak, Em sensed a small crowd gathering. She didn't care. Let them see what she could do. If someone in Blackout got wind of it and sent an op after her, all the better. At least that would be *something*.

Brak landed a punch on her solar plexus that took her breath, but she didn't let it slow her down. She ducked out of Brak's reach and got into position just in time to hit Brak hard in the small of the back. A lucky shot, but whatever. If Em hadn't already known what she was capable of, she wouldn't have even attempted to spar a Briveen. In all ways but one, she was outmatched. But that one way happened to be the finest training on this side of the galaxy, and Em was betting on that.

She felt all of that training in her blood. In her brain. She knew the counter footwork, knew how to block this type of hit or parry that kind. If she wanted to simply escape unscathed, she could evade all day long. A good tactic to tire out an opponent, but not helpful if she needed to take out a target fast.

She could fight expertly with a dozen different weapons, but she preferred this hand-to-hand showdown. It brought it all down to the basics. Down to keeping herself out of Brak's reach, so Brak couldn't use her strength against Em. And down to anticipating what Brak would do next based on the weight of her instep or the tilt of her shoulders. It was glorious. Em had never felt so magnificently alive. That she remembered, anyway.

Brak spun, a beautiful blur of power and color. Em dodged. Shifted her balance. Ducked and then bolted upright, using her entire body to slam into Brak's shoulder and knock her off-balance. They traded punches.

Around and around they went. Hitting, twisting, dodging, sweating. Em's entire being became nothing but the next attack, the next crushing blow against her own body, feeling like the bones must surely crack. And she loved it. More than she'd ever loved doing anything. She felt as if she'd been sleepwalking through life and now had suddenly awakened.

Finally, Brak stepped back against the edge of the ring, signaling the end of the fight. Honorably, Em did the same, retreating to the semi-flex barrier that ran the entire perimeter.

"Enough," Brak said. Her chest rose and fell rapidly, which Em could relate to. "Good match." She bowed.

Em returned the bow, just a touch deeper than Brak's own, to honor Brak's fantastic skill. Her own breath rushed in and out of her lungs. It seemed almost a shame that all that gorgeous ability took a backseat to scientific work. Brak would have made a brilliant BlackOp.

Some cheers and shouts of appreciation came from the crowd. Em accepted a towel from the sysops lieutenant and wiped her face with it. She was drenched with sweat, and relished the feeling of all of her muscles singing with adrenaline and fatigue at the same time.

As she dropped her arm, she caught a glimpse of pink hair disappearing around the exit doors. Before she could be sure of what she'd seen, it was gone. The incident poked a hole into the balloon of her ebullience and she felt it slowly leaking out.

She paused on her way to the locker room to give thanks in return for compliments or pats on the back. Em was amused to note that Brak had earned herself a fan club. A group of officers ringed her, peppering her with praise and questions. Brak seemed surprised but pleased. Smiling, Em ducked into the locker room.

She took a very long hydro-shower, dialing the water up to nearly scalding and letting it work on her tight muscles. The physical activity had helped. She felt more at ease, in spite of being a bit battered. Her mind felt clearer too, as if opening herself up to her physical abilities had loosened a cork and let her thoughts flow, releasing pressure.

By the time she turned off the water, her body had begun to

ache. Purple and magenta bruises mottled her shoulders, upper arms, chest, and ribs. The marks of a job well done, as far as she was concerned. But they'd only fester if she left them.

With her towel wrapped around her, she forayed deeper into the locker room, where she almost never went. A single regen-bed occupied the back room. Similar to a techbed in looks, it was sort of a watered-down version of one. It could run an auto-cycle to check for broken bones, dehydration, electrolyte imbalances, concussions, and the like. It would correct the minor conditions, and would alert the infirmary of the more serious ones.

Em dropped her towel and slid herself onto the bed. Her bare legs glided over the slightly sticky surface, but she didn't feel cold. The regen-bed had already adjusted itself to her body temperature. She closed her eyes and let it do its work. It gave her audio updates of its progress and findings. Other than what it considered to be significant bruising, the regen-bed deemed her healthy. She lay peacefully while it soothed away the bruises.

"Feeling better?" Brak's voice sliced into her.

Em sucked in a breath and opened her eyes. She'd almost fallen asleep. The regen-bed had long since completed its work. It felt warm, though, and entirely soothing.

Em stood and retrieved her towel. "Yes. All fixed up. Thanks for the fight."

Brak bobbed her head. "Thank you, as well. I found it quite stimulating."

"What took you so long out there? I've been in here probably an hour."

"I talked with people for several minutes, then took a run on the track."

Em shook her head ruefully. "A run, after that fight? You're a machine."

Brak lifted her arms slightly. "Only partly."

"Oh. I didn't mean...it's an expression."

Brak laughed, a soft, chortling growl. "I know. I was joking. Gotcha."

Em laughed as she walked back to the locker area. She pressed her palm to her designated compartment and it unlocked with a soft *floomf* of depressurization. She swung the door open and grabbed her clothes. Dropping her towel onto a bench, she began to dress with quick, efficient movements.

Behind her, Brak had opened a guest locker and rummaged around, then closed it again. As Em smoothed out the shoulders of her uniform, ensuring her insignia was properly displayed, Brak excused herself to the showers. They said casual goodbyes and Em was struck once again by how different Brak was from other Briveen.

Since the end of the day shift remained hours away, Em decided to go to her quarters and plan a nice meal for Wren. Maybe that would help thaw the ice between them and allow them to get on better footing. She hoped so.

———

EM PUT AWAY Wren's uneaten dinner and cleaned the dishes. Wren hadn't come home after work. Em tamped down her concern for Wren's safety, knowing that she must be in need of some time to adjust to what Em had told her. It was a normal thing. She kept telling herself that.

The quarters felt too still, too quiet without Wren's voice and laughter. All the familiar elements of home remained, but without Wren, the quarters echoed hollow. They didn't feel like home without her. Em wandered listlessly from the kitchenette to the couch, then around the living area in a lazy circle.

She finally sat, fiddling with the holo-projector. She didn't really want to watch anything, so she moved to the voicecom display instead. She made sure nothing work related had come up, built the relay to check for a signal, then found herself at a loss. What did she normally do when Wren was occupied? She didn't need a workout. She didn't want to work. The idea of socializing wasn't worth entertaining.

She went to her bedroom closet and pulled out her knife collection, setting it at the foot of the bed. Meticulously, she polished and oiled each weapon, admiring the fine curves and sharp edges. When that was done, she prowled the quarters again. Her eyes fell on the doorway between the bedroom and the living area. Now that she was thinking in Blackout ways, that sure looked like the perfect place for a slip—a place to hide something. Surely a BlackOp would stash some things here and there, in case of emergencies.

She retrieved a mech kit from Wren's side of the closet. Inside, it held a trove of tools, far more than the average resident would keep on hand. Perfect.

She removed the panel that ran along the inside of the door track, where it slid in and out. It wasn't easy. She gritted her teeth as she worked in the narrow space. This wasn't meant to be done with the door still in place. Which was exactly what made it a good hiding spot.

"Scrap!" Her index finger caught on a sharp edge, slicing a small cut across her fingerprint. With her other fingers, she teased away an access port and found success.

A flat case, not much bigger than an identity card, had been wedged into the tiny space. She fished it out and laid it on the bed on her way to the necessary. She retrieved a towel to wipe the thin line of blood from her finger, then opened the small case.

Three identity cards, complete with bio-info chips. All with her face. Three different names, hairstyles, and planets of origin. So she could hop onto a ship and disappear into the ether, with just a moment's notice.

After memorizing the information on the cards, she returned them to the case, then placed them back into the door and closed it up like nothing had happened. She retrieved the first-aid kit from the necessary and painted dermacare over the cut on her finger. If she didn't get it healed in the infirmary, the dermacare would take care of such a small wound in less than a day.

If she'd had any doubts about being a BlackOp, finding the identity cards would have killed them. No one else would have false documents like those. Standard PAC intelligence didn't work that way. Em would have spotted a forgery within seconds, even the most sophisticated. No, each of those identities had been official. Legitimately issued in every way, other than the fact that they contained false information.

She went back to prowling the quarters, turning her situation over in her mind. The hour grew late and Wren still did not return. Em fought the urge to go searching for her. No doubt she'd turn her up with little effort, but if Wren had wanted to let Em know where she was, she would have done so. Instead, Em called on Arin and asked him to subtly find out where Wren was and verify her safety. She didn't ask to be told where Wren was, only whether she was safe. Arin didn't ask questions, but his voice conveyed sympathy.

He called her back while she was in the shower. She hadn't needed another shower, but she didn't know what else to do with her time, and the hot water soothed her disquiet. She shut off the flow and stood dripping while Arin assured her of Wren's safety. She thanked him and promised to talk to him the next day.

She toweled her hair off, then her body, pausing to trace the odd tattoo on her stomach, as she always did. Slowly, as if swimming through a vat of industrial coolant gel, she dressed in soft lounge clothes. Every movement got progressively more difficult.

Brannin had predicted she'd feel tired by day's end, and she did. She slid into bed, refusing to look over at Wren's empty spot. She faced the wall. As soon as she let her body rest, her mind went sandy and her thoughts stuck together like wet paper. She sank gratefully into sleep.

SHE SNAPPED AWAKE. She moved nothing but her eyelids, allowing her eyes to adjust in the dark. She kept her breathing slow and steady, even as her heart rate increased. Someone was near. She knew it. The sensation of not being alone screamed in the back of her mind.

Wren? Had Wren come home?

But Wren would have turned on the lights.

Em stayed still, opening her senses as her flesh crawled with the knowledge that she was too vulnerable. Too exposed. But if she moved, she'd alert the intruder to her awareness.

There. It wasn't a sound or a movement or anything she could describe. It was a sense, an awareness of an anomaly. Her belt and stinger lay out of reach, in the wrong direction. It didn't matter.

In one movement she threw off the covers and leaped across the bed to land on the floor. She grabbed the knife she kept on the nightstand and slipped it into her waistband. Three running steps had her outside the door of the bedroom, almost smacking into the door as it retracted a little too slowly for her speed.

She clasped her hands together and swung them like a wrecking ball at the mass she sensed. The impact was solid and she heard an exhalation of breath. Good. Chest hit. That gave her a mental map of the person's orientation in the dark space around them.

Something hit her temple hard, and would have skewed her vision if there'd been anything to see. Close contact now. The other body closed in on her. Bigger than her. Stronger. Fast, too, and extremely skilled. No chance to evade. Her only hope was to take him out immediately.

She threw herself into her opponent, taking them both to the ground. While she had that advantage, she reached to the back of her waist and pulled a knife.

A crushing blow to her wrist made her entire hand go numb and the blade fell to the floor. That was it. She'd lost her advantage and knew unconsciousness or death would come before she could even lift her other hand.

She felt herself shifted and pinned beneath the body instead.

"Lights!" a male voice called.

Daytime illumination flooded the quarters and Em squinted at the man pinning her. She glimpsed dark hair and possibly human features.

"Prelin's ass, Fallon. You nearly took my head off."

He released her and stood, offering a hand. She ignored it, leaping to her feet on her own.

"Oh, don't be like that. If I hadn't known you sleep with knives, you'd have had me." He sounded amused. Placating.

Her eyes adjusted in time to see his grin.

"Good thing I used to sleep with you, right?" he added.

He was good-looking. If you liked that muscular, confident, perfect-features sort of thing. And without a doubt, he knew her. Not just who she pretended to be. This guy knew who she really was. The way he looked at her said it all. As did everything else about him. He was a BlackOp, just like her.

"Why are you here?" she asked. She sensed that he posed her no danger, but she felt wary. She moved away, putting the couch between them.

"Something's going on. Why haven't you reported in?"

"I have my orders." She didn't know exactly what they were, but surely she did have them. Who was this guy? Could she trust him?

He looked hurt. "Are you part of it? We've never had secrets. Now I can't find Hawk, and Peregrine has been off my radar for weeks. Something's wrong."

"Your coming here might jeopardize us," she warned. That was certainly true. She needed him to talk more. Help her figure things out.

He threw his hands in the air. "What else was I supposed to do, Fallon? Our team has been separated. I can't get answers from Krazinski, or even Simmons. We've never done separate assignments and now we've all been put on individual long-term gigs? I haven't even heard from you on our frequency." His voice rose. "*What's going on?*"

He was the one she'd been building the receiver for. A knot inside her came undone.

"I don't know. The truth is, I don't even know who I am."

RAPTOR SAT AT HER TABLE, eating what would have been Wren's dinner. She reclined on the couch with her feet up on the table. They were both trying hard to put together the facts they'd shared.

"So your Blackout name is Raptor. But you're also Ghost to the others of us within Avian Unit."

He finished chewing a bite and paused with another bite between his chopsticks. "Yup. You all named me that because I can get anywhere without being detected."

Which explained how he'd gotten not only on her station but into her quarters. That irritated her tremendously, but she put it aside for now.

"We also have Peregrine, a.k.a. Masquerade, who specializes in impersonation."

"That's understating it, but yeah. Basically. She almost had me convinced once she was my mom." He popped the chopsticks into his mouth and managed to chew while grinning at her. Was he joking, or serious?

Whatever. Not important. "And then the fourth is Hawk, a.k.a. the Machine. He excels in extractions." Meaning he could either get someone out of their circumstances, or make sure they disappeared without a trace.

"Among other things. But yep. That's us."

"You realize those names are mostly terms for the same kind of bird, right? Other than Hawk."

Raptor shrugged his broad shoulders. He didn't have a massive build, but his well-honed physique had an enviable V-shape. It just wasn't fair that type of physicality came so much more easily to men than to women. He also had brown eyes framed by thick lashes and shaggy light-brown hair. He was very good-looking, and no doubt he knew it.

"At least they're cool names. You could have been Secretarybird, or Vulture. I don't think I'd make a good Owl." He made a dismissive sound. "Blackout gives the names it wants to. Operatives don't get a choice. Except for our alternate names, which we invented way back in OTS."

"We go that far back?" The idea surprised her.

"Further. We got recruited as a group, and have always stayed that way. Makes us the best team there is."

"Is that your opinion or Blackout's?" she asked.

"Everyone's." He squinted at her. "None of this rings a bell?"

"No. I told you. Memory loss. Brain surgery. Thanks a lot for that punch in the head, by the way. I'm sure that will help." She rubbed her temple, which ached dully.

"Hey, you were trying to knife me."

"That's what you get for sneaking up on me."

He shrugged again. "Only way to get to you without notice. Lucky break for me that your mark stayed out. Thought I'd have to drug her or something."

She bristled at the characterization of Wren, but she said nothing. He could be right, for all she knew. She might have made a huge mistake falling for Wren.

"So why am I Fallon instead of Falcon?"

He grinned. "Administrative misprint. They fixed it, but by then the mistake had stuck. So they made it official."

She wasn't really Emé Fallon, then. That didn't surprise her, but she did wonder about her true identity.

"When was the last time you heard from the others?" she asked.

"Over six months ago, just like you. We were all put on special assignments and told not to communicate." He snorted.

"Did we?" she ventured.

"Well, I tried like hell. But none of you checked in, so I had to hunt you down. I'm kind of pissed about that, actually."

"Where are you supposed to be?"

He frowned at his chopsticks. "Long story. Let's get to that later. When I got a lead on you, I started trying to find Peregrine and Hawk."

Also known as Masquerade and Machine. Got it. "Nothing?"

His face darkened. "No. And that's not good. I know that they'd answer, if they possibly could. Would risk their lives to answer. Our unit..." He trailed off, stirring his chopsticks around in his beef and noodles. "We learned early on that we're all we'd ever have. We're family. Above all else. Even above Blackout."

She stared at him in shock. You didn't become a member of a nearly mythical clandestine department without being fully, completely, all in. Saying *anything* was above it was blasphemous. Yet she believed him. What he said made more sense than anything she'd heard since waking up in the infirmary with a freshly busted head.

He noticed her surprise and stood up, his hands going to the zipper on the front of his jumpsuit.

She took a step back. "Uh, what are you..."

But he'd already opened the suit and pulled up his undershirt, revealing a tattoo, just like hers, on the left side of his abs.

After staring for longer than was polite, she dragged her gaze back up to his face. She thought he might laugh at her for her confusion, but he didn't. He looked deadly serious. "We're close, the two of us. We go all the way back. All four of us have these, but you and I got them in the same spot. Avian Unit is a family, and no one comes between us. Not the PAC, not even Blackout."

He stared her down hard. She looked right back, not wanting him to think her less than whatever she'd been before. She didn't feel comfortable, but she did it. Finally, his stance shifted, became less aggressive. He smoothed his undershirt, but left the top half of his jumpsuit to hang at his waist. He sat down and went right back to eating, as if he'd never paused.

She had so many questions she barely knew where to start. "So you're Raptor/Ghost, but what's my other name?"

He smiled. "Fury. We wanted to go with Brainstorm, but you weren't having it, so we settled on Fury."

"Sounds kind of angry." She wasn't sure she liked the name, but it was way better than Brainstorm.

"Eh." He shrugged. "We meant the ancient Greek meaning. You know, a punisher of crimes. But it works either way." He smirked.

She fought the urge to roll her eyes, guessing that it would only encourage him. "And why do we have a second set of code names? It seems a little redundant."

His face drew up tight. "Our official names were given to us by Blackout command. Assigned. The others, we use just for us. It's hard to explain but when you rely on each other to live, and know your teammates as well as you know yourself... Well, it's not like typical relationships. It's similar to family, but more intense. So we like to keep something personal, just for us, that command didn't assign to us. You'll see."

She'd rather remember than relearn, but she'd have to take what she could get. "Okay. So what's my specialty?"

"Information and espionage. There are none better." His eyes softened before narrowing back into a hard look. "You're the leader of our unit. We thought it was crazy for you to be put on special assignment, with us not even knowing where you were. But we were good soldiers, and received our own orders. We accepted that it all must be for a good reason, because that's our job. But it's gone on too long. Something's wrong. Units don't get split up like this, and leaders of units don't disappear to do solitary fieldwork. So I disobeyed my orders to find you." His eyes softened again, and she knew he must feel quite fond of her.

He'd made a crack about them sleeping together. Did that just mean training and missions, or something else? She wasn't about to ask. If it was something more, she sincerely did not want to know. Her life was complicated enough already.

"What do we do next?" she asked instead.

"You tell me. That's your expertise."

"I have a hole in my head," she pointed out. "Which you might have made worse by whacking my already-damaged brain."

He shrugged. "You're a pain in the ass too, but you always get the job done."

Somehow, his insult touched her, when his fond look had only made her uncomfortable. She sensed that he and she had a very odd dynamic.

"When do you have to leave?"

He glanced at his comport. "I have to leave in forty-two minutes exactly. If I don't, I might not make it off Dragonfire without detection."

"How will you get out? Do you have a ship?"

He gave her a cocky grin that didn't annoy her as much as she knew it should. "Trade secret. I'll tell you about it next time I see you, if it works. If not... Well, if you look out the starport and see an unusual cloud of dust..." He fell silent, then snickered.

She barked out a laugh, surprising herself. "You're impossible."

He stood from the table and came over to chuck her gently under the chin with his fist. "Never thought I'd be so glad to hear you say that again. I like the hairstyle, by the way. Reminds me of security school."

He sat on the couch beside her. "Now, in the time we have, let's get through as much info as we can."

FALLON WOKE UP ALONE. No Wren, no Raptor. She sat up at the edge of her bed and dropped her head into her hands for a moment. Her life had taken a strange turn, and now she was surrounded with bird names. A curious coincidence.

After her tussle with Raptor, she didn't feel great about going for her morning run, but she needed to keep up her normal routine for whoever might be paying attention. Besides, a good rest in the regen-bed would take care of the bruise on her temple, and might ease the pounding in her head. So off she went.

As luck would have it, she got the track to herself that morning, and the recuperative help of the regen-bed did indeed ease the pain in her head. She'd have to check in with Brak about that, all the same. Just in case Raptor had scrambled her brain into even worse shape.

After making herself shipshape in her uniform, she visited her office to apprise herself of the night shift's activities. Then she went to ops control for her morning report.

"I need to see you in my annex," Captain Nevitt announced as soon as she arrived, barely sparing Fallon a glance.

Once seated in Nevitt's sanctum, she wondered if she'd be meeting another ship full of ambassadors. The captain quickly disabused her of the notion.

She fixed Fallon with a hard look. "I need to know what's going on."

"Sir?" Fallon asked. Like most female PAC officers, Nevitt preferred "sir" over the matronly sounding "ma'am." Fallon did as well, though most people just called her "Chief," which was even better.

Nevitt squinted just one eye, which gave her a knowing,

rueful look. "Come on, Chief. I haven't gotten where I am by not knowing something's going on under my own nose."

"I'm not sure what you mean, Captain."

Nevitt let out a long, slow breath, as if releasing a great deal of pressure. She sank back into her chair, and her casual posture looked so foreign on her that Fallon found it alarming. "Fine, I'll spell it out. I know you weren't put here just to serve as security chief. There's a reason you were forced on me. A reason far above the heads of anyone I have a connection to. Which means it came from very high, indeed." She leaned back in her chair, looking sly. Fallon suspected her estimation of Nevitt was due for a sudden and significant upgrade.

Nevitt continued, "I've been waiting it out. Waiting for you to be recalled to wherever you're really from, and waiting to get my chance to place my own officer. But you're still here. And now this thing with your head. As well as this feeling I have that something just isn't right."

Nevitt steepled her fingers and pressed them to her lips. "Whoever you are, you're in trouble. Am I right?"

What else could she say? "I believe I may be."

Nevitt pursed her lips, looking both thoughtful and satisfied. "I thought so," she intoned in a low voice. Then she stood abruptly and leaned over her desk. "Right! So I'll tell you what. I may not have chosen you, but you're one of mine, nonetheless. My responsibility. What can I do to help?"

Fallon could only stare at her.

"Close your mouth," Nevitt instructed wryly.

Fallon did.

Nevitt smirked. "Surprised you, didn't I? Well, good. I'm not the heartless career climber you think I am. Well, scratch that. I am. Just not for the reasons you think. See, I got sick of seeing the universe the way it is and decided that it was up to me to make things fair. Get help to people who need it. But the only way I can do that is to get to the top, where I can have the power to get things done. In the meantime, I spend every minute of my day pushing hard to get to where I need to be."

"I'm...sorry. Captain Nevitt." Fallon had completely misjudged the woman. Nevitt had fooled her completely.

Nevitt made a slashing gesture with her arm. "You saw what I wanted you to see. You had no reason to suspect anything else. You, though. What are you?"

Fallon shook her head slowly. "It's better for you not to know. Getting mixed up in this will not get you where you need to go."

"And yet. Here I am."

Fair enough. Fallon chose her words carefully. "My memory loss is real. I don't know exactly what I'm up against. I know that it goes all the way up, though. Something is very, very wrong." She paused, thinking. "And I know that whoever I really am, wherever I'm really from, I'm on the side of what's right. Ethical, if that's a term that can be used for what I do. I don't know the facts of what's happening, but I *know* that about who I really am. I feel it." She took a breath, watching Nevitt weigh and measure her. "So if I'm good, then that means that whatever is working against me is not. And I need to stop that."

Yeah. Hearing herself describe the situation that way, out loud, made something click into place inside her, as if she'd put a piece of her puzzle where it belonged.

Nevitt smiled, and Fallon found herself staring again. Nevitt had struck her as regal the first time she'd seen her. Never mind that she ruled from a chair like any other on the station, behind a standard-issue desk.

Nevitt broke the silence. "So I'll ask again. How can I help?"

———

FALLON FELT as though the ground had solidified beneath her feet. Not literally. The deck plates in her office remained the same as they'd ever been. But existentially, she'd been rooted into her place in the universe. She had a purpose. And comrades.

Now that she had her team, as well as Brak and Nevitt, on her side, Fallon second-guessed her decision to let Arin and Endra in on her secrets. That might prove dangerous to them, as well as herself. She'd chosen to pit herself against a colossus. She didn't want them to get caught in between.

She grimaced at the thought of Wren. It was now lunchtime the night after Wren's failure to return home, and Fallon still hadn't heard from her. Maybe their relationship was over. Wren might have decided that Fallon wasn't the person she'd married. She'd be right. She wasn't Em. She wasn't a station's security chief. She was a game piece in a galactic chess match.

With a shake of her head, she pushed the thought of Wren away. Brooding would get her nowhere. Wren had to choose what was right for her.

After her stunning meeting with Nevitt, Fallon spent the rest of the morning handling some details. The captain had given her permission to make it far easier for Raptor to let himself onto the station without detection. Their first order of business would be finding the other two members of their unit.

The alterations she'd made to Dragonfire's security wouldn't help anyone but Raptor. She'd keyed in his handprint and retina scan, as well as a DNA sample. Ghosting all of that data to an innocuous falsified trader identification had been no effort at all. But he'd be able to enter and exit every part of the station, outside of ops control and crisis ops, without any effort, and she'd programmed all cameras to fail to register him.

Of course, if he wanted to break into the ops stations he surely could. He was Ghost, after all, and he'd been the one to teach her everything she knew about programming and coding. Under his guidance, she'd engaged in a quick refresher course the night before, and was amazed at how much she'd forgotten she knew. Which was still far less than Raptor. He had a gift for what he did.

As did she, apparently, as well as her two other comrades, whom she didn't even remember. She'd been close with Peregrine and Hawk, Raptor had said. Closer than coworkers, closer than family. Blood and bone. That's what their motto was, he'd said. Before he'd left her quarters to depart the station, he'd taken her head in his hands, touched their foreheads together, and sworn, "Blood and bone, Fallon." She'd said the same, and it had felt right.

She felt buoyant, even though she *should* be feeling daunted. Terrified, even. She'd pitted herself against whoever was at the top of PAC intelligence. People who could make entire towns just disappear. Maybe even entire planets, if they wanted to. But energy zinged through her veins. Everything Raptor said had rung true. Maybe it even jibed with some vestiges of memory, if she had any. She believed everything he'd said, and knowing that part of herself, at least, had made her feel like a whole person again.

She built the communications relay and sent a heavily coded message to Raptor to let him know about her security changes. She'd even assigned him quarters, to give him a place to duck into if he needed. He'd be back in a few days. Or whenever he got the information he needed. Their first priority was to find Peregrine and Hawk. Once the four of them were reunited, then they could begin.

She dismantled the relay and pushed her chair back from her desk. She spun in a slow circle and her thoughts returned to Wren. Though the idea made her feel like a class-six shuttle had landed on her chest, she knew it would be better for Wren if Em broke things off with her. Annulled their marriage. Moved on with her life, away from all of this cloak-and-dagger shit.

Because the truth was, Fallon knew that she lived and breathed for all of that cloak-and-dagger shit. She'd never felt as alive as when fighting for her life in the middle of the night. Or even now, forcing her mind through patterns and filters, creating decision trees for whatever might or might not happen in the fight against Blackout. Fallon didn't want Wren getting caught up in all that. What had she been thinking, getting married?

She wished she knew. Though she hadn't experienced any side effects from the previous day's surgery, she hadn't recovered any memories either.

Which reminded her that she needed to let Brak know about that crack in the head she'd gotten. She called Brak's guest quarters and left a message. No telling when she'd receive it. Being on shore leave, no doubt Brak was out enjoying some recreation. Fallon could only imagine how little free time the *Onari* crew usually got.

In two more days, the *Onari* would depart. Even though that would calm things down on Dragonfire and make her day-to-day work easier, Fallon would miss the crew. Particularly Brak and Jerin. Though she quite liked Kellis as well. Arin had certainly talked about her a good bit during their daily meetings. Wren no doubt would miss her dear friend Endra. Particularly so with the state of Wren and Fallon's marriage being what it was.

She needed to stop circling back to Wren. It was time for her Deck One rounds, anyway, which ought to keep her occupied.

FALLON FOUND it curious to go through the regular routine, with so much now changed for her. The boardwalk had all the same smells, sounds, and activity. She nodded and said hello to people, and stopped to chat here and there. She checked in with shopkeeps to ensure they'd had no issues with any patrons.

No one had any idea she had become something entirely different. Well, actually, she'd always been something different than what they'd thought. She just hadn't been aware of that until

Raptor showed up. So really, she'd simply resumed being the duplicitous person they'd always known. It was kind of trippy, thinking of it that way.

Nix and Robert rose from a table on the food court as she meandered by.

"Hi, Chief!" they said almost in unison, approaching too fast and coming to stutter-stops in front of her.

"Hey, Nix. Robert. How are you two?"

"Good," Robert said, just as Nix said, "Fine." They giggled, a little out of breath from their short sprint. She knew she should caution them against running on the boardwalk, but chose not to. Youth was youth. Let them have it while they could.

"We heard you fought the Briveen yesterday," Robert said in a rush, his eyes glowing with excitement.

Ah. That. "Yes. I do like a challenge. Brak was a very worthy one."

"Who won?" he asked. "I heard she did."

Nix cut in. "No, I heard the chief did! You did, right?"

"It was just a sparring match." They needn't know about all of her very real bruises. "No one won."

They groaned with disappointment. Fallon supposed she should have guessed that the match would become a hot topic.

"What's it like to get hit by those arms?" Robert asked eagerly. Nix made a sound of disapproval and nudged him.

Fallon couldn't help smiling. The two of them were so cute. Innocent, eager, with a whole universe of stars in their eyes. She tried to imagine herself being like them, long ago, and just couldn't.

"Like getting whacked with a pneumatic hammer at full power," she admitted. "Hurts like crazy."

"Then why do it?" Nix asked, her face scrunched up in distaste.

Fallon shrugged. "Some people just live to fight. I'm one of those."

Nix shook her head. "I'd like to learn, but I don't think I'd do it just for fun."

"Learn to do all the school things first. Fighting will wait," Fallon advised. She'd rather see these two happily employed as engineers, scientists, or PAC officers. She didn't like to think of Robert growing up to take a job like her true occupation. She wanted the stars to stay in his eyes for as long as they could.

Nix nodded. "I'll get top marks. I want to do that internship you promised."

Robert's eyebrows raised, so it seemed Nix hadn't mentioned it to him. Given Fallon's uncertain future, she didn't want to discuss the internship. Instead, she employed misdirection.

"Want to walk with me? I'm headed this direction." She flicked a finger to indicate her travel path.

They beamed and fell into step with her, peppering her with questions about fighting, security, and whatever else occurred to them.

She always enjoyed her rounds, but she took particular pleasure in them today. It felt good to be with people who were only exactly what they seemed to be.

Fallon worked late that day, not wanting to sit in her empty quarters and watch every minute tick by, wondering if Wren would come home.

She accepted an invitation to dinner with Brak and Jerin. She and Brak met briefly beforehand so that Brak could check her physical condition. Brak was none too pleased about Fallon's blow to the head, but after a thorough exam with a hand scanner, she concluded that she didn't see any damage.

Brak clicked her teeth in dismay nonetheless. "I'd like to see you in the infirmary tomorrow for a more thorough exam," she said in a tone that sounded more like decree than suggestion.

"Won't that seem suspicious?" Fallon didn't want to do anything that might seem strange to Brannin, Jerin, or the rest of the medical staff.

"Not really. Brannin probably expects it. Forty-eight hours is the perfect time to take a look after brain surgery."

"All right, then."

Fallon caught a faint hint of musky satisfaction, but it disappeared when Brak asked, "No memories have surfaced?"

"Nothing. But I did get some information about my past."

Fallon told Brak about Raptor. Brak said little, only bobbing or tilting her head occasionally. A faint hint of anise communicated her concern, though. Fallon appreciated that, but she had no doubts about Raptor or their plans. She only hoped involving Brak wouldn't cause trouble for the doctor. Fallon had begun to think of her as a friend.

FALLON AND JERIN enjoyed bowls of hearty Bennite stew while trying to ignore the scent of Brak's mandren meat. If Fallon hadn't liked Brak so well, she'd have characterized the gamey odor as a bona fide stench. But the cyberneticist looked so supremely pleased as she ripped into her meal that Fallon bravely carried on.

They'd chosen to eat out on the food court, where they could watch people walking by or sitting and visiting. The food court was the popular choice for the younger residents of Dragonfire, as it provided the greatest opportunity to socialize. Visitors also appreciated it for the liveliness. The food court allowed a person to take in all the motley activity of the boardwalk while having a meal.

Fallon did notice that the table she shared with Jerin and Brak at the far end of the court was surrounded by empty tables, even though a few couples loitered at the edges, waiting for a place to sit. Non-Briveen simply didn't seem capable of appreciating mandren. Few stations stocked the meat, given the odor and the relatively few Briveen who visited. For whatever reason, Dragonfire did, and it made Brak one happy woman.

"So where is the *Onari* headed next?" Fallon asked, genuinely curious about the ship and its crew.

Jerin blotted her lips on a napkin. Maybe it was her nature as a surgeon, but she had the most graceful hand movements. They always drew Fallon's eye. As did the occasional glint of her ruby nose stud. Fallon always saw others noticing Jerin, too. With her dark, shiny hair and her green eyes that tilted up at the corners, she had a certain eye-catching appeal. Beautiful, in a way, but a unique, maternal sort of beauty.

"Not far," Jerin answered. "First, Sarkan. We have a week's worth of cosmetic procedures scheduled. Afterward, we head to the Zerellian system."

Sarkan was a few hours from the station in a ship like the *Onari*. It would reach Zerellus in three days or so, at a typical energy-efficient speed.

"A whole week of cosmetics?" Fallon had thought the *Onari* spent most of its time dispensing need-based care.

A sly look crossed Jerin's face. "Yes, lucky for us. Commander Belinsky earned himself some extra shore leave by putting in all the work to make that happen."

Fallon had met Demitri Belinsky only in passing, but Jerin's ops commander seemed efficient and reliable.

"Why is that lucky?" she asked.

"Along with the research funding we get through doctors like Brak—" Jerin nodded to Brak, who made eye contact, but kept eating, "—elective work is how we keep our fuel cells charged. Hospi-ships aren't permitted to run at a loss. We must at least break even to stay in operation. Cosmetic procedures allow us to do that."

"By 'cosmetic procedures' you mean…" Fallon trailed off, inviting one of them to fill in the blank.

Brak finally pushed her plate aside, having scraped it clean of anything but a few dark, wet smears. At least Briveen ate their mandren well cooked. "Anything not required for health or normal quality of life purposes. Such as replacement of viable limbs with cybernetics for enhanced function. Vanity adjustments. That sort of thing."

Fallon nodded. "Well, you'll certainly be missed on Dragonfire when you go."

Jerin smiled. "That's lovely to hear. I always worry we'll wear out our welcome. Dragonfire and Blackthorn are probably our two favorite ports, and between you and me, our engines always seem peppier when we get our maintenance here."

"Our mechanics are the best," Fallon agreed, refusing to get mentally sidetracked by thoughts of a particular mechanical miracle worker. "And you never have to worry about wearing out your welcome. Truth is, things can get a little stale living on a station. A visit like this is a breath of fresh air for everyone." She didn't have a long memory of her time on Dragonfire, but she'd noticed how much excitement the *Onari* boarding had brought. Spirits remained just as high as the day the crew had arrived.

"Makes sense," Brak reflected. "We like shore leave because it gives us a change of scenery and a change of pace. A break from the routine. Life on board a ship has a lot in common with life on a station."

Jerin said with a laugh, "Well, other than we can dock somewhere and get off the ship."

"Exactly. Which is why interesting visitors create such a stir." Fallon noted a rough-looking group of people coming away from a docking bay. She didn't look directly at them, but she studied their progression past the food court. She'd check on that group after dinner. There was something about them that snagged her attention.

"Of course, our ship is much smaller than a station," Jerin noted. "We'd have a very hard time staying on board for months on end without docking somewhere. I imagine our cabin fever comes on faster and more frequently, compared to yours."

"True. Ships and stations have their unique advantages and disadvantages," Fallon conceded.

Brak drummed her fingers on the table in a slow, contemplative rhythm. The sound was much heavier and deeper than flesh-and-blood fingers could have caused. "Either one is still better than living planetside."

Fallon supposed that, for Brak, anything was better than living her life on her home planet.

They chatted for another half hour, even though their plates were empty. The tables near theirs gradually filled in as the scent of mandren faded. Fallon simply enjoyed Brak and Jerin's company. She appreciated their intelligence, dedication to their work, and their senses of humor, different though the two were from one another. Jerin was warm and nurturing with an easy laugh while Brak was more stoic, but no less caring or amusing.

When Jerin excused herself, Brak did the same, saying she wanted to do some reading before she slept. The three of them stood and went their separate directions, leaving Fallon with nothing but space between her and her quarters, which might or might not be empty.

Instead of heading home, she strolled down the boardwalk, keeping an eye out for the group she'd seen earlier. When she didn't spot them, she visited the security office on Deck One.

She checked in with the officer on duty, Janson, and found that the group was just a private trade consortium. Which might or might not mean smuggling. It could be hard to tell sometimes. She reviewed the records on file but found nothing amiss.

"Keep a close eye on them," she ordered her officer. "There's something about them that got my attention."

"Yes, sir," the young man agreed, probably eager to have a

potentially interesting assignment. The truth was, working security could get dreadfully dull on a station that had few incidents. Which was fine with Fallon, but the young ones, well, they usually hoped for a little more excitement.

On the way out of the office, she ran into Arin. Instead of his uniform, he wore casual clothes. Nice clothes, actually. Perhaps the kind a guy would wear for a date.

"Hey, Chief," he greeted her with a grin. "Working late?"

"Not really. Just checking in on a recent docking. Janson will fill you in. Though you're not scheduled to be on duty either," she pointed out.

"Just wanted to check the voicecom before I went to dinner. I'd rather not end up getting interrupted if I can avoid it." He and she took turns being on call.

Fallon considered. Why not let the guy have the night free and clear for whatever he had planned? "Janson, the legate is taking the night off. I'll be on call tonight."

Arin's look of surprise made her smile.

"Thanks, Chief," he said, sounding heartfelt.

"Have fun." She grinned at him, and instead of acting embarrassed, he grinned right back.

Her smile faded as she walked to the lift. There was nothing left to do but go home. She had a bad feeling about it, like whatever she found would be the final answer to the question of her relationship with Wren. She didn't expect it to be a good one.

FALLON PAUSED a moment before activating the door to her quarters. As soon as they whooshed open, she had her answer. The quarters were different. Things had been removed from their places. Two large travel cases sat to one side of the door. Wren perched on the edge of the couch, her back straight and her hands folded primly in her lap.

Fallon stepped in and the doors closed behind her. "I see."

Wren's chin angled upward, though her eyes remained on her hands. "You can't be surprised."

"No. Just disappointed."

Wren's gaze flicked to Fallon's face, then skittered away. As if looking at her hurt.

Fallon quickly swept the room for monitoring devices, then returned, standing with her back to the kitchenette. "You were willing to stick with me even though I lost my memory. Why jump ship now?"

Wren rubbed her thumbs together. "I don't even know your name. Your real name."

"Neither do I."

Wren's shoulders tightened. "All the more reason you're not fit to be married to anyone."

"You want an annulment, then?"

Finally, Wren's eyes met hers. Bored into hers, really, with a pale glare of anger. "Annulment of what? There's nothing legal between us. Only between me and some fictitious person."

Fallon exhaled a soft sigh. She couldn't argue with that. Couldn't argue with anything Wren had to say. And she shouldn't, either. She should just let Wren go, for her own safety.

"What really bothers me," Wren added, "what keeps me up at night, is wondering why you married me in the first place. Did you actually care about me? For all I know, it was just some tactic, and the only reason you care anything for me now is that you got bashed in the head and assumed you should."

Fallon took several slow steps, moving through the space between being married and being alone. She sat in the chair angled toward the couch.

She wanted to argue. To soothe the hurt she saw so plainly on Wren's face and in the droop of her shoulders. Her instinct was to protect Wren, but keeping her close wouldn't do that. She squared her shoulders.

"You're right. All I know about who I really am tells me that my life can't be safe for you to be a part of. *That's* why you should go. Not because I don't care about you." She started to say more, but stopped herself. She wasn't trying to convince Wren to stay.

Wren looked conflicted. "Will you be all right? I feel like I'm abandoning you. Even though I know that's stupid. You probably know how to kill a person twelve different ways with a toothbrush, so it's not like you need me."

Fallon skipped the oh-so-obvious "but I *do* need you" melodramatics. That rubbish wouldn't serve either of them.

"Somewhere along the way, I chose this life. Apparently, I became one of the best at it. I'll be okay." Fallon hoped so, anyway.

Wren nodded. "I keep thinking I can stop it. Just stay here and see it through with you. But my mind goes around and around in the same pattern and I always end up at the same place I started. As crushed as I am right now, I know that I can survive it. But if I stuck with you and it turned out that you didn't marry me simply because you wanted to be married to me, it would break me. I can't choose you, only to find out you were using me." She took a shuddering breath.

"And you aren't going to spend each day wondering, waiting for the worst to happen." Fallon could respect that, objectively. But then, she wouldn't have married some weepy doormat. Nope, it all made very logical, very sad sense.

Wren looked miserable. Fallon wanted to touch her, but fought the urge. Then she told her better judgment to go to hell. She rounded the table, sat next to Wren, and wrapped her arms around her. Wren sank right in to her. She wasn't a loud crier. The only sounds she made were occasional gasps for breath.

Fallon ran her fingers through pale pink hair, probably for the last time. "I'm sorry. So sorry."

After several minutes, Wren sat up and smeared her hands over her cheeks. "I almost left before you could arrive, planning to send you a message. I knew it would be hard to go through with this if I talked to you. But I couldn't just disappear."

"Yeah." Fallon understood that, too.

"I'll be in my own quarters on the other side of the station," Wren said. "Smaller than these, but it's what was available on short notice."

"I'll be sure my staff knows to keep an eye on it."

Wren laughed, a wet, high-pitched yip of sound. "Right. Well. I guess there's that. I can expect good security."

"Do you need help getting your things there?" Fallon gestured toward the travel cases.

"No. Thank you. That would be too awkward. Endra's going to be here in a couple minutes."

"Right." Fallon didn't know what else to say.

Apparently neither did Wren. She stood, fussily smoothing invisible wrinkles out of her clothes. "I'll just put those out in the corridor."

Knowing Wren wanted to do it herself as an outlet for her nervous energy, Fallon stayed seated, until Wren hesitantly stepped back through the door, her eyes wide with uncertainty. Fallon met her halfway across the room.

"I do love you," Wren said. "I'm not even sure what that means, when you're not at all who I thought you were. If I really love *you* or just an idea of something you're not. But I know I want you to stay safe. So be careful."

"I will," Fallon promised. As careful as a person like her, in her choice of profession, ever was, anyway.

"If—I mean, *when* you figure it all out..." Wren stepped forward, putting her hands lightly on Fallon's shoulders. "Tell me. I'm not promising anything, and we both need to just live our lives from here, but...tell me. To my face. Okay?"

Fallon didn't need any more invitation. She slipped her arms around Wren and poured herself into what she assumed was the most meaningful, fervent kiss of her life. At least, if she'd ever felt anything more conflicting, she hoped she'd never remember it.

They let go and stared at each other for a long moment before the door chime sounded.

"Perfect timing," Wren whispered.

Fallon didn't trust herself to speak. She merely nodded.

And just like that, the best thing that she'd had in this fraction of a life slipped away.

———

HER QUARTERS WERE TOO quiet without Wren's vibrance. She tried watching a holo-vid to distract herself, but it didn't work. She tried an extra-long shower. No luck there. Finally she lay down in bed, hoping for sleep to take her. It didn't.

Lying on her back, staring into the darkness, something felt off. Like a picture frame hanging half a degree crooked. She sat up and slapped the light panel at her bedside.

At the voicecom display she keyed into her security settings and went through her routine of checks and protocols, looking for anything out of place. Ah. There. "Talar Prinn" had just boarded the station. Raptor.

An idea occurred to her and she smiled. She threw on a uniform and rushed out of her quarters. Given his entry time and location, she projected his most likely route and calculated the best point of interception.

No one seemed surprised to see the chief bolting down a corridor. She was security, after all. Sometimes she needed to get somewhere fast.

She arrived with ten seconds to spare. She'd selected a junction away from usual traffic. Exactly where Raptor would want to be. She pressed herself into her vantage point.

Fifteen seconds ticked by and she wondered if she'd miscalculated. But then she saw him. His footfalls made no sound, even to her acute senses. She waited until the last instant and let go, falling from the ceiling to stand right in front of him.

His hands immediately came up to fight, but he recognized her in the same instant and grinned. "Nice job. How did you know?"

"I had a feeling." She fell into step beside him. By unspoken agreement they headed to the nearest place they could ensure privacy—the quarters she'd assigned him.

"Is it smart to be seen out here with me?" he asked.

"Minimal risk. Should I appear on any video feeds, and I shouldn't, I can scrub them before they're seen."

"Worth the risk to score a point, is that it?" His eyes glinted with amusement. "Same old Fallon, whether you know it or not."

She knocked into him with her shoulder. "I owed you one for showing up in my quarters and punching me in the head."

He sighed theatrically. "You're never going to let that go, are you?"

"No time soon," she agreed.

As they entered the quarters and ensured their privacy, she felt buoyant. There was something about being with someone who truly knew her that gave her energy. And hope. There might just be someplace in the universe that she really belonged, as her true self. If she could only figure out what the scrap was going on.

———

As far as guest quarters went, the ones she'd assigned to Raptor were the low-rent variety. They were clean and well maintained, furnished with both a voicecom display and a narrow washroom that was nothing more than a commode and a sink. Space was tight. Laid out studio style, the room converted from living space to sleeping area with some clever multitasking furniture.

At the moment, it was set up as living space. A futon currently served as a couch, and a low table could be either a desk or dining space, although there was no kitchenette for food preparation. It was a takeout-only sort of room. The only personal item of Raptor's that Fallon could see was a medium-sized brown backpack that looked like someone had beaten it with a bat.

Fallon didn't mind his proximity as they sat shoulder to shoulder on the futon, with the voicecom display arranged on the table before them.

"Before we get started, tell me exactly where you've been." She was done with only having a partial picture of events.

"Aw, c'mon. You know it's better to share as little as possible. We've always worked on the basis of trust," he protested.

"And we will again. But for now, with the limited amount of knowledge I have, I need all the details to bring things into focus." If he expected her to parse data into something actionable, she needed context.

He sat back, sinking a little into the futon cushion, which doubled as a mattress. "All right, but if someone tortures my techniques out of you, I'll be really mad."

"If someone tortures me for information, I doubt your pique will be my biggest concern."

"Fair enough." He cleared his throat. "After I left here, I hightailed it to PAC command."

"I'm serious," she interrupted.

"No, really," he insisted. "If you go down to the stem section of Dragonfire and look out porthole RTG-2817 right now, you'll see an ultralight racer docked there."

Fallon had to tighten her jaw to keep it from dropping. "An ultralight."

"Yeah."

"You're telling me you crawled into one of those coffins, put on a contained rebreather and a thermal suit, then flew all the way to headquarters and back?"

The man must be crazy. Which probably meant she was also crazy. This did not bode well.

"Yep." He looked quite pleased with himself.

"That's ridiculous. One teeny meteorite and you'd be dead."

"Exactly why I avoid them," he agreed.

"Why an ultralight?"

"It's the only way to slip under command's notice. They don't routinely look for anything that small, and as long as I kill all the systems and coast into the correct range, which I happen to know, then there's nothing for them to detect. Bang—there I am, right on their hull. In the exact sort of surveillance blind spot that you have right where the ultralight is docked now."

"Other than porthole RTG-2817," she pointed out.

"No video there, but yeah. Visible if someone looked out the porthole. But no one will. It's a terrible place to dock, all the way down there."

Knowing that there was a dark spot on her security surveillance was annoying, and she'd have to install a new video feed once all this was over. He was right that no one would be down there, and even if someone *did* dock there, anyone besides Raptor would be unable to breach the station. Still. It was a matter of pride.

"So why did you want to be on the hull of headquarters?" she prompted. She had an idea, but wanted him to spell out the details.

"To exploit a fail-safe. Every twenty-six hours, the entire network backs itself up. There's a brief window when I can punch into the system from the outside and extract data without it being detected."

"How brief?"

"Two-point-three seconds."

"Wow. That's brief." To get into the system in that amount of time would be impossible for her, much less to do it and extract data.

"Plenty enough if I'm ready for it. But I have to know exactly what I'm after. If I need more than one file, I have to wait until the next backup."

"Which means you have barely enough time to get back there, if you leave within the hour," she predicted.

He grinned and bumped her on the shoulder with his fist. "You got it. See, you're still the Fury."

"Yeah, I'm still not excited about that name. Let's stick with Fallon. So what are you leaving me with, then?"

He got right back to business. "Your current active file. The real one."

Active file. That meant her vital statistics and career history, but no detailed information from further back in her past, such as officer training school or her planet of origin.

"And you want me to analyze it while you go back to get…what?"

"Peregrine's file. Then the next one will be Hawk's." His eyes narrowed.

"What about yours?" she asked.

"Already on there." He gestured toward the data chip he'd given her. "First thing I got before I came here to find you."

"So how did you know I was on Dragonfire without my active file?"

His grin came back. "Your name. Clearly, you used your code name as your surname so that I could find you. And I did."

"Emé Fallon. Right." Did that mean she'd known something strange was going on before she even arrived at Dragonfire? Disturbing, if true, but at least it had led Raptor to her.

"So while you're gone, you want me to dig through our active files and see what I can figure out?"

"Exactly. We need to find Peregrine and Hawk immediately. They could be in danger. So could we. We've got to be back together again, where we're strong." He stood.

She had so many more questions, but time would not wait. She clasped his hand, and swore, "Blood and bone, Raptor."

He repeated the motto, grabbed his bag, and walked out the door.

Fallon squinted at the screen, trying to squeeze out another scintilla of information. No luck. She'd gleaned everything she could. It had been quite a bit, though. Far less than her life story, but a lot more than she'd had before.

She and Raptor were the same age. That made sense, given that they'd been in school together. After she'd been shipped off to Dragonfire, he'd been assigned to a remote lunar location, supposedly to track some suspicious signals that might contain plots against the PAC.

She doubted his assignment had been anything legitimate. Hers certainly hadn't been, given her clandestine investigation that had come to nothing. How better to keep an intelligence officer busy? Have them investigate a squeaky-clean suspect. A good officer would assume she was being thwarted and work that much harder. But Fallon had eventually caught on. She didn't have communications logs, but the fact that she'd married Wren six months into the assignment seemed significant. She must have been certain well before that point that Wren had been innocent. Blackout had made Dragonfire her home assignment until the rest of her team had completed their own special assignments. Supposedly.

Blackout had shelved her and she'd been happy to go along with it, given her newly married status. Which also explained why she'd even been *permitted* to marry. She shouldn't have been. BlackOps couldn't afford weaknesses, and spouses and children were nothing but weakness. A soft spot for exploiting. Even having a family back home was a vulnerability, which was why Blackout had a high percentage of orphaned officers.

Fallon sighed and rubbed her eyes, wishing she had her office chair so she could go for a slow spin. Her bum and back hurt from sitting hunched forward for the past three hours.

She stood and stretched her arms over her head, arching her back. She should get back to her quarters. Keeping her regular routine was the best way to avoid suspicion, so sleeping in her own bed would be the right move. She pulled the chip from the voicecom display, then made sure she'd scrubbed the unit right down to the factory specs. She might not have had Raptor's skills, but she still had far more than even a top-shelf sysops analyst.

No one was there to see her leaving the quarters, which left her home free. She walked with purpose, just as she would when answering a security call.

She'd have to update Nevitt the next day, in a way that gave no details about what had happened, for the captain's own good, yet still let her know that Fallon was making progress. Fallon would worry about how to word that in the morning. Right now, she felt tired, all the way down to her bones.

Once back in her room, she changed into lounge clothes and fell right into bed. She quickly descended into a deep sleep, where she dreamed about hurrying down corridors and looking for Wren, only to catch a glimpse of her before she slipped around another corner.

———

WITH THE EXCEPTION of her private report to Captain Nevitt, the next day proved to be entirely routine for Fallon. She made her rounds at the normal time, then checked up on that odd group of traders she'd asked her officer to keep an eye on. They'd departed the station earlier that morning, leaving no trail of mischief behind them. Maybe she'd been wrong about them.

She checked in with everyone as usual, remained busy throughout her shift, and in the evening shared dinner with Arin and a few other security staff. Jerin and her crew were scheduled to leave the next day, which left Fallon with the decision on whether or not to fill Brak in on some of the new developments.

On one hand, the less Brak knew, the better for her. On the other, Fallon felt obligated to her, given that Brak had already taken risks on Fallon's behalf. When she considered that she might well need Brak's help in the future, and that Brak would not appreciate being left out, Fallon made an appointment to speak with her privately the next day. No sense in doing it today, since she suspected Raptor would show up again tonight with additional information.

With that in mind, she made a few programming changes to her security system, determined to detect him. In a way that only she would recognize, of course, but still. It was her station, after all, and a matter of pride. Even a ghost shouldn't get past her, as far as she was concerned.

She returned to her quarters after dinner, but didn't dress for bed. She was too on edge, waiting. But the signal she'd been waiting for didn't happen. Finally, halfway through the night, her comport chirped.

She leaped up and charged out of her quarters, slowing to a businesslike pace through the corridors to the lift. She arrived at Raptor's guest quarters just as he did.

"Hah!" He ducked in behind her and the doors closed. "Nice try, polarizing the docking clamp. Like I wouldn't see that coming."

Yeah, so that part hadn't worked. "Still got you though."

"Only because you expected me, and knew where I'd be headed. How did you do it?"

"I calculated your likely rate of speed and your three most likely routes, and programmed the computer to alert me when something matched those parameters. With a certain amount of variance, of course."

"Not bad," he allowed. "But you only found me because you

knew I was coming. And if I was really trying, I would have used an illogical route."

He was right. Still. "I would have anticipated that, too."

He laughed, then made an almost gross scoffing sort of snort. "You keep telling yourself that." He rubbed his hands together. "So, what did you come up with?"

"For one thing, that my marriage to Wren was the real thing. It worked in Blackout's favor that I was content enough to stay here and play house. I didn't marry her to protect her, or to try to get information from her. That has to mean I married her only because I wanted to."

"Makes sense." He stretched out on the couch, kicking his shoes off and letting out a groan. "I'll tell you, if I never fly in an ultralight again, I will be a happy man."

"I bet. How do you avoid getting sick?"

"My instinct tells me to be cool, but I can't lie to you." He gave her a crooked grin. "There's a reason I travel with spare clothes."

She laughed, and he chuckled with her. She wondered about their ability to laugh in such circumstances. Were they nuts? Or just hardened? Perhaps both.

"So are you going to tell the wife? Ask her to come back to you?" His expression didn't suggest judgment, only curiosity.

"No. At least not until I have the full story on my background. Or if I get my memory back. Either way, she deserves more certainty than I can give her at this point."

He nodded, but she caught a hint of something in his eyes. "What? You think that's wrong?" she demanded.

"I'm not saying that. I just wonder how she'll feel about it if you tell her months from now that you've known all along that you were for real about marrying her. Seems to me she'll be pissed."

She sighed. "Yeah. But either way, I figure she'll be pissed. So I'm going with the option that keeps her out of Blackout's way."

"Yeah." He stared down at his hands for a long time, then

repeated more softly, "Yeah." He shook his head. "No way I'm ever getting married."

"Never know. You might find someone who makes it all worth it." She sat down next to him, nudging him over to make room.

Before moving, he snaked his arms around her and pulled her in for a hug. "Nah. She's already taken."

Fallon looked at him sharply, but he burst into laughter. "Should have seen your face." He scooted over, giving her just barely enough room to sit. Apparently, he was a space hog. He had the whole other side of the couch he could move over to.

She wrinkled her nose at him.

He ignored her expression. "What else did you learn?"

"That your assignment was as bogus as mine. Which makes me think that the same is likely for Peregrine and Hawk."

He nodded.

"How are you even here? You're supposed to be on some minor moon, sifting the radio spectrum for pretend transmissions."

"It's not hard to spoof myself being somewhere else when there's no one to physically check. All the right patterns and signals are coming off that blasted moon, and all the proper responses will go back to routine inquiries. Any communications that require my personal attention will come my way here, and then I'll spoof them back over. No problem."

Actually, that did seem very doable. She could probably manage the same thing, though without his finesse.

"Do you have any idea why they'd want us out of the way?" she asked. "Surely you've thought about it."

"Of course I have. But none of my ideas worked. Maybe they wanted to replace us with another team. But why? They'd just need to give them the orders instead of us. No reason to separate us and have us do busywork. It doesn't make sense to spend years training operatives, only to waste our talents by having us do nothing."

She thought that over. "True. And if we'd done something wrong, something worth punishing, we'd either be censured or somehow find ourselves unable to breathe anymore."

"Exactly. So that means that someone *else* is doing something on the wrong side. Something they don't want us to figure out. Something that, if we *did* find out about it, would turn us against them. Right?"

"That's what I was thinking," she admitted.

He pumped his fist in the air. "Yes! Fury's got nothing on me."

She ignored him. "So what do you have for me?"

"Hawk's active file."

"Not Peregrine's?" She'd thought that was his plan.

"Missed it. I barely managed to grab his. I'll get hers when I go back."

"Then what?" she asked.

"Then I'll get whatever you tell me we need at that point. I'm hoping something about the assignments puts you on to something. An angle to work."

"Right. Well, let me see it." She held out her hand, and he placed the tiny chip into it. "When do you have to leave?"

"Thirty-five minutes. Would it be okay with you if I slept? I can't sleep while I'm flying, and—"

She cut him off. "You probably haven't slept for days. Yes." She got off the couch and pantomimed him opening it. "Sleep. I'll take this to my quarters and study it there. I'll be ready for Peregrine's when you get back."

"I know you will." He stood and gave her a quick hug, which she found oddly comfortable.

She reflected on that on the way back to her quarters. She didn't have a normal security job anymore, and she didn't have a wife anymore, either. But she did have this new partner, and hopefully two more to find very soon. She needed them, badly, to find some sort of purchase in the universe. To find her footing. To keep her from flying off into the blackness of space like a random piece of flotsam.

"You can't give me more information?" Brak asked. The *Onari* would leave at noon, and Fallon had invited her to breakfast, which they'd eaten in Fallon's office. Takeout from the Tea Leaf was surprisingly good. Fallon would have to get her breakfast there more often.

"You have the important details already," Fallon told her. "I'm just leaving out names and locations, to keep both you and my unit safe. As safe as I can manage, anyway."

Fallon smelled the onion scent of frustration. "I wish we could tell Jerin. She'd be a strong ally for you."

"That would be an unnecessary risk to her and your ship. I couldn't do that. Besides, I don't see the tactical advantage."

Brak clicked her teeth softly. "That's because you don't know Jerin as well as I do. She looks refined and sophisticated, but in her way, she's a warrior too. You've been wronged, and if anything makes her scales itch, it's when someone has been treated wrongly. And if there's an entire section of a government that's gone corrupt—" She broke off and uttered a growling, hissing sound that made Fallon simultaneously edgy and impressed. "She would be angry if you didn't let her help."

Fallon smiled faintly at the idea of Jerin having scales. Sometimes one species' idioms didn't quite fit seamlessly with the realities of other species. The meaning was clear, though.

"Okay. I'll tell you what. If, at some point, I think Jerin could be helpful enough that it justifies the risk, I'll bring her in. How's that?"

"Too many qualifiers," Brak huffed. "But I know it's the most you'll promise."

Fallon felt a fondness for the Briveen. She'd miss her. Other than Raptor, Brak was the only person she could really talk to about the serious things going on in her life. Captain Nevitt knew the basics of the situation, and had surprised Fallon with her shrewdness and social conscience. There was a lot more to the woman than Fallon had suspected before, but that didn't make her a friend.

"I'll miss you too," Brak said.

Fallon smiled. That Briveen sense of smell. No doubt they made very good lie detectors. A shame they couldn't get some of Brak's people in Blackout. Well, maybe they had, for all Fallon knew.

"We'll be in communications range for some time yet. Let me know how you're doing, in whatever vague way you can." Brak's head tilted with amusement.

"I'll keep in touch," Fallon promised.

"And if we can be of help…"

"I'll contact you."

Brak fell silent, drumming her fingers in a slow cadence on the table. "I hope so. I knew when Krazinski asked me for those neural implants that something was wrong. I was afraid of what would happen. The fact that all of this is unfolding in front of me does not feel like coincidence. On Briv we have a phrase that translates roughly to, 'An eviscerated animal does not get its guts back when no one's looking.'"

That made zero sense to Fallon, so she waited for the explanation. Brak did not disappoint. "It means that even if you regret what you've done, you can't ignore it. You must act and make things right."

"Okay, I hear you. You've made your case. I promise, if I need your help, I'll call."

Brak nodded, seemingly satisfied. "Good. Now, would you like to take a walk with me? I'd like to get a triple order of mandren to take back to my ship."

No doubt that would please her shipmates mightily. Fallon

held back her chuckle as she escorted her friend to the boardwalk.

Fallon had started to become accustomed to the quietness of her quarters. She no longer expected Wren to come walking through the door. Funny how quickly she'd made that adjustment.

She set aside an infoboard, considering what to do next. She was quite tired after her half night of sleep, but she wasn't ready for bed. Her mind whirled dust devils of thoughts around. Still dressed in her uniform, she decided to go down to the Tea Leaf and get a cup of Zerellian nut milk tea.

After receiving her drink, she decided the tea parlor was too noisy. She wanted a low, steady thrum that would wend its way into her senses along with the tea, quieting her mind and leading her toward sleep. So she took her cup with her, promising to return it to the shopkeep the next day. Not the sort of thing the average customer could get away with, but sometimes being the chief came with perks. She wasn't above taking advantage of that now and again, so long as it was harmless.

She strolled the boardwalk, sipping tea and peeking into the restaurants and shops. A pair of Trallians walked by, making her smile. There was something about Trallians that just made her happy.

Things were quieter now in general, with the *Onari* gone. But the activity level in each place she wandered by proved to be more than she wanted. Too bad Dragonfire didn't have a starport like Blackthorn Station's. She'd seen the images on the voicecom. Five decks high with theater-style seating. Incredible. She could definitely use something like that tonight.

The arboretum might suit her current mood. Not the gentle hum of activity she'd hoped for, but a peaceful place. She had just started in that direction when Cabot Layne's shop caught her eye. He looked up as she passed, waving her in.

"Hey, Chief. Having trouble sleeping?" He gave her tea a significant look.

"Just winding down," she answered. "Some days are tougher than others."

"Mm. Indeed." He nodded with understanding. "I was just about to close up shop. No business coming in at all. Mind if I walk with you?"

"I was going to visit the arboretum." She didn't really want company, but he was such a genial presence that maybe walking with him could be pleasant. Besides, she didn't want to be rude, and she did like Cabot. She probably shouldn't, but she did.

"Perfect. Probably my favorite place on the station. After my shop, of course."

"Of course," she agreed. "I'd enjoy your company."

They walked along the path, chatting pleasantly. Cabot was a shrewd judge of people, and had a prodigious ability to maintain an entertaining patter of conversation, as if he knew exactly what topics she would find most relaxing.

With her cup of tea warming her hands, Fallon wandered among the trees and shrubs, vines and flowers. She drew the scents of nature into her lungs and they grounded her. Her tension eased, leaving her shoulders and jaw feeling looser.

When they reached the far end of the arboretum, they sat on a pair of benches made out of huge tree trunks. They faced an art piece, which fit perfectly into its surroundings. Part art and part wind chime, it had been constructed of lightweight panels festooned with spheres, spirals, and circles. The shapes spun at different speeds under the ministrations of a small wind-generating device at the center of the piece. The artwork reminded Fallon of butterflies and leaves cavorting in the breeze. When the panels made contact with one another they created soft, hollow sounds like bamboo wind chimes. Fallon found it exceedingly peaceful.

She and Cabot fell silent, enjoying the moment. She closed her eyes to focus on the soft sound.

A whisper, or maybe a sense of something, had her on her feet and moving even as she opened her eyes and turned. Cabot shouted in surprise and backed away as a man clad in gray burst out of nowhere. Fallon had been ready, and instead of tackling her from her seat as he'd intended, he had to roll and pop back up to his feet. Which was more than enough time for her to grab her stinger and hit him with a point-blank burst to the chest.

Except that didn't drop him, as it should have. Didn't even make him pause. *His clothes.* He must be wearing a neutralizer. Top secret tech. Only issued to PAC intelligence and Blackout itself. Which organization he represented, she didn't know. It hardly mattered at the moment.

The time she'd taken to use her weapon had given him the opportunity to get back into an offensive position. A terrible loss of advantage for her. She flung the stinger away. She had blades in her belt and hidden in her uniform. She wouldn't draw one yet, though. This guy had skills like hers, and she might need the use of both hands.

In the split second that they sized each other up, Fallon recognized him. The tall, blond one in that trader group she hadn't liked. Her suspicions about them had been well founded, after all. He charged her again and she leaped out of the way, catching his shoulder and shoving down on it hard as he rushed past her. Off-balance, he wheeled around, and she pressed her advantage. Grappling with a bigger opponent was always her last resort, but she had little choice at this point. She had no idea if there would be others and she couldn't afford to be vulnerable if they arrived.

She got in close, distracted him with a feinting head shot, then got a grip on him for a hip throw. She followed him to the ground and punched him in the throat. He began choking and making horrible sounds. Possible trachea rupture. Damn. If so, he could suffocate before she got any information out of him. She'd hit him too hard.

She scrambled up to straddle his chest, with her knees painfully pressing the flesh of his arms into the dirt. Her hands wrapped around his throat.

She leaned down so he could hear her, while hopefully no one else could. "Move, and I'll crush your windpipe, if it isn't already," she hissed in his ear.

He stopped trying to fight her off and his body shuddered under her. Lack of oxygen. Prelin's ass.

"Cabot, I need a medical team down here immediately. Tell them it's a critical case, crushed trachea. They might need to resuscitate. Use the comport in my belt." She couldn't spare a hand to give it to him. Even in his critical state, the agent under her could not be underestimated.

To his credit, Cabot didn't even pause. He grabbed the portable voicecom, sent a terse message, and said nothing more. He retrieved her stinger and stood silently waiting. She was impressed. There might well be more to Cabot than she'd thought.

The medical team arrived and a brief argument ensued. Fallon insisted that the man, who appeared unconscious, be heavily sedated before she'd release him from her death grip.

With a few grams of trophezine in him, Fallon had no worries about him being a threat. Now she just had to hope he lived. She needed information.

After the medical team rushed the man to the infirmary, Fallon faced Cabot. He stood, watching her with new understanding in his eyes. What exactly he'd learned about her she couldn't be sure, but he was a canny fellow, and she suspected he'd realized far more than she'd like.

Her gaze caught on the edge of the wind-chime art, where an errant foot had kicked in a dent. "I'll have to see that gets fixed."

She accepted her stinger from him, annoyed that she hadn't been able to use it. Her attacker would be in perfect health now if she had.

"Yes," Cabot agreed.

"I must excuse myself to the infirmary," she said. "Thank you for the walk. Before that guy showed up, it was perfectly relaxing."

Cabot smiled wryly. "That's what I was aiming for. Certainly not a visit from...an old friend?" His eyebrow raised.

"Hardly. I don't know him." She paused. "I imagine I don't have to tell you—"

He cut her off. "No. You don't. I know when to keep my mouth shut." He nodded his head once.

"That's good." She again noted his lack of distress. He didn't even seem to have an adrenaline rush. She sure did. Her limbs buzzed with electricity. By contrast, Cabot looked just as he had when they'd been admiring the trees and flowers.

"Although," he added, "if you happen to need someone to lend an ear...well, I have two very good ears. And, on occasion, I've even been known to help a person out of a pickle."

She studied him hard. What exactly was he alluding to? She didn't have time to figure it out just now. "I'll find you. Soon."

He seemed delighted rather than intimidated. "I'll look forward to it." He gave her a courteous bow, which she returned perfunctorily, already in motion toward the exit.

IN THE INFIRMARY, she overrode the door lock utilized during a crisis to ensure privacy and a minimum of confusion.

Brannin stood over a techbed, yelling names of drugs and procedures without seeming to pause for breath. Doctors, nurses, and techs filled the space, and a cacophony of voices and equipment sounds completed the synchronized chaos.

Brannin caught sight of her and gave her a disapproving look, even as he barked an order to increase the peak flow. Or whatever he'd said. Fallon knew a great deal about anatomy, but only advanced field medicine when it came to actual doctoring. She'd uncovered that skill set just the other day, after poring through her active file.

Her attention riveted on the man lying on the techbed. He looked grayish. Not good at all. His eyes were closed and Brannin's voice rose higher and louder, even as the rest of the noise in the infirmary quieted to silence.

Finally Brannin's shoulders slumped. "Loshem, please note the time of death and prepare for an autopsy in the clean room."

The entire infirmary was designed to function as a clean room, and could be counted on to be sterile even for surgeries. The area known as *the* clean room, however, was one of the private suites at the back of the infirmary, where her surgery had been.

Brannin faced her. "What do you know about him?"

"Nothing. He came out of nowhere and attacked me." She smoothed her hands over her uniform, wondering if she had stray bits of dirt or leaves on her.

"And you never met him?"

"Saw him once. Coming off a trading ship with a group of others. Didn't like the look of them, but they supposedly left yesterday."

He seemed unhappy with that response, but he nodded. "If you'd try to find out more about him, I'd appreciate it. I at least need to notify his next of kin."

She seriously doubted she'd find any trace of his existence, but she definitely intended to try. "I'll let you know what I find out."

"Thank you. I'll do the same. We found nothing on his person. No identification, no money, no personal effects. Just his clothes."

"I'll need those, once you're done with them."

He nodded. Assuming, no doubt, that it was part of her investigation. She knew the clothes wouldn't give her any information. But they did have a stinger neutralizing field, and that might come in handy.

She hesitated, then gave a small bow and left the infirmary. Brannin had no additional information for her, and hanging around would only encourage him to ask her the questions she saw in his eyes.

Her pace slowed once she emerged into the corridor. She replayed the incident over and over in her head, but no new information presented itself. Once in her quarters, she sent a message to her staff on duty to inform them of the attack, and instruct them to see to the arboretum. She didn't even remember tossing her teacup, but she must have, and she'd promised to return it to the Tea Leaf shopkeep. If it had been damaged, she'd have to be sure to pay for it.

She ran her fingers through her hair as she paced her quarters. What now? She wished her attacker had lived. At least Raptor was due to arrive within the next few hours. She could discuss it with him.

———

"What did he look like? Did he say anything to you?" Raptor's words were tight. Terse.

They sat in the quarters she'd assigned to his alter ego, discussing what had happened since last they saw each other.

"No, he was too busy trying to kick my ass for a polite hello," she sniped as she flipped through security feeds on the voicecom. "Here." She pulled her attacker's image, turning the screen toward Raptor.

He hissed in a breath. "That's Granite. Oh, Prelin's ass, you killed Granite." He twisted to face her, his eyes intense.

"Who is he? PAC intelligence, or Blackout?"

"Blackout." Raptor sat back, letting his head rest on the futon, which left him staring up at the ceiling. "From the class ahead of us. Stone Unit. We've worked with him before. An okay guy."

"Specialty?" That might let her know what his plans for her had been.

"Assassin."

The silence in the room rang in her ears.

"Sooo," she said slowly, "we can assume I'm now marked for death."

"Yeah." His tone was flat. "And likely the rest of us, too."

"Oh, great." She said it flippantly, but her mind raced. "Well, that changes things."

"Yeah," he said again, seeming to have retreated into his thoughts.

She pressed her fingers to her mouth for a moment, thinking. "First off, you aren't going back to that moon. That's just asking to get killed. And we need to extract Hawk and Peregrine immediately."

Raptor said nothing and she poked him in the shoulder. "I need the data chip with Peregrine's information."

"Right." He opened a seam in his sleeve and handed her the tiny chip.

She inserted it into the voicecom display and began tearing through the information.

"Peregrine's in deep cover on the far side of Sarkan." Strange for her to be so close to Fallon, but maybe not so bizarre since she'd been buried under deep cover. She was so undercover she might as well be on Earth, except for the fact that she and Raptor could now extract their partner.

"So we go get her first," Raptor guessed, coming back around.

"Yes. Hawk's on a moon in the Zerellus system. We'll get him as soon as we have Peregrine."

"Shouldn't we split up? We could get them out sooner."

She bit her lip. The sooner they got their teammates safe, the better. They all had targets on their backs, no doubt. If Raptor took his ultralight to get Hawk and she liberated Peregrine, they could all rendezvous and be a complete unit again.

But she had no idea what they'd find in either location. Once Blackout realized Granite had failed, they'd try again, and this time they wouldn't send a lone assassin.

Which meant they had to leave immediately. She stood. "Is your ultralight ready?"

Raptor ran a hand through his hair. "It could use some maintenance, but it has enough juice for a one-way trip to a Zerellian moon."

She nodded. No way both men would fit on the ultralight. They'd have to get their hands on a ship to escape the moon. She'd leave that to them. She had her own problems.

She gave him the coordinates of Hawk's location and all the details that seemed potentially pertinent.

"We rendezvous on Dineb in two days," she said.

The tiny planet of Dineb was a party spot. They'd easily get lost among the hubbub of Dinebian festivities, so long as they didn't linger there.

"Easy for you. You don't have far to go," he scoffed.

"Oh, so you can't do it?" Her voice held a high degree of taunting.

"Of course I can. Just pointing out how much easier your assignment is."

She snorted. "Right. At least you know exactly where you're going. I have to track my target down."

"Aw. Need help?" He gave her big, helpful eyes full of condescension.

"Shut up and get out of here," she ordered.

"Not just yet." He clasped her hand. "Blood and bone, Fallon."

"Blood and bone, Raptor."

"Let's get our team back."

5

For someone Fallon had originally suspected of wanting her dead, Captain Nevitt had turned out to be a surprisingly good ally. She had no problem with Fallon taking the station's only class-six cruiser for a rescue mission, about which Fallon had given as few details as possible.

"I'm guessing you're going to need a sizeable leave of absence."

Fallon wasn't sure how to answer that. She didn't know if it would ever be possible for her to return to her position on Dragonfire. A part of her hoped so. At least, that it could be a possibility.

"Don't think you're getting out of your assignment. You owe me about three more years of duty. I expect you to take care of business and return here to finish out your tour." Nevitt gave her a severe look.

"And owe you, for the rest of my life," Fallon translated dryly.

Nevitt's grim expression broke into a grin. "Exactly. You and I are going to get things done. Things that have needed doing for a very long time."

Fallon wondered if Nevitt knew more about the shady dealings of PAC administration than she let on. Then she dismissed the idea. Nevitt might have very good instincts, and accurate impressions of corruption, but at her security clearance level, she'd have no hard data Fallon could use. Nonetheless, she could prove to be a powerful ally.

"What would you think about scrubbing all the data referring to the *Onari*'s visit? Making it look like it was never here?"

Nevitt's eyes narrowed and her gaze wandered to the far wall. Fallon could practically see her running through the massive undertaking. She was a little surprised the captain hadn't just snapped off a quick negative.

"Consider it done."

Fallon stared, causing a slow smile to spread over Nevitt's face.

"Oh, I get why it's necessary," Nevitt assured her. "Brak's presence here, the implants, PAC intelligence. There's a trail of bread crumbs that could be followed, and someone will definitely be looking. I'll take care of it. Including letting the crew know that the *Onari*'s visit didn't happen. We can't do anything about the other people visiting Dragonfire during that time, but most of them wouldn't have much interest in the *Onari* unless they were in need of a hospi-ship at the time. Just one more stop among many. You'd be surprised at how much it all blurs together for them. Sometimes poor recollection is a captain's best friend."

Which was a *very* intriguing statement, but Fallon couldn't afford to get off track. She had to focus on containment. "The crew's families are a potential problem."

"Wrong. Everyone here loves you. They won't know the *why* of it, but they'll know they're backing you up." A humorous light glinted in her eyes. "And you know what, my looking out for you might actually get people here to like me, for once."

Nevitt seemed to find that highly amusing, and Fallon wondered about this captain of hers, whom she'd taken to be a dull, insufferable hard-ass. She wished she had more time to get to know the real Nevitt. Maybe sometime, in the future.

Before leaving Nevitt's office, Fallon saw the captain's mouth curl up on one side. "I almost wish I could come with you. Before I started on my long climb to the top to change things from the inside, I wanted to do what you're doing."

"Fighting for your life and the lives of your team, against a special-ops outfit gone wrong?" Fallon couldn't keep all traces of disbelief out of her voice.

Nevitt grinned. "Well, not exactly that, but something along those lines. Just with less, you know, likelihood of death."

"Thanks for the vote of confidence," Fallon muttered.

Nevitt laughed, perhaps for the first time that Fallon had ever heard. "I have every faith in you, Chief. If I didn't, I wouldn't be giving you my class-six. Which I expect to get back, intact."

"I'll do my best."

SINCE FALLON HAD ALREADY INFORMED Arin that she'd decided to take a couple days of shore leave on Sarkan, she had nothing left to do but depart.

She liked piloting the class-six. It was maneuverable and fast, though it left a bit to be desired in the way of amenities. The cockpit doubled as the sleeping quarters, with the seats converted into narrow, though not horrible, beds. The washroom was as basic as it got—a sonic sink and a zero-gravity toilet. The latter being standard spacefaring equipment, since no one wanted to deal with the results in the event of an artificial-gravity failure. Fallon was unlikely to need the ship's facilities, though, given that the trip to Sarkan would only take a couple hours.

As soon as she sat in the pilot's seat, something clicked. Not only that she had superior piloting skills, which her file had noted, but something inside her immediately told her that she really, really *enjoyed* flying. She took some liberties in her flight plan, executing some maneuvers that weren't the least bit necessary and definitely wasted fuel. But they sure were fun, and gave her some inklings as to what she was capable of. She hoped she'd soon get the opportunity to pilot something with greater power and heft.

Poor Raptor. Here she was enjoying the cruiser, while he was squeezed into an ultralight. Well, better him than her.

At least neither of them had to worry about money. Raptor had worked his magic and filled fake accounts for each member of their team with many more cubics than they could possibly need. Another benefit of working with a programming genius and hacker extraordinaire, who knew where all the gems were buried. Score one for having someone from the inside. And score another one for already having an identification card she could use for her clandestine trip to Sarkan. Not too shabby on the spy stuff for someone who didn't yet remember having been one.

She locked in the coordinates for the docking station and spent the last half hour of her trip studying the specific area where she'd find Peregrine. A small island off the coast of a southern continent. Supposedly, Peregrine had been searching for a deep, deep underground hitman who had settled on Sarkan. Fallon doubted the man even existed.

She had to wait briefly to dock above the planet's atmosphere. Sarkan's docking station was a busy one, as the planet was a popular destination for tourists and vacationers. It was also large, as well as efficient, so she didn't have time to get frustrated before receiving clearance to link up to a docking bay.

Once on board the docking station, she crossed the large complex and hopped one of the three orbital elevators, which had luckily just arrived. She waited impatiently for the doors to close. Finally they did, and a slight dip in her stomach let her know that the clamps had released and the cables had begun pulling the elevator down.

She stood in a back corner, where she could see the other travelers, who all seemed entirely at ease. She was glad that none of the passengers had elevator phobia. She had the sense that she'd seen it before, and considering they were basically riding a massively shielded rocket down a cable straight toward the planet, she could sympathize with the nervous types. Theoretically.

After an hour of slow descent to clear them of the docking station, the elevator pilot ignited the propulsion system and they really began the drop. Even Fallon preferred to sit for that part. She and the others were shielded from the majority of the g-force, but it was far easier to tolerate the ride while seated.

Though the ride took the same amount of time as elevator rides always did, it felt to Fallon like an agonizingly long downtime. The weight of the universe above seemed to push down on her, unseen and foreboding. She had two team members up there, ones she didn't even really know, fighting for survival. Against a foe she wouldn't recognize if she saw it, and which likely controlled more things than she even knew. Her muscles screamed to be in motion, to be getting the job done. Instead, she had to sit here. Waiting. Inactive. Lacking any apparent measure of control. She barely managed to hold herself still.

Finally the elevator cut the propulsion and glided to a seamless stop. The doors opened and Fallon burst out into the transport station, alive with the need to move, to run, to get the job *done*. Was this how she always felt on a mission?

She took a deep breath, her lungs filling with the fragrant freshness that only planetary atmospheres had. She drew it in over and over, until she deemed herself at risk for hyperventilation. Outside the station, the air would smell and feel even better, with just the right touch of natural humidity and gentle floral breezes. She itched to get out and soak it all up.

But first she had to make it through all of her transport. She had only a brief layover before boarding an air tram, so she proceeded directly to the boarding point. She pushed through the throngs of people, who were a study of organized chaos. Moving sidewalks and staircases hustled travelers toward their destinations, but that didn't keep some individuals from striding forward, squeezing past others in an attempt to hurry their trip along. Too often, the hasty ones bumped the patient ones with their bags and parcels, eliciting some dirty looks and now and then a muttered curse.

Not that Sarkavians were unpleasant. Quite the opposite. The cranky ones all appeared to be visitors to the planet. True Sarkavians didn't need to rush. They lived in a virtual paradise, and could afford to take the time to enjoy life and take inconveniences in stride.

Sarkan was like an entire world modeled after Earth's Hawaii, more or less. The planet's double suns were situated perfectly to gently warm it and encourage prodigious growth of flora.

Even as she skimmed through the station, nimbly dodging groups and stragglers, constantly calculating the quickest route, Fallon tried to imagine growing up on such a planet, and found she couldn't. Maybe because she had no frame of reference for her own growing-up years. She could definitely imagine retiring on Sarkan, though. If she managed to grow that old, it would be the ideal place to settle in. But she didn't really want to start calculating the odds of her reaching such a point.

After her first air tram, Fallon boarded three more, then took a taxi from the tram station. More impatient waiting. More agonizing slowness.

She arrived at a small boat-rental marina, along the edge of a beach resort, with a sense of relief. As the taxi drove away, she stood still for just a moment beneath the suns. *Now this is air.* Genuine sunlight floated down from the universe and sank into the skin of her arms and face, a sensation almost as tangible as a touch. And finally, she could get to work. Both sensations felt incredibly satisfying.

She adjusted the small backpack she wore over one shoulder, in the local fashion. Along with her lightweight pants, hiking boots, and breezy blouse, it would mark her as one of the many people who had settled on Sarkan and become locals. Since retirement didn't seem likely for her, she'd just have to make the most of this little experience of pretending.

―――――

"You sure you're familiar with one of these?" the marina's boatman asked with a friendly smile. "They're a little more complicated than the basic pleasure boat."

She admired the islanding craft. A powerful outboard motor with a backup and responsive controls to go from leisurely to serious speed in seconds. Oh, yes, this was the ride she wanted.

"Yep. Been taking these out for years," she assured him, pressing her hand to the infoboard for the transfer of cubics. It could be true. The controls certainly looked familiar. "Good for the soul, ya know?" She gave him a sunny grin, just like a native-born Sarkavian would. Falling into character had been completely intuitive. Even the way she held herself had changed, shifting from a rigid posture and quick steps to a loose, languid way of moving. Yes, she'd certainly done this sort of thing before.

The man smiled, relieved. "That's what I always say. Does me good to see people who still know how to pilot a real boat, instead of one of those." He jerked a thumb at the tourist version. Slow, simple, and difficult to screw up.

"At least they're boats and not hovercrafts with automated controls," she chuckled.

"I heard that."

They shared a smile, then she hopped in and he untied the boat, helping her ease down the dock. Once she floated clear, he tossed the ropes to her and she started the engine. As she gently powered away, she waved back to him.

It wasn't just talk. She really did love boats. She wondered if she'd liked them before marrying a Sarkavian, or if that had come after. Either way, she had an affinity for being on the water. Given how much she'd also loved piloting the class-six, maybe she just liked driving.

As she focused on the mission objective directly ahead, her adrenaline spiked. It didn't make her feel jittery or nervous. It gave her a laser-tight focus, sharp eyes, and the feeling she could chew through the hull of a ship with her bare teeth.

Once at a safe distance from the dock, she increased the power. She took a wide, indirect approach toward the tiny island's beach, giving herself the opportunity to scan the land. She noted no obstacles or traps, but made a mental map of the most protected approach to the tiny building in the center of the island. Not that the trip inland would take much time. She judged that she could have hiked from shore to shore in less than twenty minutes.

Fallon cut the motor and coasted toward the island's surprisingly well-maintained dock. She moved to the port side of the bow and stood waiting, hoping she'd judged the angle just right. As the boat nosed up to the pier, she extended her arm and deflected the approach, avoiding a hard collision. The adjustment slowed the boat's momentum and she guided it in as it gradually slowed.

She loved this old-school stuff. Wood. Rope. Docking up with your own arms and muscles. She quickly tied the boat up to a post, grabbed her backpack, and carefully leaped up to the pier.

Wasting no time, she strode toward the shore while adjusting her pack so that it hung comfortably. She scanned the island from end to end, looking for hazards. All she saw were tropical trees swaying in the breeze and playful water birds chasing each other through the air.

She heard a splash and pivoted, only to see one fish right after the other break the surface, spend a couple seconds in the air, and crash back into the water. Listerfish. She turned her attention back toward the tiny cottage, and immediately felt like something had changed. She couldn't put her finger on anything different, but she had that growing presence in her chest that suggested that she was not alone.

She slowed her pace, scrutinizing every tree, every shrub, anything that might conceal a person. She kept shifting her orientation and looking side to side, keeping a three-hundred-and-sixty-degree awareness.

"Relax, Fallon," a voice rang out from nearby. "If there were a combatant on my island I'd know it. We're clear, at least for the time being."

Fallon didn't recognize the voice, but it could only belong to one person. She saw movement to her left and part of a tree trunk twisted away from itself, revealing a woman dressed in mottled shades of brown. Her skin had been painted in the same palette, with the cracking effect that the tropical trees on the island had.

Silhouetted against the larger island backdrop, the woman had a thick, athletic build that Fallon envied. She herself had plenty of lean muscle, but she'd never be able to put on the bulk that Peregrine had, unless she took hormones and steroids. Which she wasn't about to do.

Fallon and Peregrine walked directly toward each other, and when they met up, Peregrine said, "Let's get inside. I need to know everything. Immediately."

What they really needed was to get out of there, not sit around talking shop. But they could fight over the sequence of events once they had sufficient cover. "Right."

"Follow my steps. I've laid out a few surprises for unwanted visitors."

She fell in behind Peregrine, obediently planting her feet exactly where Peregrine had walked.

Peregrine accessed the cottage with a palm scan and a coded voice-ID check. Clearly, she was no less paranoid than Fallon herself. Though she likely had good reason for her caution, just as Fallon did.

The inside stood in stark contrast to its rustic outside. Every surface gleamed with video screens, metal, or high-durability polymer. The place was practically a mini ops-control room combined with a sysops lab, then condensed into a tiny space. A kitchenette adjoined the room, which had one doorway, probably to a small bedroom.

"What's going on?" Peregrine wasted no time with hellos, and that suited Fallon just fine. The sooner they got off Sarkan, the safer they'd both be.

"I'm here to get you off-planet. Raptor's doing the same with Hawk. Someone at Blackout has decided to take out Avian Unit. We don't know why. But someone tried to assassinate me, in a very public way. We need to leave immediately."

Peregrine's barklike face moved, but it was hard to make out her expression with the patterning.

"I haven't seen you in a year, and I don't even know why. Before I lift a finger, I want to *at least* know what the plan is."

Fallon hadn't anticipated resistance to her rescue. Damned inconvenient. She wondered if Peregrine were always so contrary, or if she had just been saving up her pain-in-the-ass moments for right now. "The plan is to get the scrap out of here. Immediately. Forget your assignment. It's probably bogus. We need to grab everything useful you have here and bolt, then meet up with Raptor and Hawk."

Fallon had expected a demand for more detail, but Peregrine only said, "Understood. There's a backpack and a couple of duffels in that compartment." Peregrine pointed to a trunk-like storage table. "Load up the tech I have. I'll get clean and changed, pack my supplies, and we can go."

Now that was more like it. Action. Movement. Fallon tore open the trunk and began breaking down the voicecom and surveillance tech. She packed everything they wouldn't be able to easily get their hands on. She'd just about finished when Peregrine re-emerged, looking entirely different.

She'd dressed similarly to Fallon in pants and a blouse, along with boots. Her long hair, which was right on the dividing line between honey blonde and light brown, had been pulled back into a simple ponytail. Fallon recognized from the active file the round face, the brown eyes, and the narrow lips with a tendency to frown.

Peregrine dropped a backpack and hefted a large duffle onto a table. She pulled out a hat and put it on, stuffing her ponytail into it. She settled a pair of sunglasses on her nose, then shrugged into a jacket with a masculine cut.

Fallon had to smile. Dressed thus, with her build, the casual eye would see Peregrine as a man. Three looks in less than ten minutes. No wonder they called her Masquerade.

Peregrine yanked a blonde wig out of the bag, but before she could hand it over, Fallon spoke. "Not yet. After we return the boat. If I don't return it, the boatman will report it missing, and that might bring Sarkavian officials here sooner rather than later, and there's no telling who they might discover here. I don't want innocent people to get hurt. After we return the boat, then you can disguise me."

Peregrine nodded, stuffing the wig back into her bag. She crossed the room, opened a drawer, and put several more things into the duffle. She cast a quick look around the cottage, then nodded. "I'll arm some booby traps on the way out, in case someone comes looking."

Fallon liked the way she thought. She waited at the door while Peregrine input some commands, and they were headed to the pier less than twenty minutes after Fallon's arrival on the island. Not bad, considering most of the time had been spent on Peregrine de-treeing herself. Still, Fallon itched to get moving. To get off the planet.

The boat ride back to the marina gave them a few minutes to

talk. Fallon filled Peregrine in on the basics of the situation. She had questions for Peregrine too, lots of them, but they'd have to wait.

"Back so soon?" the boatman asked genially as he came to help tie up the boat.

"Happened across an old friend," Fallon answered, keeping her tone amiable and full of shoot-the-breeze. "Decided we'd go get some lunch."

"Nothing better than a meal with good company," agreed the boatman. He really seemed quite nice. Normally that would make her suspicious, but on Sarkan, it just made the guy a local.

Instead of getting a taxi, they rented a rough-terrain buggy wheeler. People usually used them for recreation, but given their versatility and the fact that Fallon could drive it herself rather than hiring a driver, a buggy would do quite nicely.

After they'd gotten some distance from the marina, they stopped and Peregrine kitted Fallon out with the pale blonde wig and light-colored makeup. Finally, she poked pale contacts into Fallon's eyes. After they stopped watering and Fallon got a look at herself, she had to admit she looked like a native Sarkavian. Even the shape of her eyes was different. Weird. But a Sarkavian woman and a man of uncertain origin would not stand out, and no one would see a Japanese and a Zerellian woman together at the transport hubs.

At the air tram station, they left the buggy in the return area, where the boatman would look for it later. Then they hopped on the first tram they could. It took them in the wrong direction, but that was fine. A somewhat circuitous route wouldn't hurt. Especially if they changed their disguises partway through, which Fallon was sure Peregrine intended to do.

On that tram and the three that followed, they chatted about their nonexistent kids, the weather, and the rising cost of jujafruit. Mostly lies and fabrication, designed for anyone who might overhear, though the jujafruit conversation actually proved interesting. Peregrine told her how imported Earth trees, like coconut and pineapple, had grown rampantly over the last decade, and begun to choke off the local jujafruit trees. Conservation efforts were in progress, but it would take another decade to reverse the damage.

"A shame," Fallon tsked. "I grew up having juja every morning with my toast and tea. I hate that transplanted species are causing such a problem."

Fallon had to work hard at appearing benign and banal. Underneath, she vibrated with adrenaline and the urge to move, to do, to fight. Taking some punches, she could happily do. Sitting around when there was so much ahead of her proved exceedingly difficult. She wondered if Peregrine felt the same. Surely she must. How could she not?

Before they left the final tram station, they ducked into a necessary. In just a few minutes, Peregrine transformed herself into a woman with black hair, and then turned Fallon into a teen with soft brown curls.

They rode the elevator up to the docking station in near silence. Fallon fidgeted and drew imaginary shapes on the wall with her finger until Peregrine gently chided her.

Once on the docking station, they went straight to Dragonfire's class-six cruiser. They were so close to escaping Sarkan, and Fallon felt like demons were nipping at her heels. She wouldn't be able to relax until they got out of Sarkavian space. Well, she wouldn't exactly relax then either, but her hypervigilance could ease down a notch or two to mere paranoia.

The docking security disregarded her wig, contacts, and juvenile dress. It cared only about her facial structure, voice print, retina scan, palm print, and security code. Docking security was no joke, for which Fallon was grateful.

She didn't relax until they'd cleared the docking clamps and set off in the wrong direction. After they got a few light-years away, they'd adjust to their real course. Dineb. Where, hopefully, Hawk and Raptor would be waiting for them.

With privacy and nothing to do but wait, Peregrine, sitting in the other chair, turned and fixed her with a no-nonsense look. "Now. Tell me what the hell is going on."

Peregrine paced around the cruiser's narrow interior. Back and forth, back and forth. Fallon was glad she wasn't prone to travel sickness. "So you're saying you don't remember me at all? Not school, or our missions or…anything?" Peregrine's voice rang with bewilderment.

"No. Or Hawk or Raptor, either. Or my own wife. All of my memories are less than a couple weeks old."

"But you can fly a cruiser? Pilot a boat? Take out a Blackout assassin?" Emotion crept into her eyes. Peregrine had known Granite, too.

"My core memories, as the doctors call them, are intact. That information is in my brain, and I can tap into it when it becomes relevant. I have my skills. It's just my life I don't remember."

"Oh, is that all." Peregrine sat and dropped her head into her hands, making a sound that was half-sigh, half-groan. "Why would you *marry*?"

"I don't know. But I believe it was genuine." She filled Peregrine in on her discoveries, as well as the basics of her relationship with Wren.

"That is so messed up." Peregrine slouched in her chair. As they talked, she'd removed their disguises. Fallon felt much better not being dressed as a teenager. She now wore a sleek black bodysuit, which Raptor had given her. Peregrine had changed into the same thing, so it appeared to be their team uniform.

"You have no ideas who's behind it all? It has to be at least one admiral. Maybe more. No one else could manage all this." Peregrine nibbled at the pad of her thumb, deep in thought.

"One of the doctors I've been working with is a friend. A Briveen cyberneticist. She believes Krazinski is involved."

"Krazinski? That doesn't sound right. He's always been one of our biggest backers." Peregrine frowned. "Why does your friend suspect him?"

Fallon told her about the admiral's request for neural implants.

"Why risk the PAC? Memory augmentation isn't worth the peace and stability the PAC provides." Peregrine continued to bite her thumb. Apparently it helped her think. Or maybe it just helped work off her nervous energy. Fallon got the feeling that Peregrine didn't like to sit still. "The evidence is circumstantial, which means there could be another explanation. There's got to be."

Fallon started to wonder if Peregrine was going to draw blood from that thumb.

"You think they tried to implant you, don't you?" Peregrine's words were almost accusing, but her tone only conveyed bewilderment. "And maybe the accident caused something to happen?" Her eyes narrowed. "Or was there someone on that shuttle with you, who did the damage there and then?"

"I don't know." Fallon didn't want to talk about herself anymore. She'd said most everything she could, and she'd wondered all these what-ifs too many times to count. Right now, she wanted to know about Peregrine.

Fallon asked, "So what happened to you? Why were you out on your island, already in disguise? Who were you watching for?"

"Someone tried to kill me last night. I handled it, but I thought they might try again when they realized they'd failed. I'd assumed it must be my target, having gotten wind of my search for him. I never would have thought it was Blackout." Peregrine's face showed her sense of betrayal and disillusionment.

"So you didn't recognize the assassin?"

Peregrine shook her head, which caused her long ponytail to swing back and forth like a pendulum. "Might have been from a younger class. Newly brought in."

"Or Blackout has agents even we don't know of."

Hell if that wasn't an awful thought. That would be a whole new layer of trouble. She and Peregrine exchanged a grim look.

Peregrine checked their ETA. "Two hours down, twenty-five to go."

"Too long," Fallon muttered.

"Yeah. I need to hear that Hawk's okay. My guess is that they put simultaneous hits out on all of us. Raptor ducked it because he wasn't where he was supposed to be. But what about Hawk?"

Fallon said nothing because there was nothing *to* say. They could only wait until they arrived at the rendezvous point on Dineb. Fallon was back in the position of having so much she needed to do, but having no immediate means of doing anything. She wished she could be out there, running whatever gauntlet Raptor was going through to get to Hawk. Better to be in the thick of it than to be sitting helpless and waiting.

She decided to use the time to get reacquainted with Peregrine. At least that was something useful.

"So tell me about these tattoos." She traced her finger over the black cloth covering her abs, where her ink was. She'd noticed Peregrine had her own on her left shoulder blade.

Peregrine's face showed surprise. "Raptor didn't tell you?"

"We had very limited time. We were trying to get the data we needed to find you and Hawk. I kept meaning to ask, but didn't get the chance."

"We got them when we got recruited for Blackout. When we knew we'd be a unit."

"After OTS, or during security school?" Fallon asked.

More surprise from Peregrine. "Uh, no. During the academy. Near graduation."

But that meant... "We were recruited to Blackout when we were teenagers?"

"That's the way it works, most of the time. They want teams training together for years before their first field op. They use standardized testing to pick out the potentials, then cross-check the results against academic records and achievements. They locate the trailblazers early and bring them in. Some wash out, but most of the early-identified stick."

"So you know my real name, then. The one I had before Blackout."

Peregrine blinked. "No. Well, yes. I know the name that you went through the academy with. But it wasn't the one you were born with."

"What do you mean?"

"Early-identified intelligence candidates are the ones intended for clandestine ops, whether for central intelligence or Blackout. That means they don't want those candidates to have pasts. So when you arrived for academy, at sixteen years old and fresh faced, they spoofed your name. Gave you an official record for people to track, but that was a ghost. The real you had a brand-new name and background that you presented from then on."

Which made perfect sense. And meant that the family and personal information in her active file had all been fabricated. She could actually have family still alive, somewhere.

Fallon tucked that highly intriguing bit of information away, then prompted, "What do the tattoos mean?"

"Outwardly, they're just a symbol of our devotion to one another. Just like our motto. Blood and bone. They're a stylized version of ancient Atalan hieroglyphs that mean just that. Blood, and bone."

Which meant the story she'd told Wren about her tattoo had been a lie. Not that some story about tattoos was worse than all of Fallon's lies of omission, but knowing she'd looked Wren in the face and told her a fake story just sucked. All the better that she stayed away from her until she knew all of the facts.

"You said outwardly. What else are they?"

Peregrine smiled. "Trackers. A sort of transmitter. Raptor devised teeny little tracking modules. Microscopic, but tons of them, embedded in the skin. We got the tattoos to hide the trackers."

Fallon had an urge to laugh. "How close do you have to be?"

"About the size of a small continent."

"That means different things on different planets," Fallon pointed out.

"About ten million square kilometers. Depending on the natural minerals in the area."

"So if I'm within that distance, I could find the three of you?" That would have been nice to know when she'd been tracking Peregrine down.

"Easily, with a receiver. You just—"

But Fallon cut her off. Now that she knew to access that information, her brain resurrected the info. "Right. I got it." She'd need the right equipment, but it was basic tech. The coding and the correct frequency were the tricky parts. But there the information was, just waiting for her to come looking for it. Another thing pulled from her core memory and into the active memory.

With the major bases covered, Fallon now had a chance to get a better idea of her personal history and her background with Avian Unit. At the moment, they had a lot of time to fill, and the more background she had, the more material she had to work with in figuring out what was happening to them.

"So," she said. "Tell me everything you can about Avian Unit."

"And when he woke up in the morning, all his chest hair was gone." Peregrine managed to get the words out around the laughter that kept bubbling up. As soon as she finished talking, she erupted into a big hooting laugh that filled the entire cruiser.

Fallon laughed with her. "Well, he deserved it. But I'm sure he didn't let that go without answer. What did he do back to me?" She cringed, waiting for whatever horrible thing Hawk had done for payback.

"Nothing yet. But it's coming." Peregrine snickered. "That's the great thing about Hawk. He's a slow-simmering sort."

Silence descended on them as they both remembered that if Hawk's would-be assassin had succeeded, that reprisal would never come.

"He'll be fine," Fallon said. "We both managed."

"Barely, in my case. In truth, I got lucky. My antipersonnel devices were what saved me."

"Doesn't matter," Fallon insisted. "You made it, and so will Hawk. He and Raptor will already be on Dineb, waiting for us. From the sound of it, they wouldn't want to let us beat them there."

A hint of Peregrine's smile returned, though tinged with wistfulness. "No, they wouldn't."

The way Peregrine had described it, the four of them enjoyed competing with one another, as well as playing minor practical jokes. Well, maybe more than minor, but a Blackout unit was hardly a group of people designed to be reserved and placid. Too much ambition. Too much ego. Too much adrenaline left over after risking their lives doing this or that. It made sense that they played as hard as they worked.

Over the hours, their conversation followed that pattern. Enthusiasm and amusement punctuated by withdrawn periods of deflated energy. It was such an in-between place they existed in. Either a whole team still, or only half of it. Or three-quarters might be an option, if only Raptor or Hawk showed up. Fallon decided she didn't like fractions.

The cabin seemed too small to hold their combined energy

and worries, and when Dineb came into view, they both breathed a sigh of relief. Judging from Peregrine's face, she felt the same stab of dread that Fallon did.

The Dinebians offered both excellent security and anonymity. Since it was a party planet, it provided privacy for those who didn't wish to be tracked down while having a good time.

They took the elevator down into the atmosphere. Peregrine had brought a receiver to monitor for Raptor and Hawk's trackers. Fallon wished she could wear her stinger, but she wasn't going to Dineb as a PAC security officer. She was going as a private citizen, off to dance the night away. Or whatever people did here. Which was their own business, as far as she was concerned.

They didn't bother with disguises, since Dineb didn't allow recording devices except for in marked security areas. They did wear light jackets over their black outfits, which made them look less like what they were and more like important people enjoying an opportunity to go incognito. All the better for them, as people would be eager to help them, in the hopes of earning a gratuity. Fallon was prepared to tip or bribe anyone she needed to, equipped as she was with her stolen funds.

Fallon paid close attention to her surroundings as they made their way toward the place Raptor had decreed as the meet point. Dineb was a planetary oddity. Once you got off the elevator you were stuck with ground travel only. Plus, only licensed cabbies could operate groundcars. It was safer, from a crazy-partiers-don't-use-good-sense perspective, and the planet had an excellent safety rating to show for it.

As Fallon and Peregrine approached the coordinates, the receiver stayed stubbornly quiet. They knew long before they arrived that Hawk and Raptor had not beaten them to the rendezvous.

"Doesn't mean anything," Fallon said as she dropped her gear and sank onto a too-squishy couch in their rented suite of rooms. "They had farther to travel, and who knows what kind of ship they managed to grab to get off that moon. Could be a busted-down cargo ship with barely any engine power."

"They'll be here," Peregrine agreed, kicking off her shoes and sprawling onto the couch with a groan.

It had taken them nearly a full, sleepless day—or perhaps more than one, depending on the planet—to make it from Sarkan to Dineb. Their suite, decorated in bright pinks, greens, and oranges, had only three bedrooms. They'd been lucky to snag it on such short notice, but once they were four again, someone would have to sleep on the couch. Fallon didn't plan on it being her, never mind that she was the smallest of them. The thing folded out. Any one of them could be just as comfortable as the next on it. But Fallon valued her privacy.

"I can't decide if I'm more hungry or more tired," Peregrine sighed. "I've been on alert for two days straight now."

Fallon hadn't had much sleep lately either, with her late nights with Raptor. She heaved herself to her feet and crossed the room to rummage in the minibar, which had both a mini-cooler and a heat-ex. She found a sleeve of cookies, a container of some sort of yogurt, several packets of mixed nuts, some protein-supplement packs, and various drinks. Not a lot to choose from.

She shoved all the food, along with a couple fruit juices, into a punch bowl and carried it over to Peregrine. Because what party room would be complete without a punch bowl? She snorted.

While Peregrine went first for the protein supplements, Fallon grabbed the yogurt and detached the disposable spoon from its side. She ate it quickly, barely tasting it, then moved on to some of the nuts. They were salty, so she drank the fruit juice. She was sure she needed the hydration and electrolytes, anyway. Finally she took a protein pack, ignoring the cookies as a junk food her body didn't need. She chewed the protein, combined too loosely to be called a bar and too tightly to be called a cereal. It had a faint taste of oatmeal and sweetness, but little else. She didn't care for it, but she wasn't in a position to be picky.

After she finished off her juice, she stood. "Now I can sleep without being woken up by hunger pains. I'll see you in ten or twelve hours, unless Raptor and Hawk arrive."

"Make it fourteen," Peregrine groaned as she stood.

They grabbed their bags and Fallon headed for the bedroom closest to the shared necessary. If she woke up to pee, she didn't want to be stumbling through an unknown space to get to it. Peregrine took the bedroom on the other side of the necessary, just a little farther from it. *Great minds think alike*, Fallon thought. It always paid to be tactical.

"In fourteen hours, then," Fallon agreed before closing her door.

Just before it shut, Peregrine called, "Hey!" and she swung it back open.

"Yeah?"

"I'm glad to see you again," Peregrine said with a tired smile.

"Same here. Even if I don't remember seeing you before."

They stared at each other, and burst into tired guffaws. Fallon closed her door, dropped her bags next to the bed and didn't even bother bending her knees. She belly-flopped right onto it, kicking the blankets down and then yanking them over herself, clothes and all. Bathing could wait until tomorrow.

―――

FALLON AND PEREGRINE didn't panic when Raptor and Hawk didn't show up the next day, though Fallon's concern intensified. When they didn't show up the day after, Fallon became straight-up worried. Being a day overdue was not a good sign. All she and Peregrine could do was wait and bide their time.

They ordered room service the first day, talking and staying in the suite so they could be there as soon as the men arrived. But by that evening, they both had cabin fever. They ordered some standard Dinebian-style partygoer clothes and had them rush-delivered to their room, then laughed at each other. It felt good to let go of some of their tension, if only for a moment.

Fallon wore a hot-pink-and-orange sarong, with stupid little strappy sandals that wouldn't last a second in a fight. Peregrine wore a flowy maxi dress in shades of blue, along with a ridiculous floppy hat. There was no way she could wear that thing inside some local hotspot. Which was fine. Fallon had no desire to visit some building full of pounding music and bodies packed shoulder to shoulder, all attempting to impress one another with inept dancing. No thanks.

Instead, they took a walk, waving and returning cheery greetings to other people. One thing you could say for Dineb, everyone was far too happy to be rude. Every new person was a chance to meet your new friend, lover, or whatever. Except, of course, for Fallon and Peregrine, who were careful to avoid getting entangled in any invitations. Fallon did notice Peregrine looking at a particular blond human with interest.

"Feel free, if you're up for it," Fallon suggested. No doubt Peregrine could use a good distraction. "I can hold down the fort and contact you if anything happens."

Peregrine's eyes tracked the guy, strolling down the walkway with a group of other young men.

"No," she said with a tinge of regret. "I don't want to be hung up somewhere if the guys show up. *When* they show up."

They stopped at a stand selling frozen custard and each got a dish of the creamy dessert. Fallon let the berry flavor melt on her tongue as they walked along, pondering the irony of enjoying such an indulgence during a tense waiting period. The nature of the confection also amused her, as it contained a variety of berries from disparate planets. Funny how an entire universe could come together into one small cup of custard. She could almost get philosophical about it.

Peregrine had fallen silent too, and by unspoken agreement they sat on a bench alongside the parkway, watching streams of people pour out of one set of doors, only to enter another a block or two away.

In backward fashion, after they finished their desserts, they went in search of a quiet spot to get some dinner. No luck. Instead, they ordered some Zerellian takeout and returned to their bench.

They arranged the containers on the bench beside them and dug in with their chopsticks. After several bites from one container, Peregrine passed it to Fallon. "This one's really good. Try it."

Fallon put down the spiced chicken she'd been eating and accepted Peregrine's offering. She pinched a bit of the brown noodles and vegetables and quickly shoveled it into her mouth.

"Mmm," she mumbled in appreciation. The noodles were thick, but not tough, giving them just the right chewiness. The brown sauce on them was simultaneously sweet and acidic, tearing into her taste buds and making them take notice. Fallon ate several more bites as she watched the passersby, then handed it back to Peregrine. "Thanks."

"Hendaya has always been one of my favorites." Peregrine dug right back into the dish, expertly popping noodles into her mouth.

"I can see why. Maybe it's one of mine, too." Fallon chuckled.

Peregrine turned her head toward Fallon. "What's it like? Not knowing your own life?"

Fallon lifted the shoulder nearest her partner, then let it drop. "Like being incredibly young, I guess. As far as my awareness goes, I'm only a couple of weeks old. But I came with all of these preloaded programs, so I know tons of stuff. I don't even know what all I know. And somehow other people know more about me than I know about myself, but whenever I find something out about my past, it makes perfect sense." She wiped her mouth with a disposable napkin, which she found terribly wasteful, but that was how Dineb worked. Everything disposable. No worries about the consequences of tomorrow.

She continued, thinking as she spoke. Having to put her thoughts into words made her analyze them more than she had previously. "It's a little eerie sometimes. I feel like I'm a brand-new person, but I'm exactly like the version of myself that existed before the accident. A mirror. I'd have thought some things might change. That without memories of the events of my life, my basic personality composition could shift. At least a little, here and there."

"But no?" Peregrine had paused with a dumpling in her chopsticks hovering just beyond her lips.

"Nope. I'm exactly what everyone tells me I am. It makes me want to rebel sometimes. Do something that people wouldn't expect of the Fallon they know."

Peregrine smiled while chewing a large dumpling, making her look rather goofy.

"What?" Fallon asked.

"Nothing. You'll get mad," Peregrine said from behind her hand, her words loose and juicy with spicy sauce.

"I'll get mad if you don't tell me. So go ahead."

Peregrine swallowed. "I was thinking that it sounded just like you to want to go against the grain. To be different just for the sake of being unpredictable. Very typical Fallon behavior."

"Gah!" Fallon rolled her eyes and made a sound of disgust, though she found it mildly amusing. "I guess that's part of being a team. Being known so well."

"Yup." Apparently the dumplings were as tasty as the hendaya, because Peregrine stuffed an even bigger one into her mouth and still didn't offer the container to Fallon.

"Give me those." She grabbed the container out of Peregrine's hand. "You're about to eat them all."

"But you don't—" Peregrine began.

Too late. If a flavor could be a stench, that's what was filling her mouth. "*Auuugh*," she groaned as her taste buds rebelled. She could only describe the flavor as rot and dirty running socks rolled into one. With a very spicy hot sauce, but not nearly enough to cover the evil stench-taste.

There was nothing else to do. "*Pleh.*" She spit the dumpling out right into the walkway in front of her. "Oh, Prelin. So gross."

She hung her mouth open, trying to air it out as she scrabbled for a napkin, then wiped her tongue with it. Peregrine pressed a recyclable drink bottle into her hand and Fallon gulped the oddly refreshing cucumber-mint juice.

"Ahh," she pulled in a breath. "Oh, that was so bad. Rastor dumplings, right? As soon as I tasted it, I knew."

Peregrine's laughter grew louder and louder until she sat holding her stomach and hooting with tears running out of the corners of her eyes.

Fallon sighed, feeling foolish, but a reluctant snicker wrested its way out of her.

Peregrine gasped for breath, still giggling, wiping her face. Fallon supposed she should be embarrassed, or angry at being the butt of such laughter, but it pleased her to see Peregrine so relaxed. Her features had been so tight and strained up to this point that she hadn't been able to see how attractive Peregrine was. Not in a beautiful way, or even pretty in the strictest sense of the word. Her face had so much strength, and a lack of the high cheekbones and full lips that typically equated to beauty, but her eyes sparked with intelligence and her features were so full of character. No doubt her partner could make herself up as a beautiful woman, but in Peregrine's own style, Fallon found her quite appealing. A unique, interesting person. Someone she wanted to know more about.

She smiled at her partner, feeling truly connected to her for the first time, as if two components had suddenly clicked into place together.

People walking by grinned at them, having witnessed Peregrine's big crack-up. The two of them smiled back, but didn't invite conversation. Fallon took a napkin and scooped up the offending Rastor dumpling, then dropped it into a rubbish bin. Visitors who made a habit of leaving messes behind would find themselves without visiting privileges. Not that anyone knew her true identity here, besides Peregrine, but not cleaning up after oneself was quite rude on Dineb.

After eating, they grabbed a couple more frozen custards to take back to the room. This time, Fallon chose chocolate flavored. There was nothing philosophical about chocolate, unless one wanted to do an in-depth analysis of indulgence and sin. Not being the religious sort, Fallon did not.

In the living space of their rented suite of rooms, they both set down their dessert cups and did a security sweep, then returned and sat—Fallon on the couch and Peregrine on a recliner chair that looked highly comfortable. Fallon made it a priority to snag that seat next time.

They ate their custard slowly, and mostly in silence, though occasionally one of them remarked on something or other.

Fallon decided to suggest a holo-vid. There was little else for them to do, and she'd tired of peppering Peregrine with questions about her past. She had to accept that getting answers would take time, and some of them might never come.

"Do you—" she began, but Peregrine's leg made a shrill noise and she cut the words off.

Peregrine dropped her cup and spoon to the table with a clatter and lifted her dress to midthigh, where Fallon saw a belt holding a pair of wicked-looking knives and the tiniest stinger she'd ever seen. More Blackout tech, no doubt.

Peregrine tugged a tiny receiver from the belt and squinted at it. "They're coming. Or at least one of them is. Heading our direction, moving fast. Probably a taxi."

Fallon sat up straight. "Finally."

Peregrine just nodded distractedly.

Fallon stood. "We should prepare food, water, and medical support. Then get into tactical positions." No telling what condition their other two partners were in, or who might be on their heels.

Peregrine blinked at her, then gave a jerky nod. She jumped to her feet. "I have a Blackout medkit in my gear."

"Good. I'll get food and water ready." Fortunately, they'd found a bodega and stocked the mini-cooler, as well as the cabinet.

That done, they both grabbed weapons and took up defensive positions. Peregrine chose the window, while Fallon selected the hallway adjacent to the stairwell and lift. Fallon had her stinger and knives, and her eyes widened when she saw what Peregrine held. How had she fit so much into the few bags she'd taken away from the island?

Peregrine held a military-grade personal laser cannon against her shoulder, using the scope to look at long-range targets out the window.

"No way," Fallon said. "How did you get that through the docking station?" She'd thought she'd been clever in smuggling her stinger down to the planet.

"In pieces. Lots of them. Disguised to look like small electronics."

"Niiiiice. I've got to get one of those."

"You have three," Peregrine answered without turning to look at her. "But I'm guessing you won't make it to your quarters at central command anytime soon."

Fallon hadn't even given any thought to where she'd called home previously. She still had quarters somewhere else, where her previous self had lived? She *had* to get there at some point.

She'd at least get some insight into her life, and maybe even finally manage to jog her memory. A sudden burst of total recall would sure come in handy about now.

"Blood and bone, Peregrine."

This time, her partner turned her head to give her a steely look and a nod. "Blood and bone."

As she crouched in the hallway, Fallon was surprised by how easy it was to stay motionless for a long period of time. Peregrine had estimated arrival in ten minutes, but fifteen ticked by and still Fallon remained, her weight on the balls of her feet, ready to leap at any second. Her ears strained for any sound.

Finally she heard it. The faint whine of the lift's motor, a tiny squeak, and a pause. She clenched a knife in one hand and her stinger in the other.

The doors hissed open and out stepped Raptor. Practically carrying a burly guy whose legs seemed to be made of rubber. Hawk. *Scrap.* Hawk was injured.

She waited until they cleared the lift and the doors closed, guarding their rear, before rising to her feet and making a gentle whistle like an ocarina bird. Raptor and Peregrine had ensured that she knew the signal, which they used among themselves. She didn't want her teammates to turn around and shoot, thinking she was the enemy.

Raptor didn't stop hauling Hawk toward their room, but stole a glance behind him. "Fallon," he said with relief. "Help me out here. He made it planetside, but then started to really go downhill."

At least it wasn't unusual to see someone not quite in control of their faculties on Dineb. The taxi driver and others would have simply thought that Hawk had guzzled a few too many high-octane beverages.

Fallon rushed to Hawk's other side, putting her arm around him and taking some of his weight. She imagined her spine filling with polymechrine to make her strong. The dude was *heavy*.

His eyes rolled and his skin was a horrid chalky gray. "Shit," she said. "What happened?"

"A few troubles getting out. Guessing something's ruptured," Raptor huffed, out of breath.

At the door, Raptor did a quick knock pattern that Fallon had not previously been apprised of, and then Fallon went through the security process, opening the door as quickly as she could.

They stumbled through the doorway together, Fallon twisting awkwardly sideways because the three of them did not really fit all at once.

"Hawk!" Peregrine lifted her head from the cannon, which had been leveled right at them. "All clear?"

"All clear," agreed Raptor. "As far as I know."

Peregrine nodded, then seemed undecided. "Should I keep up guard, or help with Hawk?" She looked at Fallon. Well, of course she did. Fallon was their leader.

"What do you think?" she asked Raptor. "Did you come in hot? Any pursuit at all?"

"Lots. But none left living." He didn't seem to have breath enough for many words.

"Come help," Fallon told Peregrine.

Together, they stripped their partner down to his underwear and went to work. He had three stinger burns on his back. They eased off a plaster that had been slapped on his chest and revealed a deep slash across his left pectoral that was gushing blood. His hands had tiny cuts and burn marks, and his left wrist had clearly been broken.

Fallon administered painkillers, antibiotics, and immune boosters while Raptor stopped the bleeding and sealed the gaping slash with a skin knitter. He seemed quite capable at it, and she'd already seen his high rating for field-medic skills. Fallon knew she couldn't have done nearly as neat of a job, though as she watched Raptor, she realized that she did know how.

Meanwhile, Peregrine tried to keep Hawk conscious. A losing battle. His eyes kept fluttering closed, which would cause Peregrine to bark at him. She resorted to cursing, which revived Hawk briefly before his head lolled to the side again.

"He's lost too much blood," Raptor muttered. "Did what I could on the ship, but they were on us the whole way. I only took out the last ship an hour before we docked, and I had to spend that time forging our papers and authorization, as well as arranging an express taxi to get us here."

Fallon rummaged through the medkit, pulling out a single packet of universal synthblood. Not enough, but it would have to do. She slapped it into Raptor's hand and watched him break open the seal and expose the needle.

"This is going to hurt," he said between gritted teeth.

Just as well Hawk wasn't awake then, but his color and shallow breathing worried Fallon. He was in bad shape. They could lose him.

Fallon applied a heal-pack to Hawk's thick, muscled chest. She had to slick away blood with her palms to get it to attach. The pack would keep delivering painkillers and immune boosters, as well as nanopods that would aid in Hawk's healing. She could only hope the nanopods could handle the blood loss.

Finally they all sat back on their heels, surrounding Hawk on the floor of the living room as he fought for life without making a sound. Raptor watched him intently, waiting for his vital signs to stabilize.

Fallon looked at her hands, covered in her partner's blood. She hadn't even gotten to say hello to him yet, and she might end up having to lay him to rest. "I'll go clean up," she said in a low voice. At least that would be a productive way of spending the next few minutes, rather than sitting and holding her breath.

In the necessary, she quickly scrubbed off the blood in the hydro-shower and removed her party clothes, which looked even more ridiculous now. Shameful, even. She'd been eating frozen custard when Hawk had been struggling for life. She should have been there with her partners.

She balled up the clothes and shoved them into the processor. She wore a towel to her room, then yanked on the black bodysuit that felt like a second skin to her. In this, she felt better equipped to save Hawk.

Not that there was anything for her to do for him now. Her attention shifted to Raptor as she rejoined the others, only minutes after she'd left. "What about you? Any injuries?"

He still sat next to Hawk. He looked up at her, his face lined in a way she hadn't seen before. He looked older. Exhausted. "Just some scratches and bruises."

All of Hawk's visible injuries to his front side were gone, as though they'd been erased. Fallon looked over Raptor's shoulder to see the readout from the medical scanner. It was a woeful substitute for a techbed, but it showed a steady heart rate and breathing. Hopefully they would stay that way.

"We need to roll him and get those stinger burns, now that he's stable," Peregrine said to Fallon.

The three of them rolled him onto his stomach, and Fallon cringed at the three burn marks in Hawk's back. They weren't life threatening where they were located, but they must have been hideously painful. As Raptor worked on Hawk's back, Fallon sat next to them, her hand on Hawk's shoulder.

She leaned down. "Hang in there," she murmured. "We've got you. Blood and bone don't quit."

When she straightened, she saw a surprised expression on Peregrine's face. Raptor, too, had frozen, his gaze riveted on her.

"What?" she asked, defensively.

"What did you just say?" Peregrine asked.

"Just...blood and bone don't quit."

"Why?" Raptor asked.

"I don't know. Just seemed like the right...thing." She shrugged.

Peregrine and Raptor exchanged a look.

"*What?*" Fallon asked again, annoyed.

Raptor went back to working on Hawk.

Peregrine answered her. "That's what we've always said when one of us is hurt or things are really looking bad."

Fallon felt everything inside her go very still. She could recover skills when she knew to try, but she'd never recalled specific things like words or phrases. But maybe the phrase was more than just an encouragement that had occurred to her on the spur of the moment. Could it be an actual memory?

———

Throughout the night, no other memories surfaced. What she'd said to Hawk might have been nothing but a coincidence.

Fallon sat up with him, watching him breathe. Peregrine would take over in two more hours, ensuring that they each got half a night's sleep. When there was nothing left for Raptor to do for Hawk, Fallon and Peregrine had insisted he shove some food into his face and then sleep. He'd protested, but the quickness with which he capitulated proved his exhaustion.

She still didn't know just what had happened to Hawk. Only that assassins had been sent for him too, and getting off that Zerellian moon had not been easy.

She lay next to him on the foldout bed in the living area. They'd decided not to move him farther than they had to, both for his comfort and theirs. Hawk was a huge dude, and seemed to be filled with iron. She kept herself propped up on one elbow, measuring his every breath from half a meter away. He seemed to be out of imminent danger, but Raptor had warned about a pulmonary embolism, which could kill Hawk in minutes. They had no monitoring equipment, only the scanner, which she used every quarter hour to get a read on the basics. A doctor could not have done much more for Hawk than Raptor had, and they sure could have used a techbed.

It was a shame she didn't have Brannin, Jerin, or Brak to look after Hawk. She was certain Jerin and Brak would have refrained from asking too many questions. But they were days of distance away, and she'd agreed with Raptor and Peregrine that taking Hawk to a medical facility on Dineb would be like shooting a flare right to Blackout, cueing them in on Avian Unit's location. Even worse, Dineb had no medical staff that they could trust to do some off-the-books doctoring.

So they could only watch and wait. At least the medkit had included a sonic cleaner, which had allowed them to get the blood off of Hawk. The smell of wet metal and dirt, permeating the entire suite, had bothered the three of them. After getting him clean, they'd increased the cycling speed of the air purifier, and the stench had cleared out in minutes.

She shouldn't have been surprised, but when they got him clean, she'd recognized the tattoo, just to the outside of his left nipple. Just like the ones she, Raptor, and Peregrine had. It made her feel suddenly more connected to this big bear of a man.

They'd covered Hawk with a light blanket, but his skin had grown hot and Fallon had pushed it off him. Raptor had warned her it would happen, as his body recovered in ways that only it could accomplish at this point.

She touched her hand to Hawk's forehead, then rested it on his chest, gauging his body heat. She left it there, feeling his heavy heartbeat against her palm, ensuring that it stayed steady. It felt oddly intimate, lying next to a nearly nude person, watching him sleep. Listening to his breathing as she would a lover's. And she did feel a connection to him. Something sort of *like* a lover, but without the sexual component. Was it just empathy and a shared tattoo, or some actual remembrance of him? She hoped it was a memory.

She flexed her fingers against his chest, lightly touching the tattoo beneath them. Funny to see what she considered a piece of herself on another person.

"Stop groping me, pervert." The words were as rough and rusty as an ancient hunk of metal, but she heard them clearly.

She yanked her hand back and sat up, peering down into his face. His eyes opened, revealing the blue-gray she remembered from his file. Up close, they were much prettier, like a cloudy sky with a hint of rain.

His lip twitched, causing his full beard to move in tandem. He worked his jaw, keeping his eyes fixed on Fallon.

"I feel like shit," he rasped.

"You smell like it too. Especially your breath," she answered.

The mountain of a man who'd been near death only hours ago grinned at her. "Good to see you, Fallon."

She hopped off the couch-bed and retrieved a pouch of biogel. He glanced at it as she returned, folding her legs under her to sit next to him.

"I hate that rubbish. Get me bourbon."

"Forget it." She punctured the pouch and pressed it to his mouth with gentle fingers that were completely at odds with their barbed words.

He obediently drank it down until she withdrew the depleted packet and dropped it next to the bed. He cleared his throat.

"Feels better, at least." He'd lost the raspiness, but his resounding bass voice still seemed to come from deep within his chest. It suited him, given his hulking physique. In contrast to Raptor, he was all bulk and muscle. The male equivalent of Peregrine, she supposed.

"Good. We were worried."

His thick arms, previously so inert, surprised her by grabbing her suddenly and pulling her down across him, into a bear hug. "Man am I glad to see you. I like the hair. Like the old days." He reached up and tousled it.

"Thanks. You're looking much better." She rolled away and sat up to study him. His color had returned, pinking up what she could see of his cheeks above his beard. The facial hair had a way of highlighting his eyes and his full lips, giving him the look of a cherubic lumberjack. His reddish-brown hair matched his beard precisely. He was just handsome enough to be eye-catching, but earthy enough to be charming and disarming. A potent combination, she was sure.

"Raptor?" he asked, his eyes gone serious.

"Fine. Just exhausted. I can't wait to hear about whatever happened."

"I've already heard about what happened to *you*. Didn't hear much of Raptor's blather when I was trying to sleep, but I did catch that part." He pushed himself up to sitting, groaning a little.

"You okay?"

"Damn back hurts." He awkwardly reached around himself, probing his back.

She slapped his hand away. "Stinger burns. Healed, but the new skin will be tender. Why weren't you wearing a stinger dissipater?"

He scowled at her. "I didn't have any reason to expect trouble. I was sleeping when they showed up."

Well, that answered that.

"Bet you didn't expect to have to perform your own emergency extraction." She stood and moved to his side to assist. She braced her shoulder into his side and put her arm around him.

"Good thing Raptor showed up when he did. They had me pinned down. Five of them." He accepted her help without complaint, resting his arm on her shoulder. It felt like a boulder, but a warm, gentle boulder.

"Where are we going?" she asked.

"The necessary. I'm about to burst."

He did fairly well, only bobbling twice. She served as a small anchor, and his arm tightened on her each time briefly, until he'd steadied himself.

She helped him all the way into the necessary, where he let go of her and rested a hand on the sink basin for surety.

"You good on your own?" she asked. Surprisingly, the idea of helping if he needed it didn't bother her.

"I got it." He shuffled to the commode and Fallon watched him to be sure, then stepped out, letting the door slide closed behind her. She remained poised, listening, in case he called for her.

The door hissed back open and they resumed their previous situation. On their way back to the bed, he asked, "Any chance of some food? I'm starved."

"That's a good sign." She made sure he was seated before going to the kitchenette and throwing a variety of high-nutrition foods onto a tray.

He'd arranged himself sitting up with a cushion behind his back, so she set the tray next to him. He wasted no time in tearing into it.

"So you don't remember me at all, huh?" He watched her sit next to him while he chewed.

"I saw your active file," she answered. "So I know everything from there. But from my own personal knowledge, no. I don't."

"Ah, yes. Your memory. Eidetic, or whatever." He put his hands in the air at each side of his head and waggled his fingers. Then he reached for another protein pack. He seemed to like them.

"Not quite. But close."

"Never knew you to forget anything." He uncapped a bottle of juice and tipped it back for a long drink that nearly emptied it. "Well, until now."

"Irony." She shrugged. "I'm managing."

She considered waking Raptor and Peregrine to let them know that Hawk was up, but quickly decided against it. They needed their sleep, especially Raptor. She'd keep Hawk company until Peregrine came to relieve her. She was glad to get the chance to meet this fourth partner, her final teammate.

They talked like old friends, which they were, though Fallon didn't recall it. He told her about his escape from the Zerellian moon. They'd barely gotten off the rock, and Raptor had had a hell of a time shaking off the pursuers.

"Could have used your flying skills," Hawk noted, starting on his fourth protein pack. They'd need to stock back up the next day. Unless they were leaving. She didn't know yet. If they were, then they'd need a whole slew of supplies. Some of them might not be accessible on Dineb. She started making a mental shopping list.

"Why mine?" she asked.

"You're the best of us, by far. You don't know that either?" He snorted, as if scoffing at her stupidity.

She smirked. "I know I love flying. I also noticed my flight rating was higher than any of yours."

"Could have been a fighter pilot for the PAC if you'd chosen." He smashed the protein-pack wrapper between his hands and reached for a tango fruit.

"Did not know that." That reminded her. "So I'm both the intel-slash-tactical person and the pilot. Raptor is the programmer-slash-hacker and medic. You're the extraction specialist and what?" It only made sense that the pattern followed throughout their team. Each of them with skills that, when added to those of the others, made them a fully contained unit.

"All-around good guy." He gave her a cocky smile.

"I'm serious."

"So am I. Everyone loves me." His smile held.

At her baleful glare, he sighed. "Fine. I'd hoped you'd be more fun this time around. Should have known better. Well, we're all top-notch fighters, though we each have our own tactical style. I'm sure you knew that."

She nodded and twirled her finger in a "keep going" gesture.

He relented. "I have a network of people who can help out with things on a not-so-official basis."

"Like what, smugglers?" She selected a bottle of water for herself and opened it, taking a sip.

"For starters. Forgers, smugglers, thieves. You know. Helpful folks."

"Criminals." She grimaced.

"Don't be so quick to judge." His tone was joking, but there was an underlying seriousness. "Sometimes the line between legal and illegal is faded and blurry. Like us. What we're doing, going off book, makes us criminals. Traitors, technically."

She hadn't thought of it that way. She'd thought of it as her team rooting out what had gone bad in Blackout to restore it. That double negative, in her mind, had equated to Avian Unit still being a positive. The good guys.

"I guess you're right." She sighed.

He bumped her shoulder with his fist. Even in his weakened state, and even though he was clearly being careful, it felt like she'd stumbled and smacked her shoulder on a bulkhead.

"Course I am. You remember that, at least. 'Hawk is always right,' you always say."

She laughed. "You'll never get me to believe that."

He affected a wounded look, then stuffed the last of the fruit in his mouth, making loud slurping sounds against the juicy flesh. The sweet smell of it made Fallon want one, but they were officially out of them now. Something else they'd need to get the next day.

"How are you feeling?" She reached for the hand scanner and ran through the routine biometric checks.

"Better than when I woke. Worse than yesterday."

"Your white count is a little low. When Raptor wakes up, he might want to give you some injections."

He sighed and pushed the tray away. All that remained were empty packets and bottles, and one lone container of water. He picked it up and twisted it between his hands. "I hate injections."

"You'll survive it." She swung her legs off the bed and took the tray back to the kitchenette. She shoved the wrappings into the recycling tube and left the tray on top of the mini-cooler.

When she returned to sit on the couch, Hawk continued as if there'd been no break to their previous thread of conversations. "Peregrine's our gadget person, if you didn't know. She can refit anything in less than the standard spec time. She doesn't do big things like engines or anything, but with contained systems like surveillance, scanners, and the like, she's a pro."

Made sense. "She made me into her daughter for the trip off Sarkan," Fallon confided.

Hawk grinned. "She made me into her dad once. I bet I liked that even less."

"Yeah. I could see that." At his sharp look, she added, "Not liking it, I mean. Not that you look like you could be her dad."

He smiled fondly, scratching at the beard just under his chin, which made a gross, scritchy sort of sound she didn't like. "She comes up with some fun ones sometimes." His last word morphed into a yawn that grew surprisingly big.

"Think I'm getting sleepy," he mumbled.

"It's the middle of the night," she reassured him. "You're supposed to be."

"I want to talk more. I haven't seen you in a year." He frowned at her. "I have a lot of questions."

Still, he lay back when she put her hand on his arm and guided him. "The four of us are back together now. We're going to stay that way. We'll get caught up."

He yawned again. "All right." His eyelids drifted shut and she smoothed a lightweight blanket over him. His eyes popped back open. "Stay with me?"

Somehow he managed to sound like an eight-year-old child, in need of mothering. "Yeah. I'll be right here."

To prove it, she lay down next to him and stretched out her arm to rest her palm on his shoulder. He fell asleep almost immediately, but she didn't move her hand.

Fallon woke up tired. She rubbed the sand from her eyes and, yawning, left her room to join the others in the living area.

"There she is!" announced Hawk, eating again, but this time sitting up at the small dining table. His color was good. To look at him, she wouldn't know he'd been in such bad shape the day before.

Peregrine and Raptor sat with him. Peregrine looked sharp and alert, even though she'd spent the second half of the night watching over Hawk.

Fallon joined them at the table, aware that this was the first time, in her memory, all four of them had been together. The others didn't seem to notice, though. To them it must have been just like old times. Other than Hawk's recent distress and her own memory loss. But maybe such hurdles were normal for a unit like theirs. Just another day at the office for a group of BlackOps.

They made plans over breakfast. Over Hawk's protests, Fallon assigned herself and Peregrine to go out and get whatever supplies they could find. Food and other basics would be easy enough to obtain, but they'd need to look elsewhere for some of their other, more specialized, needs. Unfortunately Raptor had lost the ultralight during the confrontation on the Zerellian moon. He insisted they watch for an opportunity to acquire another one, but Fallon had reservations about allowing them to be split up again. That seemed like a terrible idea. To pacify Raptor, she agreed that they'd all be on the lookout for an ultralight.

After they'd eaten, she and Peregrine set out together, buying food, clean comports, and basic living supplies. As they walked back to their suite, laden with bags and with deliveries to follow, they talked about Hawk. They could have hired a taxi, but they both appreciated the opportunity to be outside and stretch their legs.

"Is it weird for you, dealing with Raptor now?" Peregrine asked, shifting the conversation.

"What do you mean?"

"Since you got married," she said. "None of us ever expected to marry."

"Why Raptor in particular?" Fallon had a bad feeling about this line of questioning.

Peregrine's face betrayed nothing, which of itself betrayed *something*. "Since you two were always so close."

"Are you saying something was going on between him and me? Something more than partner behavior?" Fallon shifted one of the bags on her shoulder.

"No. I just don't know how things are to you, with that gap in your head. I'm trying to imagine it."

"I don't feel weird with him, or any of you. I feel like I belong. Even though I don't remember our history." If it weren't for all the things that had happened, she'd distrust that feeling of belonging. But given the way everything had played out, she felt lucky to have a team on her side. A family.

"I'm glad." Peregrine carefully stepped over an uneven spot in the walkway, pointing to it to make sure Fallon didn't trip. "I don't know what the rest of us would have done if you didn't want to be part of Avian Unit. Or had a tough time trusting us."

She nodded her thanks for the trip-hazard warning. "Well, I sure don't know. I'm just feeling lucky I have anyone on my side at this point."

Peregrine's sad look said it all.

"Hawk, will you be strong enough to leave tomorrow?" Fallon glanced from Hawk to Raptor.

"Of course. What am I, a newborn lamb? Come on. I'm the Machine."

Peregrine smirked. "Right. You only came in here bleeding like a hunk of butcher meat. Why would you not be completely well?"

"He'll be okay," Raptor said. "Just needs to take it easy and rest as much as possible for a few days."

Fallon nodded to Raptor. She trusted his medical opinion. "Then we'll leave at checkout time. That'll be the most crowded the transit stations and the elevator will get, and we'll have the most cover. Just in case anyone's looking."

"That leaves the remainder of the day to rest, to plan, and to reacquaint ourselves with one another," Peregrine noted.

Fallon talked as much as she listened in the subsequent hours, always hoping that something would jog out a memory, one that would confirm that her remark the night before had been an indicator of something. But no. Though she learned a great deal, particularly about the strengths and preferences of her teammates, she didn't get a single feeling of déjà vu, or intuit anything she shouldn't have known.

Though disappointed about that, she felt comfortable with her team, and deeply gratified to have them. That might not seem like much to others, but for Fallon, it was everything.

Late the next morning, Avian Unit packed up, paid their room bill, and got themselves to the elevator and up to the docking station. With some makeup, wigs, and clothing, Peregrine made them all into different people. Each of them walked alone, but within sight of the others, with all now equipped with a new comport.

They arrived on the docking station without incident, though none of them would be able to relax until they'd boarded their ship. Fallon piloted Dragonfire's class-six. They left behind the small but speedy ship Raptor and Hawk had stolen. A shame to lose it, but the thing was tainted goods. Nothing positive could come from keeping an association with it.

They'd paid a month-long docking fee on Dineb, along with some extra cubics to keep the stolen ship's registry number off the records. Before that time was up, Hawk would contact an acquaintance who could make sure no one at the PAC ever associated the ship with Dineb. That left them able to put Dineb, as well as the team's separation, behind them.

Their destination was a definite, though calculated, risk. Raptor had looked like he wanted to argue when she announced her plan, but he'd said nothing. She appreciated that. She just hoped it didn't come back around and bite her in the ass.

Space on the shuttle had been tight for two, and for four, it was truly unpleasant. They took turns sitting in the two chairs. Fallon sat on the floor with her back against the bulkhead and her knees drawn up to her chin. Hawk kept bumping into things, then cursing prodigiously.

When Dragonfire Station came into visual range, they all sighed with relief. Fallon patched into the station's security feeds and worked her magic, ensuring that their approach went unnoticed. At least for anyone not looking for it. She'd told Captain Nevitt what to watch for.

Fallon docked the shuttle right where Raptor had docked his ultralight, then led her team through the station. After a short but exciting journey that included a close call with a mechanic, she led them to a cargo bay that would go unused that day. Closed for maintenance.

She signaled their presence to Nevitt, then sent another message and prepared to wait.

Only twenty minutes later, Cabot Layne arrived.

"Chief. So good to see you back. And you've brought friends." Cabot surveyed each of her teammates in turn with a shrewd gaze. She was pretty sure he knew exactly what they were, and that they'd gone off book.

He gave her a deep bow, which she returned, then extended his hands. A gesture reserved for close relationships. She accepted, wrapping her fingers around his. They were in it together now.

"I need your help," she said, watching him intently. He didn't bat an eye.

"What do you need?"

"A ship. Big enough to get four people halfway to the Zerellian system. Fast enough to do it within a day."

Cabot nodded, as if such a request were perfectly commonplace. "I see. Is there a monetary restriction?"

"None."

His eyes sparkled and a smile curled the corners of his mouth. "Excellent. And when do you need it?"

"As soon as possible. No more than four hours from now." More than that and they risked having BlackOps come for them on Dragonfire, if they weren't already there. She'd known this was a big risk.

"A tall order," Cabot mused, rubbing his chin with his forefinger. "But I think I know just who to talk to. I'll be back shortly." He bowed, politely but hurriedly, then turned smartly on his heel. Just before slipping out the door he called in a soft voice that still manage to carry, "Don't worry, Chief. I've got you covered."

With him gone, she faced the task of explaining to her incredulous-looking team why a Rescan trader was the one she trusted to help.

CABOT PROVED true to his word. In less than an hour he returned with the entry and command codes to a run-down Rescan cargo ship. Nearly a hundred years old and falling apart from the look of it, but it had passed all of its safety checks. The number of cubics required to purchase it would provide the previous owner with a class-four cargo ship. Heck of an upgrade.

Whatever. Fallon didn't need more than a scow. Cabot had assured her that their seller wouldn't mention a word of the transaction. Along with keeping Cabot's good opinion, the seller had a vested interest in giving the appearance of being an up-and-comer in the trading world, one who could afford an upgrade. The boon to the seller's career would be worth many times the ship's actual price, in time. *If* that person was smart enough to leverage it.

Fallon sent Captain Nevitt another message, informing her of their imminent departure. Cabot would go to Cargo Bay Seven, then bring the scow down to Fallon's location. He'd re-enter, and Avian Unit would depart.

She hadn't expected to see Nevitt appear in the cargo bay while they waited. The captain looked cool and relaxed, with that new friendly expression that Fallon had a hard time getting used to.

"Chief," Nevitt said with a courteous bow.

The title made Fallon a little sad. It reminded her of a life that wasn't hers, and now seemed too small for her to fit into. It had felt right, until Raptor had shown her how much she hadn't known about herself.

Fallon returned the bow. "Captain. Thank you for your help."

But Nevitt wasn't looking at her. She was eyeing each of Fallon's teammates, who studied the captain with equal interest.

"I won't even ask for introductions. Seems like a bad idea for all involved." Nevitt smiled.

"Agreed." Fallon didn't know why Nevitt had come, and didn't know what more to say.

"I wanted to tell you, in person, that I'm not replacing you. I expect you to come back at some point and fulfill your assignment here." Her smile broadened when she saw Fallon's surprise.

"I thought all you wanted was to pick your own second in command."

"I did," Nevitt agreed. "Because I wanted someone I could count on to help me climb the ladder. And then I found out that the second I already had was higher up than anyone I've ever met."

"That's not true," Fallon argued. "You know lots of admirals."

Nevitt clucked her tongue derisively. "Yes, fine, admirals. Someone like you is above even them. Changing things from the inside—that's exactly what I want to be connected to. So you owe me, Chief, whatever your name really is and whoever you really are. I intend to collect on that." The look on her face was radiant with triumph and amusement.

Fallon knew she should be annoyed, but she admired Nevitt's ambition and guts. It took a lot to deliver a speech like that to a BlackOp.

"I'll do what I can, Captain."

"I'll inform Arin that you've taken an extended medical leave, and he will be acting chief in the interim. It'll be good experience for him."

Fallon nodded.

"Would you like to see Wren before you go?" Nevitt asked.

Fallon froze, and felt the eyes of her teammates burning into her. "No. There would be too much to explain. Things that aren't safe for her to know."

Not safe for Nevitt either. Fallon saw the unspoken knowledge spark in Nevitt's eyes. "Don't worry about me, Chief. I'm ready for anything."

No doubt she was. Fallon answered, "I'm only worried about anyone who tries something on your station."

Nevitt grinned. "You got that right." She stepped back and

bowed toward Fallon's three companions. "Good luck." She turned and marched out before anyone could return a bow.

Hawk let out a low whistle and Peregrine said, "I *like* her."

Fallon smiled ruefully. "Yeah. So do I." She caught movement out of the corner of her eye and saw their raggedy new transport come into view. At three times the size of a class-six cruiser, it wasn't nearly as concealable. No matter. They'd be out of here in minutes.

They jetted for the airlock, where they met Cabot. Fallon offered effusive thanks, which Cabot waved aside.

"Least I can do, Chief. Now stay alive, and come back home." He grasped her hands again, gave them a gentle squeeze, and was gone.

She turned to Raptor, Peregrine, and Hawk. "Right, then. Let's move on to the next phase."

FLYING the trading ship was like piloting a very large potato. Fallon wouldn't seek to repeat the experience, given any alternatives. But at least the ship got them to the starting point of what she felt would be a long, treacherous journey.

The *Onari* looked different from within the scow. Bigger. Bolder. Stronger. They docked, and Fallon felt Avian Unit's collective relief in disembarking from the Rescan ship. Though it had two small crew quarters, it had been less than adequate space for four people for nearly two days.

When the airlock opened, Fallon saw friendly faces. Jerin. Brak. Kellis. Trin, the physical therapist she hadn't yet gotten to know very well. He gave them a strange finger-gun point that she assumed was a friendly gesture. Behind him stood Endra, looking angry. Scrap. That was going to be awkward to deal with.

Fallon had new breath in her lungs as she stepped on board

the *Onari* for the first time. Breath full of hope. Breath full of purpose.

She turned and watched as the unpiloted scow undocked and fell away into space. Raptor had scrubbed it clean and she'd overloaded the power core. It wouldn't explode or anything dramatic like that, but by tomorrow it would be just another scuttled piece of Rescan flotsam floating through space.

Jerin looked both grave and welcoming. "Shall I show you to your quarters?" she asked.

"Yes!" Hawk practically shouted before Fallon could speak. "There was no shower on that thing, and you do *not* want to socialize with us just now. Especially Peregrine." He screwed his face up into a comical grimace.

Peregrine shot him an annoyed look. Jerin simply smiled, though Trin and Kellis laughed. Endra still looked pissed. Fallon sighed inwardly. A truly bittersweet arrival.

HAWK DIDN'T GET his shower right away. Fallon ordered him to the infirmary first. To her surprise, he capitulated, merely grumbling under his breath as Jerin led him away. She hadn't quite gotten her mind around the idea of being the commanding officer of this team of elite specialists. She'd need to work on that. When things got gritty, and she had no doubt that they would, she had to be fully prepared to throw down orders. Their lives were in her hands.

For the short term, Fallon was just glad for a chance to get clean and in fresh clothing. The *Onari* only had sonic showers, though, and she missed hot, steamy water. Life on board a ship would be an adjustment.

She'd have plenty of time to adjust to her new surroundings. She'd chartered the *Onari* for the next four months. Keeping a low profile, Avian Unit would accompany the ship on its previously scheduled route, which would ultimately take them to their destination—Earth.

Though Fallon would have preferred to burn straight for their target, the extended downtime would get Blackout off their trail. Four months could have gotten them all the way out of the PAC zone, into unregulated space, if they'd chosen. Blackout would have no idea at all where to look for them. And they'd be looking, of course, but a net could only be spread so wide before it was full of massive holes the size of solar systems.

Meanwhile, Raptor would be tapping into every data port along the way to scour for intelligence on Blackout. Finding out who was talking to whom, if any surprising deals were in the works, and if Blackout had any theories on where Avian Unit might be.

Thanks to Nevitt, Dragonfire's records wouldn't show the *Onari*'s recent visit, so there was nothing to connect Avian Unit to the ship. Blackout wouldn't suspect a meandering hospi-ship, wending its way from system to system. That sort of passive, low-energy situation would have a unit of BlackOps itching to get out of their own skins in no time. Fallon knew it, her teammates knew it, and Blackout would, too. Short-term suffering for long-term gains.

At least the company would be excellent. Fallon looked forward to getting to know Brak better, as well as Trin, Kellis, Jerin, and others. This crew of anomalies somehow seemed like an ideal community to her. Maybe she could while away the months ahead by teasing out the mysteries of these people. She'd definitely need *something* to keep her busy.

Her quarters, and those of the others, nestled alongside the crew residences on Deck Two. A quick look around revealed a small but well-designed space. No kitchenette, but it did have its own necessary, thank goodness. To her, the quarters seemed like an upscale version of the low-rent quarters on Dragonfire. The couch was a real couch, rather than a convertible futon, and a small desk and chair sat in one corner, along with a voicecom display. With the chair pushed aside, there was just enough space to pull the desk out into a bed. Fallon recognized the design. Surprisingly comfortable, but pricy. When she woke, she'd fold the bed back up, accordion style, into a desk. A brilliant space-saving solution.

The only other distinguishing feature of her room was a small closet. Fallon opened the door and looked inside. Hangers, and a pair of crisply folded pajamas. She had no interest in the pajamas, but she could put the hangers to good use. She opened her bags and unpacked her meager belongings. Might as well make herself at home. She hesitated before unpacking the last item, wondering if she'd been a fool to waste precious space on the thing.

She held the wedding photo in her hands, debating. Finally, she set the image on the corner of the desk. After a lingering look at Wren's face, Fallon straightened and strode out of the quarters. She needed to check on Hawk.

———

"I TOLD him I could take care of the scars, but he said he likes them," Jerin said, looking somewhat mystified.

Fallon arched an eyebrow at Hawk. He grinned, managing to look both cherubic and wicked at the same time.

"Badges of honor," he said, hopping off the techbed on surprisingly light feet for a man his size. "I feel great, Doc. Thanks."

"How is he?" Fallon asked.

Jerin frowned. "I don't know what happened to him, but he seems to have had both serious stinger burns and a stage-four laceration. I'm guessing he hemorrhaged, because his blood volume was too low, and his white cell count too high. An indicator of immune boosters, which I also detected, in extreme amounts. Then there are the nanopods." She cast an appraising look at both Hawk and Fallon. "Very interesting to see those used in what appears to have been a field medicine situation, when most hospitals don't even have them yet."

She stopped talking, looking at Hawk with a speculative expression, then began again in a lighter voice. "I'm leaving the nanopods in for now. I'll remove them tomorrow or the day after, if all goes well. I compensated for his blood volume and returned his body to normal levels of immune activation and electrolytes. And I did a lot of other technical, medical-ly things, too." A smirk haunted her lips.

"Medical-ly?" Hawk repeated. He looked at Fallon. "I think I'm going to like her."

"You will," Fallon confirmed. "And I already do, so, seriously, don't piss her off."

Hawk affected a look of hurt. "Would I do that?"

"Entirely possible."

The hurt look vanished, replaced with a grin. "Not on purpose."

Jerin arched an eyebrow. "I want to keep a close eye on you for the next couple days, and would prefer to keep you in the infirmary. But I already know how that conversation will go, so can someone at least keep tabs on him?"

Fallon nodded. "I'll make sure of it." She gave Hawk a hard, warning look.

He showed her his palms in a gesture of surrender, then gave Jerin a deep bow of respect, in the way of PAC officers and officials. "I'll do my best to be a good patient."

A spark of surprise lit Jerin's eyes. "You needn't bow to me. Or anyone here, really. We don't stand on much formality. But thank you for the honor." She returned the bow, making the gesture look smooth and elegant. The woman had style.

"*Now* can I go shower?" Hawk asked, sounding like an anxious schoolboy. His eyes flicked from Jerin to Fallon.

Jerin nodded assent.

"Yes," Fallon agreed. She gave him directions to his quarters, which were only a few steps from hers. Such proximity would be convenient in keeping an eye on him. She liked the setup for more than just its convenience, though. Fallon and Raptor had worked hard to get the team back together, and now that they were, she planned to keep it that way.

"Thank you," she said to Jerin as Hawk left. "We were worried about him."

"I bet." Jerin had the tone of someone who was holding a lot of questions back. No doubt she'd have to get used to that. There were too many things that she shouldn't know. Bad enough she knew that they were BlackOps. Fallon didn't want to put her or the *Onari* in danger any more than they had to, but she felt confident in Avian Unit's ability to protect the ship and its crew. Plus, the massive transfer Raptor had put into Jerin's accounts would help Jerin take care of a lot of people. Which made Fallon feel doubly good about her plan.

There was one thing, though, she needed to take care of before she could truly be comfortable. Once she got back to her quarters, she would send a message asking Endra to meet with her. Fallon needed to clear the air about a few things with her sort-of-former-wife's best friend, and hopefully knock those daggers out of her eyes. That kind of hostility would be tough to travel with for months on end.

"Well," Fallon said. She and Jerin had been staring at each other wordlessly for officially a few seconds too long now. "I don't want to keep you from your work." She turned to go.

"Why don't you and your friends join me for dinner? I'll invite some people you know, and some people you ought to get to know." Jerin watched her with intent green eyes.

"We'd love to." At least *she* would. If the others had a problem with it, then too bad. She didn't think they would, though.

That gave her several hours to kill before dinnertime. What

would she do with all the hours between now and four months in the future? She'd need to find things to keep her busy. Maybe upgrade the *Onari*'s security system? That was an idea, if Jerin would go for it. She'd need to find ways to exercise, too. Not having a gym would be an obstacle.

Back in her quarters, she sent the message to Endra, asking to meet after dinner. The sooner she got that confrontation over with, the better. She wasn't eager to hear all the names Endra was likely to call her for marrying her best friend under false pretenses, though.

Fallon prowled around her small quarters restlessly. Since her team had only just escaped the confines of the scow, she wanted to give them some time to themselves. So then, what?

She contacted Brak on the voicecom, expecting to leave a message, but the cyberneticist actually answered. Her face filled the screen.

"Are you settling in well?" Brak asked.

"Too well. I'm bored already. Any chance there's anything at your lab I could do to help out?"

Brak tilted her head to one side. "There are always things to do here. How are you at wiring?"

"Excellent." She didn't have any memory of wiring anything, but her mind filled with diagrams on doing so. She was satisfied that she'd have no issues with such a basic task.

Maybe she could apprentice with Brak for a while. Help Brak to help others and learn some basics about cybernetics along the way. It seemed a good use of her time.

FALLON RUBBED HER EYES, then took a drink of her iced tea. Hours of staring at microcircuits had made her nearly cross-eyed. She'd have to get better at that. But she'd learned a lot, and the time had passed quickly.

She sat with Jerin, Kellis, Trin, and Raptor. Hawk and Peregrine sat with Ops Commander Demitri Belinsky and Brak, plus a couple others she didn't know. She recognized the faces, since she'd already memorized the entire ship's crew. Getting to know the ship's systems would take longer, due to their complexity, but the task promised to chew up plenty of hours, which worked for her. She'd prefer anything over sitting around and being idle.

Fallon cast a look over her shoulder as the other group broke into laughter. The little restaurant was cozy and pleasant, and apparently doubled as a bar. No fine dining here, just a place to relax. Which suited Fallon perfectly. She'd ordered comfort foods and enjoyed them immensely. She'd felt like she hadn't eaten in days, but now, with a comfortable fullness in her stomach, that was just a memory.

Jerin and Trin were telling Peregrine about their next stop, another vaccination run, and Fallon let her thoughts drift. It felt nice to have the time to do so, without the weight of an imminent problem pinning her down.

Too soon, the get-together ended. Everyone had finished eating hours ago, and eventually the crew had to excuse themselves. Their shifts would come early the next day, and they couldn't afford to be exhausted. Fallon had started feeling tired herself, but she still had something to do.

After saying her goodbyes and promising to see Brak in her lab the next day, Fallon reported to Endra's quarters.

The doors opened, revealing a hostile-looking Endra. The woman halfheartedly waved her in. Fallon braced herself and walked into the fray.

"What do you want?" Endra didn't sit. She paced the room with her arms folded.

Fallon chose an armchair next to a side table and affected a position of earnest sincerity. At least she hoped it struck Endra that way.

"I don't know exactly what you think of me, or what I've done, but clearly it isn't good." Fallon hadn't prepared a speech, and paused to consider her next words. "First, and most importantly, I want you to know that I sincerely care about Wren. Someday, if and when I figure out who I really am and what's going on, I hope to be able to reunite with her. Maybe we can't put things back together, but it's a top priority for me to make sure that she's okay in the long run. As important as anything else I'm doing." She let her genuine feelings display themselves on her face, feeling naked and exposed, but wanting Endra to understand.

Endra leaned on the arm of the couch, half-sitting. Well, at least it was an improvement over the stiff-legged stance from before. "You're PAC intelligence, right? Are you on the run? Have you done something wrong? Is Wren in danger?"

Fallon took it one question at a time. "I am with intelligence. But I can't give you details, for your own good. I couldn't give Wren details for the same reason. It's not what she thinks, but I can't tell her what it really is. For one thing, I'm not entirely certain, and for another, it might paint a target on her back." She paused, considering how to answer the next questions. "I don't believe I've done anything wrong but be in the way of someone who wants to do something bad. That's an oversimplification but it's the best I can do. I *am* on the run, in a manner of speaking, because it's up to me and my team to figure things out. Set things right."

Endra's brows pulled down, and her mouth tightened into a pout of deep thought.

"I know it's a lot to consider. It might even be hard to believe. But my unit and I are the good guys. We want to keep the PAC working like it's supposed to, and not let some corrupt official hurt innocent people. We'd even like to remain among the living, if we can work it out that way," she finished dryly.

"Is this ship in danger because of you being here?"

"I don't think so. If anything, you're currently the most protected ship in this sector of the galaxy."

"Is that woman your lover?"

A stab of surprise lit Fallon's chest. "Who, Peregrine?"

A hard look from Endra indicated a yes.

"No. So *very* no."

Endra's eyes softened, then her posture loosened, like frozen custard left melting in the sun. She slid over and sat on the couch with her legs folded under her. She let out a huge sigh.

"This sucks," Endra decided.

"Agreed."

"How could you marry her when you had all of this stuff right behind you?" When Fallon opened her mouth to answer, Endra held up a hand and cut her off. "No, I know. You have no memory, so you don't know, right?" She sounded more frustrated than accusatory now.

"Yes. My memory loss is real. I wish I knew what led up to my marrying Wren. I wish I knew what happened on that shuttle when I lost my memories. And I wish to Prelin I knew that when I get all of this figured out—and I *will*—that things with Wren will tie up into some tidy package. But I don't know any of that."

A long silence stretched between them.

"What *do* you know?" Endra finally asked.

"I know that I'll do whatever it takes to make things right. I know that I'm a good person. That my team are good people, too."

Fallon took a breath, thinking further back. "I know that I woke up with people telling me who I was, and that from the start, I thought they might be wrong. I know I can trust my instincts. I know my feelings for Wren are not just some figment of my imagination. I also know that staying away from her is the best thing I can do for her. But I already said that."

She fell silent for several long moments, then thought of something she hadn't yet said. "I know that I'm with the right people, moving in the right direction. Someone's tried to kill my team, and I won't let that go unanswered."

She felt like she'd just let loose her entire identity and left it, exposed, dangling between them.

Endra's jaw set, as if she'd made a decision. "I guess it's a start."

A grudging acceptance, but Endra was right. Fallon had managed to hit the reset button on the events that Krazinski, presumably, had started. She and her team now had a chance to make things right. She didn't yet know Raptor, Hawk, and Peregrine as well as she wanted to, but she would. Avian Unit would get there, wherever *there* was, together. Eventually. She had a lot of time to wait out on the *Onari* beforehand. She knew that their adversary in Blackout would be working in the meantime, but there was nothing she could do about that. Yet.

At least she had the *Onari* and its crew, and people like Nevitt and Cabot, who'd proven to be more than they seemed. Most of all, she had her team. She was anything but alone in the universe, and that was a long way from where she'd been on the day she'd woken up in the infirmary with a hole in her head.

She said goodnight to Endra and left the quarters. Once in the corridor, she allowed herself a small, hard smile. Explaining things to Endra had clarified the situation to her, as well.

This is what I'm meant to be doing, she thought. *Blood and bone don't quit.*

MESSAGE FROM THE AUTHOR

Thank you for reading!

Please sign up for my newsletter at www.ZenDiPietro.com to receive updates on new releases.

Reviews are critical to an author's success. I would be grateful if you could write a review at Amazon and/or Goodreads. Just a sentence or two would mean so much to me.

If you're ready to find out what happens next in the series, check out *Fragments*. Now that Fallon has rediscovered her team and her purpose, life in the PAC is about to heat up. The next books have plenty of action, some pretty good explosions, and more surprises.

I hope to hear from you!

In gratitude,

Zen DiPietro

ABOUT THE AUTHOR

Zen DiPietro is a lifelong bookworm, dreamer, and writer. Perhaps most importantly, a Browncoat Trekkie Whovian. Also red-haired, left-handed, and a vegetarian geek. Absolutely terrible at conforming. A recovering gamer, but we won't talk about that. Particular loves include badass heroines, British accents, and the smell of Band-Aids.

www.ZenDiPietro.com

Printed in Great Britain
by Amazon